F

So far Boring, Oregon was living up to its name. Misty had never seen so many trees, and she was seeing a lot more horses than cars. She sighed and continued to look out the window, searching for something other than an endless green and brown blur, broken up only occasionally by white spots she assumed were houses but could never be sure.

Her mother was a ridiculously fast driver.

"Honey, there's really a lot more here than just this. It'll be alright, I promise." Christina Montoya gave her daughter a big smile and patted her on the leg.

You're a lousy liar, mom. She had been fuming, and doing a good job of hiding it (at least she had thought so) for the past state and a half. At least you have people at your job. It's not like you have to go to a new school with a bunch of rednecks.

"Yeah, whatever." Misty squinted. Could that be an actual mall up ahead? If it was, it sure wasn't much to look at.

Her mom had noticed it, too. "See, shopping!"

"Great."

The road wound its way out of the town and into the outskirts, where there were only houses on one side of the street, the other being nothing more than a hill that sloped steeply downward. Large thorny blackberry bushes grew haphazardly on this side, inviting pricked fingers and purple tongues. Misty tried remembering if she liked blackberries or

1

not, decided that she had better not, and added them to the growing list of things she hated about Oregon.

"Story of my life," she muttered, looking at her hands. Lately she had taken to biting her nails, and they were chewed nearly to the quick.

"What did you say, dear?"

"Nothing." Misty lifted her eyes, and saw more green, again.

Something was strange about this green blur though. Not really a different color, though Misty had never been very good at telling her shades apart. Her junior high art teacher used to point that out. Out loud. To the whole class. God, how many times did they have to mix colors, and how many times did he have to make that stupid crack about her mastering all the many shades of mud?

And then he would follow that up with a joke about the superb red she had managed to achieve on her face.

Just another wonderful middle school moment. When she told her dad, she had to make him promise not to go to her school and embarrass her with some scene. Unlike a lot of dads, he kept his promise. He kept all his promises.

"You have special gifts, Misty," he always used her first name, and never used any baby talk—no "honeys" or "princesses" or "pumpkins"— "you just have to find them. When you do, you're going to be the person you were meant to be, and I can't wait to see it when it happens." Then he would wrap her in a big bear hug, and she always felt better.

Still looking, dad.

2

"We're here, honey." Her mother's voice woke her from her reverie, breaking the memory.

By the time she got out of the car and stretched the long miles from her back, she had forgotten completely about the strangeness of the woods. Now it looked just like any other forest: a whole bunch of trees, each one just like the other, or close enough it didn't really matter.

And by the time she saw her new house, her body had totally lost that eerie sensation, that feeling people sometimes get when someone, or something, is watching them.

Misty walked with her mother to the back porch, wondering whether it was okay to like the crunch of the gravel driveway under her feet, or if that would be against the rules of engagement for the private war she was waging against this move. She decided to stick to her guns, and stubbornly hated every step she took on the tiny rocks, picturing the driveway as not leading to a house, but away from her home. Her friends, her school, and her father, buried hundreds of miles away from where she now stood.

"It's nice, isn't it," asked her mother, her smile erasing years from her face.

Misty took it all in, the smell of new wood and paint, the huge barn where a normal house's backyard would be. And behind the barn, where she was expecting a fence, was nothing.

Just an open field, brown weeds where there should be grass, a small pond. *Too dirty to swim in. No thanks.* Beyond that another forest stretched into leafy and branchy darkness. She remembering the realtor telling them that the previous owners kept horses, but the barn was empty now.

It was the forest that kept drawing her eye, because that strange feeling was suddenly back. It was dense enough that she could not see beyond the first few layers of trees, and even that was hidden in the shade. It was, in fact, the same color as every other group of trees that she had seen, so the weirdness was all in her head. But, in her mind or not, it wasn't going away. It was almost as if the line of trees represented a barrier of sorts, and that on the other side would be a place where different rules applied.

Her mother shook her from her silent thoughts. "Oh good, they're here now."

While Misty and her mother were standing on the back porch the moving truck that Christina's law firm had arranged for had pulled into the driveway, and large, sweaty men were already moving the furniture into the house. She envied the grace with which they maneuvered even the heaviest objects through the garage and into the house.

So Misty tried to shake the feeling that the trees beyond her back field held more than just squirrels and the occasional deer. But she didn't want to give voice to her feelings or the fact that she was interested in anything other than going back to California, back home.

"I guess."

***

Misty had never had a bigger bedroom. The window stretched across an entire wall and faced the small front lawn, and the narrow street beyond. She could just barely see those blackberry bushes growing over her neighbor's front fence. Seeing them again, she suddenly decided that she had in fact loved blackberries ever since she was a kid, but that they only really became ripe in August.

Maybe she could make just one exception.

It was August now, and the school year was creeping closer. Misty had been looking forward to senior year ever since she was a freshman, perpetually lost and surrounded by people a lot taller than her. Now it was going to be freshman year all over again, except the first time around everyone at least knew somebody from the eighth grade. She wasn't even going to have that.

"Settling in?" Christina knocked softly on the door and entered to find her daughter surrounded by moving boxes.

"Mom, isn't it weird for people to have fences around their front yards and nothing around their back ones?"

"They're not very high fences, Misty."

"I know, but it's still weird."

Christina smiled patiently. "If you say so. I wouldn't say it out loud, though. Different people have different ways."

"It sounds like something dad would've said," argued Misty stumbling over the last words. It was still hard for her to talk about her father in the past tense. It was so easy to believe that he had just stepped out, or gone on a trip, that he would be coming home any minute.

"He did. All the time." Christina closed the door, leaving Misty alone with her thoughts.

Misty spent the better part of an hour looking out the window, thinking of blackberries, her father, the first day of school (*In two weeks!)* and the events that had led her from San Jose to this little nowhere town.

No one had told her that her dad was sick. To Misty, he was the same clown he had always been. She never saw the grimaces that would come over his face when he tried to fight the dizziness that came every time he would chase her around the house. She never questioned the long absences, when he would have his chemotherapy appointments. She had accepted his joking comments about old age when he began to lose his hair.

"But you weren't aging, dad," she whispered to the blank walls of her new room, walls that waited for posters and pictures of happier moments.

Suddenly the new room wasn't so great, the house didn't smell quite so new, and she knew that if she stole outside and plucked blackberries from her neighbor's bush, they wouldn't taste nearly as sweet as they used to.

Welcome to Oregon

The sun was already shoving its light through Misty's curtains when she woke. Looking at the alarm clock, the only thing she had managed to set up the day before, she saw that it was already ten in the morning. Her mom would have already gone to work. Rubbing the rest of the sleep from her eyes, she yawned, stretched (actually she did both at the same time,) swung her legs over the edge of the bed, and looked around.

Her room looked like someone had tossed a clothing grenade into the room and closed the door. Her skirts, which she had remembered carefully folding, came out of the boxes looking like used napkins. Her shirts and jeans weren't much better. In fact the only items of clothing that had escaped the carnage were an old pair of gym shorts and a sweatshirt with the mascot of her high school: the Pirates.

My old high school now. Pulling the baggy thing over her head, she headed out into the hallway to find the laundry basket. With any luck, her mom had hooked up the washer and dryer before leaving. She could spend the morning straightening her room while her clothes were being cleaned.

Misty found the note while on her way to the laundry room.

Honey, I'm going to be a little late tonight. I'm having dinner with the other partners. Sort of a "Welcome to Portland" thing. I left some money. Buy groceries, please.

Love, Mom.

PS. Something Green (not Mint Chocolate Chip Ice Cream!)

Misty found the money under the note and left it there. She had a plan for what to do with her morning, and she was going to stick with it. The groceries could wait. It didn't matter that there was no food in the house, that the pizza from the night before had been completely devoured, and that her stomach was rumbling. Once Misty had told herself she was going to do something, she did it, even if it was silly, or stupid, or really not that important. Here, in the middle of a strange town in a strange state, she had to maintain some sense of normal. Otherwise, she'd go nuts.

Two hours later, the laundry had been neatly folded and placed in the dresser, or hung up neatly in the closet, coordinated by color. The dresser was placed against the far wall and she had moved her bed next to the window. In short, everything was nearly perfect.

Well, at least in one room of the house.

Her stomach rumbled again, this time more loudly.

"Okay, okay, I'll go." She grabbed the car keys on her way out. Misty had been promised the old car ever since her mother had found out about the move and the promotion to partner, which came with a company-purchased Mercedes. It wasn't the newest thing on the block, but it was mobility, and Misty needed that, now more than ever. It was going to take her half an hour just to get to the nearest Starbucks, and they were supposed to be all over the place.

She supposed she had better find the grocery store first.

***

Getting into town took a lot longer than expected. Christina had done all of the driving from Eugene, several hours south of

Portland, and Misty had not thought to get her bearings as they were getting to the house. So she was not surprised to find that she had gone down the same street three times.

On the third time back to town, just as she was finally remembering the way, she heard the jarring sound of a patrol car's siren and, with a groan, saw the flashing lights in her rear-view mirror. Glancing down at the speedometer she noticed that in the act of repeatedly getting lost she had steadily allowed the car to gain more speed.

Mom's going to have a fit. Silently berating herself, she pulled the car over. Then, the realization hit her. There are still California plates on this car. Misty had heard stories about the Oregonians' dislike of all things California. She prayed that it would be different this time. As the officer sidled out of his car, and drew up to his full height, which Misty guessed to be at least six and half feet, the dim wish that this would end in a relatively easy manner began to trickle away. As he approached the side of the car, she rolled down the window, taking time to note the name on man's chest.

"Hello, Officer Green," she said, in as polite a tone as she could muster. Her mother had told her that the best way to handle getting pulled over was to be as nice as possible about the whole thing. She could just hear her mother's voice now: "It can never hurt, and you never know; they might let you off with just a little warning." Yeah, right.

Of course, her mother had a lead foot, which was why Carlos Montoya had always argued vehemently against his wife purchasing the newest, fastest BMW, stating, quite correctly, that "the old Honda runs just fine, and besides, you'll just end up with a whole lot more points on your record." He ended up winning that argument.

"License and registration." Well, there was nothing friendly about this particular patrolman's voice. So much for nice.

Misty pulled out her license, wrinkling her nose in disgust at her picture. Bad hair day. Did every driver's license photo have to look horrible? Was it some sort of grand rule of the universe? Her hair had been pulled back into a severe ponytail that day. It used to be long, straight, and a rich chestnut brown, her father's pride and joy. He said that it matched her eyes. It also tended to get in her face when she drove, and she didn't want to take any chances during her test. Of course, that was before she cut most of it off, right after her father's funeral. Now it barely brushed past her shoulders, but it was easy to maintain; Misty no longer had the patience to brush it out and style it every morning. She had left it long mostly for her dad anyway.

She also had his nose, which was slightly crooked. Naturally the photo had centered on it, displaying all of its majesty. Her mother had offered to get it straightened for her, and Misty had been seriously considering it. No longer.

The license said that her eyes were brown, but if so they were the lightest brown you ever saw. They were all her own, and they were the one part of her that she had never considered changing, had never wanted to alter or fix.

The officer took a while responding, merely taking both documents. The silence allowed her to think about her mother's company car, which was bound to be a lot faster than this one. I'll be completely orphaned by Christmas. Despite the slight chuckle this gave her, Misty truly was concerned about her mother's speeding. She hoped that now it was just the two of them alone, her mother would be more careful.

The first words from the man's mouth brought her out of her reverie, and dispelled the little hope Misty had of a relatively easy time of it, maybe being let off with just a warning. "A little far from home, aren't we?" Was that an actual Southern drawl in his voice? Maybe, but there was also something more, something not so nice.

"I just moved here," answered Misty, as politely as she could. She wasn't going to give anyone the pleasure of seeing her upset.

"Well then, let me be the first to welcome you to Oregon," answered the policeman quietly, but with an air of menace oozing into his voice. Misty shuddered but tried to stay calm. "We obey the speed laws here." He signed the ticket with a flourish, pointed out the court dates available should she choose to contest the speeding charge, and without so much as a good morning, strolled back to the squad car, whistling off key.

Well, it could have been worse, I guess. At the time, though, she didn't know how. This was her first ticket. Carefully turning on the engine, she shifted into drive, looked over her shoulder, and slowly pulled out into the street. The police car pulled behind her, so she made it a point to check the speedometer every five seconds, keeping it five miles under the limit all the way to town, where she found a Safeway.

The police car followed her through every turn, right into the parking lot, and then just as quickly drove away.

Creepy, Misty thought, grabbing her purse from the passenger seat. As she walked from the parking lot into the store, Misty kept hearing the man's odd voice in his head, and each time it gave her a shudder. There was something about that man, and it wasn't quite right.

***

"Paper or plastic?" The question came from the end of the checkout line.

"Plastic, please," answered Misty, turning her head from the screen to face the new voice. At first glance the teenage girl who was bagging her groceries (and not paying particular attention to the fact that she had just placed a jar of mayonnaise on top of a loaf of bread) was just the same as anyone else in the store. Then she looked again.

Since entering the store, she had finally felt a sense of serenity and familiarity; every Safeway was pretty much like every other Safeway. They all carried the same food, and even organized it in the same way; she didn't have to look very hard to find her favorite cereal. *Cinnamon Toast Crunch. It's even on sale! Oh, happy day!* The employees were all dressed the same, in that black smock. For the hour she had spent strolling the aisles, Misty almost felt like she was home.

But this girl at the line was different, and it wasn't her looks. She had red hair, cut short and curly; slight freckles, was of average height, and wore that same silly apron, and the feeling Misty was getting had nothing to do with any of that. It was a complete mystery. Then she caught it.

She was smiling, truly smiling, and no one ever smiled while bagging groceries!

Misty returned the smile, a little nervously at first, then more warmly, and glanced down at the girl's nametag. It read "Kelsey" and underneath it was printed "Employee Since 2012." Oh, I get it; she hasn't been around long enough to start hating her job.

"I'm just happy to have a job," Kelsey spoke up.

Misty jumped back about ten feet. "Did you just read my mind or something?"

Kelsey laughed, and even that was genuine. "Well, it's that or you're starting to talk to yourself without knowing it." Kelsey paused, looking overly dramatic, then continued, dragging out each word. "I'm thinking it's option B." She said this not in the sarcastic tones Misty was used to hearing from her jaded classmates, but with real warmth, as if Misty was not the butt of some private joke, but a willing participant.

Somehow, that made it okay to laugh, so she did.

"I'm Misty Montoya," she said, taking a chance; she was not in the habit of introducing herself to strangers. In fact, her mother actively discouraged it, but there seemed to be very little harm in this girl. "I just moved here."

"Wait let me guess," muttered Kelsey, in mock concentration. "California! Right?"

"How did you know?"

Behind Misty, the clerk cleared her throat impatiently, waiting for Kelsey to finish putting Misty's bags in the cart.

Kelsey ignored her. "Half of the people who come here are from California. That's why a lot of people don't like them. Buying up all the land, at least that's what they say. Heck, it gets so that even Californians that move here start to hate other Californians after about five years."

"Is that right?"

"Pretty much," answered Kelsey, shrugging. "Not all of us though. What part of California, anyway? Sometimes that can make a difference."

"Near San Francisco," answered Misty quickly. Although she loved the Bay Area, she knew that it had a reputation outside of California as the epicenter of the "Fruits and Nuts" population.

Kelsey raised her eyebrows, and grimaced. "Oooh."

"That bad, huh?" asked Misty, disappointed. She had wanted so much for things to go easily at school, and she was beginning to sense that they wouldn't. She looked back and saw that the line had grown by three carts, and many of the people waiting were staring at her, not bothering to hide their dislike. Not knowing if it was because they had overheard, or because her cart was still in the checkout aisle, but hoping it was the latter, she moved her groceries along. "Is it because. . ."

Kelsey cut her off, "No, not that. It's because so many Bay Area people sell their houses for a bazillion dollars and then come up here and buy up forty acres and sometimes even the mule."

Misty was crestfallen. "Oh, I see."

"Oops, guess that would be you, huh?"

"Yes, I guess it would."

"Well I won't hold it against you," promised Kelsey, "but I can't speak for the rest of the state. Apologies in advance."

By this time, a mound of groceries had begun to accumulate at the end of the counter, threatening to topple over the edge into linoleum oblivion. "Whoa, better get going. Welcome to Oregon!" she called, as Misty was walking away.

It took several minutes for Misty to realize that she had made her first friend, and on her first day. Not bad. She wondered, briefly, if they would be attending the same school. In a town this size there was a very good chance.

It was the second welcome she had received that day, and it went a long way towards erasing the bad taste of the first. But not all the way. As she was putting the bags in the trunk of the car, she couldn't shake the feeling that someone was watching her. From time to time she would quickly straighten up and look around, but there was never anyone there.

"Just nerves," she tried to reassure herself, as she slid into the driver's seat.

By the time she made it home the feeling had disappeared.

***

Her first exploration of her "backyard" was the complete opposite of what Misty had always thought of as walking in the woods. Each sound became magnified many times over as it bounced off the trees and into the foliage above her head. That she was totally alone made the noises seem even louder and eerily out of place.

She had decided, after putting away the groceries, to explore as much of the land that her mother purchased as possible. She had remembered the agent talking about the forest that ran in back of the house, and how a great deal of it belonged to them. She felt it only right that she get some use out of it; it was unlikely that her mom would find the time. And the sense that it was more than a forest had not dissipated with the passing a day. Misty had always been a reader, and many of the fantasy stories she read as a child had mysterious forests in

15

them, often filled with something dangerous, sinister. Yet when she thought of this one her curiosity was far stronger than her fear. So far.

Besides, the thought of Misty's mother, all five feet, two inches of her, delicately picking her way through the bushes was laughable.

So it was up to Misty to explore the land, and see what exactly they had purchased with the sale of their San Jose home.

She only managed to make it ten feet into the trees before she stopped. It was not a physical barrier that halted her footsteps—she knew that if she put her mind to it she could continue as deeply into the woods as she wished—but something was not right.

It took a while, but eventually the truth imposed itself: the wrongness that was now in the woods was her; she was not welcome in that place.

Right at that moment it didn't really matter what the property deed said; the silly little manmade lines that told her "from here to here is yours" were as nothing. The trees, which previously filtered the sunlight through their boughs, creating beams of beauty, now held shadows Misty had never noticed before. The ground became harder, and everything, even the birds that until two minutes ago were chirping merrily, was silent and still.

Misty began breathing rapidly, vainly attempting to let logic hold sway. Nothing has changed. Nothing has changed. "Nothing has changed." She stopped when she heard the sound of her voice. If she was really talking to herself then maybe things really had changed. Change had never been good for her, and it was feeling more and more like a bad thing now.

Misty wanted to turn around, wished for nothing more than the strength to run out of there. But she knew that if she turned her back on the forest something would spring out from the now-menacing trees and ride her down before she got ten feet. That was how it always happened in nightmares. Rule number one: don't turn around. Rule number two: never take a shower, but Misty didn't think that was very applicable.

Maybe it was behind her right now.

"Get a grip. There's nothing behind you," she whispered. She remained afraid, though. "Okay, slowly." That was another rule: if you ran you were sure to be chased, so you backed away slowly. Actually, Misty's father had told her that, but he was talking about angry dogs, not phantoms in the woods. But Misty was sort of thinking that it made no difference.

The next thirty seconds seemed to take ten times that. Not sure whether she should turn around or back away, Misty did both, spinning in a slow circle as she exited, praying that no one was looking into their backyard at the time; she felt like an idiot, and probably looked like one as well.

When she reached the sunlit field and felt the heat penetrating her body she nearly collapsed with joy. Behind her were the woods. Never again, was her first thought. Her second was a deep and profound gratitude that her bedroom window faced the front yard and not the back.

***

The rest of the day passed.

At 2:00 pm she began to put the dishes in the cupboards.

At 2:48 she started on the books.

At 4:01 she took a nap.

At 5:00 she started making dinner (spaghetti). She made enough for herself and her mom, with a little extra for the next day.

At 6:00 dinner was ready.

At 6:59 dinner was gone.

At 7:28, after cleaning and putting away the dishes, she sat down on the couch to read.

At 9:00 she watched an old horror video. For two hours a disfigured man with a really large axe chased around a bunch of teenage camp counselors; no one survived to make it to the credits. She felt satisfied in that this particular film deviated from the normal pattern of letting the lead actress live.

At 11:00 she fell asleep on the couch. Her mom had not come home.

At 11:42 she dreamed.

She was sitting on the wooden fence that extended from the barn in the backyard, and she was staring out across the fields, past the foul-looking, horse urine pond and into the forest. Someone was there, just on the edge of the green, watching her. She couldn't make out his or her features, as they blurred in convenient dreamlike fashion. After a while, this person waved. So Misty waved back. She heard her name being called, echoing as if through a long tunnel.

Running across the field, she moved far faster than possible in the waking world. The ground did not move under her feet so much as fly under them. It was only seconds before she found herself facing her father.

"Poppy?" she asked. It was her special name for him.

Sometimes when Misty dreamt she was unable to speak, or to hear, or to do something that came naturally when she was awake. It was, she felt, her mind's way of reminding her that what was happening wasn't real. This time it was different. Her father changed when she came within a few feet of him: she could speak clearly, could see everything. She was able to hear him speak, and for the first time in a long time, his voice possessed the strength she had remembered. There was none of the weakness of cancer working its way into his lungs.

"Hello, my daughter." He had always called her that when he was joking with her, always acting so playfully serious whenever she was trying too hard to grow up. These two words had always made her laugh when she was younger, but she had forgotten that.

Hearing her father's voice again made her realize how much she had missed it. There was nothing childish about it at all now. And only at this time, in this dream, did she realize that there never was. It had been a bond between them, father and daughter, and she had broken it.

Perhaps, she thought, she would remember this time when she woke up. But she knew she wouldn't. She had forgotten once, and she would forget again.

But it was okay for now; he was here, and it was going to be just like it was, maybe even better. He had even found them, somehow, in Oregon.

"No, I'm afraid not," said Carlos regretfully. "I am sorry, Misty, but this will not last, and I am really gone.

"But you're here," she protested, her voice breaking.

"I am. For a little while," answered her father. Then, all at once he began backing into the forest. Or the forest came forward and began to envelop him. It was hard to tell.

"No!" Misty ran forward, trying to reach him, but for every step she took her father disappeared more and more into the trees, until it became impossible to tell where the forest ended and he began. Finally, she sank to her knees, feeling every tiny rock and grain of dirt on her bare knees. "I can't do this again. Please don't leave." There was no one to hear her plea, as only the woods were there now, and she dared not venture any farther, for dreaming did not diminish her remembrance of the day before and the certainty that this place held nothing good.

"Wake up, Misty." It was her father's voice again, and though she could no longer see him, it drifted through the trees and reached her ears.

She would have been content to stay there, captured between the waking and sleeping world, but her mother's hand was on her shoulder, shaking her.

"Misty, get up. You can't sleep on the couch. It'll ruin your back."

"Hunh?" It always took her a long time to fully wake up. When she opened her eyes, she noticed that she had kicked one of the couch cushions to the floor, but she was having difficulty recalling when that could have happened. Already the dream was being stolen from her.

"It's two o'clock, Misty. I just got in," said Christina.

Misty stretched. "Must have been the longest dinner in history." She didn't bother trying to keep the irritation out of her voice. "I made spaghetti."

"Oh, God," Christina put her hand to her mouth. "I'm sorry. I should have called. I forgot. Dinner went so late, and everyone was having such a good time—they really are friendly people. I can't wait to introduce you to them—and we decided to go to Charley's—he's the senior partner—and have drinks, and by the time I---."

"I get it, mom," said Misty irritably. "Any more explaining and you're going to start sounding like me. I just want to go to bed."

"Oh, okay. Well, I'll see you in the morning then."

Misty was already down the hall. "Fine."

Here Comes the Weekend

Instead, there was another note.

Misty knew as soon as she saw the paper on the table that her mother had already left. Must be real convenient having a daughter for a pen pal. She tried not to let this latest irritation affect her as she poured the milk onto her cereal. All the same, when some of it spilled over the bowl and across the counter she consciously made an effort to ignore it. It would serve her mother right to have to clean up.

Christina had not bothered to thank her for straightening the house and getting the groceries. She had, in fact, said nothing at all.

The milk and cereal box had been opened before Misty got to them, and one of the bowls that she had put away the day before was now in the sink. Well, she certainly noticed the food. Left me some dishes too. How thoughtful.

Misty avoided reading the note for two hours, instead taking her time finishing her breakfast and getting dressed. Finally, having exhausted all her possibilities, she forced herself to look at it. This one was a lot shorter.

Got a call this morning and have to go to a meeting. *I never heard the phone ring.* **Don't know when I'll be back.**

And at the bottom of the page, almost like an afterthought:
Why don't you go to the mall and buy some school clothes. There's money in the usual place now.

Misty went to the freezer and looked under the ice bin. Sure enough there was an envelope. Misty took out the bills and crammed them in her purse.

Fine, she would go to the mall, and she would shop. Maybe it wouldn't be so bad. After all, it wasn't called the Boring Mall.

***

Misty had found in her extensive shopping that most malls were pretty much the same. This one was no exception.

Well, there was one: where someone might have expected a fountain, or a Santa Claus (in December) or an Easter Bunny (in April), there was an ice rink. And it was open, so all the shoppers could see you fall on your butt.

No thanks. Misty made a silent promise to avoid the rink at all costs. She had never understood why people would go through the trouble of strapping knives to their feet and trying to cross, as quickly and as dangerously as possible, what was clearly intended never to be crossed.

For the next two hours she contented herself with wandering in and out of the stores that existed in every shopping mall across America.

It was as she was trying on a pair of hip-hugger jeans that the day started to get a whole lot worse.

"You really don't have the waist for those, you know."

Misty, reddening, saw a small group of girls about her age watching her. They were giggling, and not trying very hard to hide it. The one in front, the speaker, looked as if she came from a page torn out of the latest fashion magazine. She had blond hair, which curled slightly and was clipped back. Her sweatshirt was from Abercrombie and Fitch (actually, all of the girls wore something from that store). And plastered on her face was an incredibly insincere smile.

Misty hated her on sight.

Nevertheless, she tried to be calm. "I'm sorry. I didn't quite get that."

The girl continued on, oblivious or uncaring. "You're a little skinny for them, that's all. No hips." The girls giggled again. Clearly, this was not the first time they practiced this routine.

"And who are you?" Misty was horrified. This girl was straight out of a cheesy 1980s high school movie. She couldn't believe that people like this actually existed; it was so two-dimensional. "I don't recall asking your opinion."

"Well, I was just trying to help. It's pretty clear that you're new here," sniffed the girl. "We're here every weekend, and I've never seen you before."

"And what does that have to do with anything?" Misty could not believe how rude this refugee from cheerleader camp was being.

"Come on, Briana," one of the other girls said, "let's just go."

Briana smiled again, but this one was nastier. "Fine." She walked away, and then looked over her shoulder at Misty, who was beginning to visibly shake with the effort of controlling her anger. "I was just trying to help her out. If you're going to try and fit in, you should at least know what you're doing." The other girls nodded in agreement as one.

Misty snapped. "And what would you know about the latest fashion, anyway."

The silence was deafening. Slowly, Briana turned around, hands on her hips. "What is that supposed to mean."

Misty returned her glare, and pointed delicately at Briana's sweater. "My grandfather's favorite store was Abercrombie and Fitch. That was sixty years ago." She said these last three words really slowly.

"You don't know what you're talking about."

"Yes I do. They used to make shorts and swimsuits," replied Misty, getting nasty herself. "Maybe if you spent more time reading and less time at the mall you would have known that. Of course," she continued, letting her voice really start to drip with venom, "that would mean you would have to start thinking for yourself. Are you sure you're ready for that?" Leaving the group to stand speechless, Misty walked away, smiling.

That felt really good. She was right though; I am a little too skinny for these pants. Shrugging, she replaced them on the rack.

As she was loading the bags into her trunk, Misty thought about her time in Oregon so far. She had managed two days in a strange place without her father, or her mother when it came right down to it, to help her. Maybe she was going to be all right. However, she knew the incident with Briana and her clones was affecting her more than she was ready to show, and the way her luck was going it was a sure bet that they would be attending the same high school. Her life was just working out that way.

By the time she had turned the ignition and was preparing to pull out of her spot Misty was no longer smiling. She had managed to meet two very different people in two days. There seemed to be something in Kelsey, she realized, a genuineness that was everything

25

that Briana was not. She privately hoped that the redhead, at least, would be going to her school.

Well, there was one way to find out. Now that Misty had begun to find her bearings in town, she was able to find the Safeway where Kelsey worked much more quickly.

Not wanting to look like a total loser, so desperate they'll go to a grocery store just to say hello to a person they met once (though that was exactly what Misty was doing) she made a pretense of walking the aisles, picking up a few items that she had forgotten to get the day before. She also made sure to pick up some Mint Chocolate Chip ice cream, taking a secret pleasure in purchasing the one thing her mother had asked her not to.

When she reached the checkout, she looked at all of the baggers, trying to locate Kelsey's distinctive head of hair. It was nowhere to be found. Feeling a little stupid, she paid for her items and walked out the doors, just missing Kelsey, who was at that moment opening the break room door and tying her smock, newly washed, around her waist.

"Hey Sue." Kelsey waved to the lady who had rung up Misty a few short moments ago. "What's new?"

"That girl was here again," answered Sue, swiping groceries across the scanner as fast as they came to her.

Kelsey started bagging. "Which girl?"

Sue snorted. "The one that kept you from bagging my groceries."

"Oh," replied Kelsey, subdued. Taking the hint, she started bagging even faster. She didn't mean to get distracted so easily; it was just in her nature to be friendly. And that girl looked like she could use a friend.

Misty's car was just at that moment leaving, and if she had turned her head to the left, she would have seen Kelsey busily working, and perhaps she would have stopped. But she only looked straight ahead, and never slowed down as she accelerated out of the parking lot.

Misty had no way of knowing, but at that same time Kelsey was wondering about the girl from California, who she was, and if they would ever meet again. There was a connection between them that Kelsey could not quite understand. She knew, though, that whatever it was, it was important, and therefore Misty was important in some way.

She just couldn't explain why.

***

The rest of the day went uneventfully. Misty made sure to eat an extra-large bowl of ice cream, then, having nothing better to do, she worked on finishing the book she had started the night before. It was one she had read several times before, but she never got tired of it. It was *The Mabinogion*, and it held tales of everything she had dreamed of as a little girl: giants, magic, fairies, wizards, knights, and princesses. The stories took place in Wales, a land with which Misty, whose family had lived in California when it was still a part of Mexico, had no cultural attachment whatsoever. Despite this, her imagination had been fired by the stories, even more so when she learned that much of the legend of King Arthur sprang from this book. One of her favorite movies was Disney's The Sword in the Stone, and she devoured anything else that related to Arthur, Merlin, and his knights. From this she had begun to

27

branch out into Celtic folk stories, studying both its history and mythology, never understanding why this culture had such a pull on her. Carlos Montoya often did a poor job hiding his chagrin at his daughter's lack of interest in La Llorona and other tales of Mexico, but he accepted Misty's passion as he accepted everything else about her: wholeheartedly and without reservation.

This book had been a parting gift from her English teacher last year, something to help ease the pain of leaving, and Misty had gratefully added it to her growing collection.

She ate dinner alone that night, again, but stubbornly refused to admit to herself how much her mother's absence was bothering her. Instead she managed to finish her book just as her eyelids were beginning to lose their battle with gravity.

Christina found her in the same place two hours later, sleeping in an awkward position and muttering softly to herself. She frowned slightly, debating whether or not to wake her daughter like she did the night before. She finally decided that it would be better to leave her where she was; she didn't want to deal with having to give excuses again. She would just make it up to her, she promised. Somehow.

She did reach into the hall closet to grab a blanket, one of Misty's favorites. It had little polar bears stitched all over it, and was a gift from a family friend, who had made it especially for Misty. Misty had called it her "Maggie Blanket" for as long as Christina could remember, and though her daughter had outgrown it long ago, it was still the first one pulled out when the nights became cold.

Wrapping the blanket gently around Misty's shoulders (it wouldn't reach to her feet,) Christina smiled, remembering younger, more carefree days, days that were gone past all recovery now. Misty mumbled a little more, and squirmed, but she stayed sleeping.

***

Misty woke to wetness.

She had been having this wonderful dream. She had won the Nobel Prize for Literature, and was in the process of receiving the award, and thanking all of the friends and family, her colleagues, her adoring fans. Briana had been in the audience as well, crying, and that made Misty even happier.

Then the presenter started licking her.

"Ewww! Gross, what are you doing?" Then she was awake.

She opened her eyes, slowly and carefully. Her entire vision was filled with a big black nose. Occasionally, a pink tongue would snake out and she would be drenched again. She pulled back, and confirmed her suspicion that it was indeed a dog that had been treating her to a morning slobber bath. Checking her memory, Misty recalled that they did not own a dog, which meant that....

"MOM!," she called, putting all the volume she could into the yell, which, being that she had just woken up, was not much.

"He's cute, isn't he?" yelled Christina, from back in the kitchen. "His name's Niko."

"What is he?" groaned Misty, wiping her face.

"He's a dog."

"Thank you, I can see that," retorted Misty, "but what breed is he, other than a really hairy one." Already snowy white hair had begun to accumulate on her nightshirt. "And is he planning on being an inside dog as well?"

Christina walked into the living room, a cup of steaming coffee in her hand. "Well, which question do you want answered first?"

"All right, Mom, just the breed. I guess I don't really care if he stays in the house or not. Actually it might be nice."

"I agree," answered Christina. "He's a Samoyed. I read that they're just lovely dogs, really gentle and really friendly."

"Hmm, well this one is at least," admitted Misty. "But why did you get a big one?"

Christina came to sit next to her daughter. Niko immediately moved to nuzzle her outstretched hand. "He's not that big, only a year old. But he's already housebroken; you're going to be busy with school and I, well I'll probably be up at the office a lot of the time, so I don't have time to train a puppy."

Misty's mood darkened. "Is this supposed to be some sort of compensation?" It would be just like her mother to try and fill in the gaps. But this dog, no matter how cute he was, couldn't replace her father, and certainly couldn't fill in for a mother who didn't seem to have time for her only child. She stopped stroking Niko's white coat, and he whined softly in protest.

"No, it's not," said Christina, trying to see things from her daughter's point of view. After all, she had been forced to leave everything she had known, and that so soon after they had lost Carlos. *They*, she reminded herself, though she had been able to absorb herself in her work.

Still, she was ready to explode; Misty was that determined to test her. She took three calming breaths, and looked at her daughter, taking her gently by the arms. "I know it must seem that way to you, but

I've wanted a dog since as long as I remember. But your father and I were both working, you know, and even though I promised that I would walk it every day, your father knew me too well." She laughed softly to herself, remembering her husband's gentle reminder that soon enough it would be he who was walking the dog.

Misty wiped a tear that was leaving a trail down her face, telling herself at the time that it was dog drool (and that's the first thing to do today: shower!), becoming more and more angry with herself. Angry at her behavior towards her mother, who really was trying her very best, and angry at the fact that every time she remembered her father she cried.

"It's okay now, Mom. Oregon's a great place for a dog. Maybe even for two or three of them." She was right, of course; the open fields would be heaven for animals. She allowed herself another look at Niko. "He is pretty. Where did you find him?"

"At the pound," said Christina, scratching behind Niko's soft ears. He rolled over, exposing his stomach to his new friends.

Misty knew enough about dogs to recognize this as a sign of trust, and began to rub his belly. "Someone actually didn't want him. Why?"

"He's blind in one eye," said Christina simply. "To some people, that matters."

If Misty's heart had not been lost to Niko already, it was then. "It doesn't matter to me." She bent down and saw now that the Samoyed's left eye had suffered a trauma of some sort. There was some old scarring, and the eye was clouded over. "Mom, it doesn't look like he was born blind."

31

Christina knelt down. "No, I noticed that too. Something happened to him."

Misty felt her stomach clench. What kind of human being would hurt a defenseless dog? "Well, he's here now," she stated, perhaps with more firmness than she had intended. "You hear that, boy?" She gently took the dog's head in her hands, staring into his gentle face. "You're safe now?"

Maybe Niko understood. Maybe he didn't. Whatever message he received from his new friend, it was enough to set him to licking her all over again.

"Yechh! Okay, that's it, I'm going to take a shower now." Misty ran into the bathroom with Niko, who was fully convinced that this was a new game, chasing her.

"Why don't you take him for a walk in the woods," said Christina, calling after her fleeing daughter. "You haven't gone out there yet, have you?"

Misty felt her stomach go numb as she was closing the bathroom door, recalling her last (and only) trip into what was technically her backyard. "No, Mom, not yet."

Maybe with Niko it would be different.

***

"All right, fuzzball, let's go." Misty struggled to get Niko's leash over his head. Christina had insisted on buying a chest harness for him, reasoning that no dog liked to be choked as he walked. While Misty would have preferred to allow the dog to run free, the far reaches of the property would not be fenced until the following week, and Christina felt that it would be safer to keep Niko leashed, at least until he came to recognize this place as his home. Niko, whether through excitement, a desire to play, or unfamiliarity with this new device, managed to drag out Misty's attempt to leash him for a full ten minutes. One minute he would be sitting still, then just as Misty was starting to adjust the straps he would take off down the gravel driveway, kicking up dust and barking at nothing in particular.

"Come on, doggy, give me a break," pleaded Misty. Either he heard and understood her, or he was tired of playing the new game, for he came trotting up to his new owner, tongue lolling happily from the corner of his mouth. "That's a good boy," she praised him, attaching the leash to the harness. Five seconds later they were heading through the old steel cattle gate (never once used for cattle) and approaching the woods, Niko faithfully keeping close to Misty's side.

This second time in, Misty felt none of the fear that greeted her before. Instead, she allowed herself the luxury of looking closely at the different types of trees. Redwoods, quite large but still growing, dominated despite being few in number. Redwoods grew extensively in California, and some of Misty's fondest memories were of the camping trips she would take with her parents on weekends, and of the hikes that would occupy those long summer and autumn days. She was hard pressed to identify the others, although she did recognize Douglas fir trees and other conifers. She felt proud of herself that she had managed to do that much. Yet in her identification one niggling fact kept scratching at the back of her mind: she knew that these giant sentinels of the forest had lived for possibly hundreds of years and had seen things she couldn't possibly fathom. And this worried her, for no logical reason at all.

Yet by the time she had gone a hundred yards into the forest, some of the wonder that nature held began to seep back into Misty's consciousness. She had at first been afraid of repeating her first experience, and when that failed to happen, her joy at that fact had occupied the rest of her concentration for a good while. Now, she was just letting things be. The sound of footfalls other than her own were comforting to her senses; despite being unable to communicate in any meaningful way with Niko he was still a living, breathing thing, of this world. What was more, his easy gait and total lack of barking told her everything was fine, just fine. Funny, I always thought dogs chased anything that moved.

As if on cue, Niko stopped in his tracks and let out a whisper of a growl.

Misty's breath caught in her throat. "What's wrong, Niko?" She looked down at the dog; his fur had begun to rise, but his ears were forward. It was like he recognized that they were no longer alone, but was unsure of what that could mean.

Suddenly, his right ear swiveled to the side, his nose, head, and the rest of his seventy pound body quickly following. Sniffing anxiously in the direction of whatever it was that had caught his attention, he let out a cross between a bark and a plaintive whine, and Misty, though she had known him for mere hours, understood instinctively what that sound meant.

Niko wanted to play.

Misty felt the woods go silent. Even in the trees above, the squirrels had ceased in their endless pursuit of whatever it was squirrels did up there. Misty could feel her heart pounding in her chest, but it was not fear that she was feeling, not this time.

Suddenly, Niko burst from her grip and went speeding off. "Niko, come back!" Misty called desperately, breaking into a run. If she lost him now, on his first day, she knew her mother would never let her get another pet as long as she lived. Not even a goldfish. Ahead, she could still hear his barking, but it was growing fainter. Niko, with his four legs, could easily outdistance Misty, forced to muddle along with just the two. Still, she had to try, and as more time began passed she managed, between gasps, to silently thank her tenth grade P.E. coach, Mr. Tognolini, for making his class begin every day by running a mile. And to think she had thought it useless at the time!

The trees had become an endless blur by the time Misty realized that in this case it really was useless and started to slow down. Unfortunately, at the same place the ground beneath her began to take a serious, not to mention steep, downward turn.

And at that exact moment she was remembering the talk she and her mother had had with the real estate agent. They were going over the bounds of the property, and the agent was pointing out the far end, and joking that it was unlikely they would ever be able to fully explore it, due to a large ravine that cut across its length.

Not From Around Here

Christina peeked out the kitchen window, watching Misty and Niko walking across the field and into the woods, and for a long time after she continued to stare. She hoped that the new addition would lift the gloom from her daughter's spirits, and would be a welcome companion in the days to come. Her new job was demanding more time than she had anticipated, and they had only arrived two days ago. It seemed unlikely that things were going to change. With Misty attending a new school in a week, things were not going feel normal for a long time.

But what choice did I have. Stay in San Jose and struggle to pay the bills? I had to come here. This chance wasn't going to come again. It was true, but so what? It didn't feel any better. Maybe, she realized, she really was trying to compensate, but she didn't know for what. Misty was a grown girl; she should be able to take care of herself. She would have to.

The phone rang.

"Hello."

"Christina, hi." It was Charley, the senior partner at the firm. It was Sunday, and that couldn't be a good thing.

"Charley, how are you?" she asked, already knowing the answer, but needing and dreading to hear it at the same time.

"Bad news, Christina, we need you in the office today. Our newest client, Keller Construction, they want to meet all the partners, you especially." Christina suspected that it was a little more than that. Charley was acting a little too tense.

"It's Sunday, Charley," Christina pointed out.

"Yeah, well the guy's flying out to London this afternoon, and he's gonna be gone for a while. He just wants to see the new face before he signs anything is all," explained Charley. "You can make it, can't you?" His tone made it clear what her answer needed to be.

Christina looked out the window. Misty and Niko had not returned from their walk. Sighing, she gave the only reply she could. "Okay, I'll be there as soon as I can."

"Great, Christina, great. Hey, listen: business attire, okay."

"Charley, the guy's in construction," said Christina. If she had to give up her Sunday to see some high-strung client, it would at least be nice to not have to dress up.

"He owns a construction firm, and I don't need to remind you how large it is. He's not really 'in' construction," corrected Charley. "See you in an hour and a half." He hung up.

Christina gritted her teeth, slamming the phone down. She had never been acquainted with the famous Thomas Keller, but she knew enough of him to understand that his insistence on meeting her had nothing to do with getting to know the new face and everything with looking over the only female partner her firm had, to see if she was cold-blooded. He was old school. None of his executives were women, and the senior vice president of the company was his own son.

And it just cost me my daughter for another day. Realizing that there was nothing she could do but hop to Mr. Keller's demands, and reminding herself, and failing, to try not to hate every moment between now and when she walked in her door again (whenever that is) she stormed into her bedroom and rummaged through her closet in search of her most formal business suit. She chose one with pants, knowing that it would annoy Mr. Keller. It was a small act of defiance, and Christina should have been rightly proud of it. And she was, a little.

She just didn't admit it to herself.

By the time she had managed to dress and do her hair in a severe bun, thirty minutes had already passed. Still no sign of Misty. She couldn't wait any longer. Hating herself for taking this job, hating Charley for being such a pushover, hating Keller for being just a prick, and hating Carlos, a little, for leaving her to handle things along, she jammed the key into the ignition and turned it violently. If she hurried, she would make it just in time.

As she was pulling out of the garage, and shifting into drive, she felt a gentle tug at her heart. Every part of her was urging her to stay, to not leave her daughter. It was the one thing she wanted most to do, and the one thing she couldn't.

"Damn it!" she yelled. In a cloud of dust and gravel she sped out of the driveway. Maybe the car would get dinged up enough and the company would have to go through the trouble of getting it fixed.

It would serve them right.

Exactly an hour and twenty-five minutes after Charley had destroyed her Sunday, Christina was walking briskly into the conference room, where Charley and Mr. Keller were already waiting. Trying not to convey the fact that she had rushed over, but had just happened to be in the neighborhood and just happened to be wearing a full business suit, she strode up to her newest client and shook his hand firmly. The man's hands were soft, not those of a person who had spent their entire life building things. Of course, Thomas inherited the company from his father, and had been slashing costs and lowering quality ever since. He had, in fact, retained Christina's employer for that very purpose; he was said to be interested in moving as many of his operations to cheaper, foreign, shores. And while he gave lip service to the goal of diversifying his company into a world market, he was really just looking to add to his profits, regardless of the jobs that would be lost by workers at home.

He was going to pay her bills, though, but that did not stop Christina from disliking him from the first moment she had heard he had hired the firm, and her in particular, to do his bidding.

"Christina Montoya, Thomas Keller," began Charley, a bit nervously, trying to dispel the tension. Christina was doing an admirable job of trying to hide her annoyance. She was not necessarily succeeding, but she was giving it all of her effort.

"Glad to meet you, Tina," said Thomas. His voice had a slight Southern twang, despite the fact that he had been raised in upstate New York. It was just another phony piece of a man made from lies. Christina had read enough of the man's file to know that much at least.

"Christina. It's nice to meet you as well," she said. "Shall we get down to business? I know you are a busy man," she hinted, subtly pointing out that it was she who had been rushed around for him, not the other way around. "What can we do for you?"

"Well, I have these papers I need you to look over." He shoved over a file box that had been resting on the table next to Charley. "Contracts and such. Frankly, they're chapping my hide and I need to find a way out of them. Can't start up the Malaysia branch until I get this mess back home untangled." He leaned back and smiled. His teeth were yellow with years of smoking. He had a lit cigar in his hand at that moment.

As much as Christina found the man unlikable, and that amount was growing by the minute, she couldn't find it in her heart to wish cancer on the man. Not after Carlos. Instead, she choked down her first thought, which would have almost certainly led to her dismissal and said "Oh, I thought you were just in construction, Mr. Keller. What do you have planned for Malaysia?"

Mr. Keller stiffened, then relaxed, settling even deeper into his chair, looking nothing at all like a man with a plane to catch. "Construction. Other things," he answered. "But that really isn't your problem. Just look those over, kid, so I can get going there. I'm paying you by the hour, aren't I?"

"That you are," broke in Charley, a bit too cheerfully.

Why don't you just get down on all fours and lick the man's boot, Charley? Christina closed the box. "I'll just set this in my office and get on this as soon as possible, Mr. Keller."

The owner of one of the world's largest construction companies (and other things) stood up then. "Right away, Tina."

"Christina."

"Whatever. Well, Charley, golf in two weeks. Better let me win." He smiled and walked out the door. At that moment, Christina noticed his belt buckle. It was gold, studded with diamonds, and incredibly large. There was only one legitimate way to acquire such a buckle.

"Where did you win it?" asked Christina.

"Excuse me?"

"Your buckle. In what tournament did you win it?" she asked again. She loved horses, and if she could forge some connection with this man, any connection, it might make it easier to deal with him. She knew she was going to have a hard time getting free of this one.

"Got it in a Cracker Jack box," he said, guffawing. It sounded so well-rehearsed he must have told that joke a thousand times.

Just one more thing about you that's fake. "I see, a Cracker Jack box. That's funny. I'll have to remember that. Good day, sir," she finished, taking up the box and beginning to walk to her office. Behind her she heard Charley wish Mr. Keller a safe flight.

Apparently it was a short conversation, because he caught up with her before she reached her office door. This meant that he was able to open it for her, but she knew that that would be the only good thing about him coming after her.

"Hey Christina, I know it's a real pain, but I need you to start working on those right away." He sounded apologetic, but also relieved that it wouldn't be him having to take the stuff home.

Christina dropped the box on her already cluttered desk. "These files aren't even organized, Charley!" she yelled, finally allowing herself to blow off steam.

"I know, I know," he agreed, holding his hands in front of him as if trying to ward off an imaginary blow. "But he's going to need it when he gets back in two weeks."

I haven't even eaten with my daughter yet. Christina dug her nails into her palm. Finally, she was able to find control. "Is this going to be par for the course?" she asked through gritted teeth. She was afraid that if she bit down much harder she was going to cut herself.

41

"It's just a weird week, Christina. It'll calm down once you're settled. Trust me," he said, not sounding at all convinced. "Look, I have a lunch thing. I'll see you tomorrow."

***

Misty woke to wetness.

The first thing she saw upon cracking open her eyes was a huge pink tongue. It was the second time that day she had been treated to a dog alarm clock.

"Ugh, Niko! Gross!" She pushed herself up to a sitting position and looked around. Beside her Niko sat at attention, ears pricked forward. He was whining softly. "Okay, boy, thanks for caring," she said, reaching over to scratch behind his ears.

"Excuse me, but could you possibly lend any assistance in getting me out of here?" The voice came from nowhere. Well, actually, it seemed to be coming from a large pile of branches and tree leaves. Misty looked up the ravine. The sides were not as steep as she had first thought. She was in one piece, after all. Still, she had managed to take out a great deal of foliage during her descent, and a lot of it followed her down, ending up in the messy mound next to her.

None of this explained why the branches were talking to her. Niko sprang forward, barking energetically. Soon he started grabbing some of the smaller limbs with his mouth, trying to pull them away from the larger mess. His entire body tensed with the effort, and it was apparent to Misty that he wasn't going to be able to do it alone.

"Hold on, Niko, I'll be right there. Ow!" She had tried to get up and discovered that much of the force of the fall had been taken by her rear. "Oh, crap, that hurts," she muttered, rubbing her sore bottom. She managed to clamber to her feet, slowly, working out the ache. Looking up at the heights from which she fell, she moaned, "How am I supposed to get all the way back up there?"

"I am sure you will find a way. You managed to get down here easily enough," the stack of branches said. "But if you will be so kind as to help me first, it would be highly appreciated." It certainly was the politest pile of sticks and leaves she had ever met.

"Uh, yeah, sure," said Misty, moving as quickly as she could and bending down. She began removing the branches on the top. Niko tried to help, but succeeded more in getting in the way than in providing any actual assistance. "How did you get under here, anyway?"

"You tell me. I was standing here admiring the sunlight as it played among the trees and played upon the water," Misty looked and noticed that there was indeed a small creek wending its way through the ravine, and that it did look quite stunning in the filtered noontime sun, "and suddenly a forest lands on me. Had I known that this would happen I assure you I would never have left the clan."

Misty frowned. Clan? While she had managed to dislodge a great deal of sticks and leaves during her tumble, she doubted that they quite added up to a "forest." Actually, the pile was rather small. "You sound very grown up for a child," she noted.

"I am not a child," protested the voice.

Misty turned scarlet, embarrassed. "Oh, you're a little. . .I mean a midg. . .a, well, you know." It was just like her to offend someone she had just physically injured.

"I am afraid I do not know. I am considered quite tall, actually," he—for Misty determined that it was a male voice, if slightly high

43

pitched—sniffed. "I do not know what clan you are from, but it must be an exceptionally tall one."

"Clan? I'm sorry, I don't know what you're talking about," she said, confused. "Hold on a minute, I've almost got you loose." She strained at the last large branch, which had become intertwined with several smaller ones. Underneath she could just make out a figure. He was small, that was sure, and whatever clothes he was wearing must have been green or brown or a blending of the two, for he was difficult to pick out from among the leaves. Beside her Niko started to whine again.

"What a strange manner of speech you possess, my lady. I must confess I have never heard its like before now—dear gods!" Misty had finished pulling the last piece of debris away, and revealed the prisoner. "Fomorian!" he screamed, scrambling as far away as he could go. He moved fast for a little man, for that is what he was. But he was unlike anything Misty had every seen.

"Connell! Siobhan! Back to the village! Now!" he screamed, sprinting away, his little legs pumping so fast Misty could barely see them.

In a brief instant he had crossed the creek and had vanished into the trees. Misty could see that his body was perfectly proportioned, almost as if he was a fully sized adult, but one shrunk into half-size. His clothes were formal, much too nice for a forest walk. And they were antiquated. Who wore a hat and tie anymore? And everything about him, right down to his boots, seemed surrounded by an unnatural and faint glow.

"Wait!" called Misty, running after him, "I'm not going to do anything." He was already gone. To her side, she heard rustling and before she could think to turn she sensed rather than saw two other shapes whisk by. "I just wanted to ask you about, oh never mind," she whispered, for there was no one left to hear.

All this time, Niko had sat stock still, not bothering to give chase. "Great help, fuzzball," she said, walking back to him. She finds something interesting, and before she even gets a chance to investigate, it's gone. Still… "They went that way, boy. Think you can sniff them out?"

"Burf!" answered Niko, trotting forward and crossing the creek.

Misty followed. "Slow down," she said, taking his leash again, which until this time had been dragging along behind him. "We don't want to hurt them."

Misty followed Niko as he pounced through the thick undergrowth, occasionally getting stuck on a branch and having to free herself before continuing. Every time she did this, Niko would stop, sit down and give her a look of incredible patience. Well, as much as a dog was able to give any kind of look other than one that said: Feed me. This happened at least five times as the pair made slow progress in their pursuit. All in all, Niko demonstrated incredible perception for an animal, and Misty found herself wondering whether all dogs just acted dumber than they really were, or if Niko was some sort of mutant superdog.

"Well, are you, boy?" called Misty, finally untangling herself from the latest thicket that had grasped and torn at nearly all her clothes. "Are you a mutant superdog?"

45

Niko, at that moment turning in circles in an attempt to catch his own tail, didn't hear. Finally, giving it up for a bad job, he lay down, rolled over on his back, and exposed his stomach, begging in no uncertain terms for a bellyrub.

It seemed that the search was over.

Laughing in spite of herself, and the fact that she had no idea where she was, how far she had come, or how she was going to climb out, oh, and that the sun was steadily making its way downward, Misty dutifully administered a scratching. Niko rolled on the dirty ground in pleasure, almost guaranteeing that he would be needing a bath before Christina even let him come within sniffing distance of the house.

"You really don't know what hassle you're causing me, do you?" she complained, giving his sides a final pat before pulling herself to her feet.

He growled contentedly, rubbing himself even more vigorously into the dirt.

And he was off again, this time he was running back the way they had come.

"Niko, wait!" He stopped, again sitting quietly, and stared back at her. Something was different about this look, and as he began to whine, Misty saw that it lacked patience. If ever a dog could appear urgent, Niko did at this time.

"What's wrong?" asked Misty, moving closer to him. She put her hand on his head, and he was shaking. "What's gotten into you, anyway?" Misty looked around, but the woods seemed the same as when she had first started chasing after that mysterious fellow. No, actually, they weren't. "Niko, there's something weird about this place, isn't there?"

Niko whined again, and started sniffing and pawing the ground. Misty let him be and walked a little further on, trying to take in every detail. The trees here were of the same type as those that bordered on her fields. Exactly the same type actually. They were even the same size. No, that wasn't the difference. They seemed older, though. Was that the right word? Maybe not; Misty had seen old trees before. She couldn't remember how many times she had traveled with her parents to Yosemite. She had even been to Yellowstone once; her mom must have used the term "scenic overkill" a hundred times as they drove through the park and the rest of Wyoming. Her father had nodded in agreement every time, chuckling softly to himself. In any event, these trees couldn't be older than the ones she had seen before; their trunks weren't wide enough. So what was it?

All of a sudden, it was clear. Yosemite, Yellowstone, all the campsites she had gone to, they all shared something in common: people. People are all over those places, and the trees never get any peace. But here, in this place, people didn't venture, and these trees, no older than any others she had seen of felt before, were different because they were pure. Misty, for all that she tried, found herself not knowing how this knowledge came to her, what it meant, or why it mattered.

But it did.

"Who's there!?"

Misty whirled around. Crashing through the brush were two men. Both were wearing camouflage, but it wasn't doing much good with all the noise they were making. Each one held a long rifle in his gloved hands, and the taller one had a scope attached to his. As they came fully into view, she was able to get a closer look at them. The taller one, who Misty assumed must have been the one who had spoken, had on clothing that was more faded, more "worn in." The shorter one (though there could not have been much more than two or three inches between the two) wore greens that still showed the creases of the clothing rack. They both had binoculars dangling around their necks and canteens jutting from their hips, and during the time Misty was checking them over the smaller one took a long drink from his.

They had stepped right out of a sporting goods catalog. Misty tried not to chuckle, but didn't completely succeed. Behind her, Niko was alternately growling and ducking behind her legs, sticking his head out for only as long as it took to growl again.

"Asked you a question, girl," said the tall man without a hint of friendliness in his voice, and Misty recognized at once to whom it belonged.

Apparently, Officer Green got around.

"Never seen her before, dad." The relationship between the two stood as clear as the sky after a morning's rain. Misty was surprised she hadn't noticed immediately; the two were carbon copies, right down to the aggressive jut of their jaws.

Still, as best as she could tell, this was still her property. "I might ask the same of you," she replied, in as cold a voice as possible. She still hadn't forgotten the ticket from two days before. "You're on our land."

48

The cop smirked. "Your land, is it? Get a load of this one, Nick," he said, nudging his son and pointing at Misty as if she were a prize horse. "Her land."

Misty stood her ground, finding strength in anger. "That's right. And I think you had better go back where you came from. I imagine," she added, snidely, "that from all that stuff you're wearing you must have hiked oh, one, two miles." Her mother would have a fit if she knew that she was addressing perfect strangers this way, but it felt so good to recover some of the power that her encounter with Officer Green had stolen from her.

"Jackson never minded us hunting his land," said Nick, speaking up, and sounding a little petulant. You could tell he wasn't too happy about a girl telling him and his dad where to go.

"True enough. He didn't" agreed Officer Green. "But he ain't here no more, is he?"

Misty nodded her head, resolute. "No, he isn't. Goodbye." Without turning to look back she grabbed Niko's leash and began the walk back to where she had first fallen down the ravine. With any luck she could find a gentler slope on which to ascend.

Officer Green wasn't quite through. "Girl! Hey, girl!"

Misty stopped, not bothering to look over her shoulder. "What?" she snapped.

"I've been walking these woods some time now, since I first come from Alabama. Nick here's just started."

Misty turned around then, hands on her hips. "And what's your point?"

She started to walk away again. "Hey wait, I just wanted to warn you, seeing as you're not from around here." Misty ignored him, and he called out after her retreating figure, "There's things in these woods! You should be careful."

I just met the only two things in these woods to be careful of. But that wasn't totally correct. Her encounter with the unkind man and his son had shaken her from her true purpose, and now she had no chance of going back and searching, not with those two still in her woods. Throughout her encounter she felt the same sense of wrongness that had permeated her first meeting with Officer Green, except this time this feeling was magnified.

It looked like his son Nick was a chip off the old block.

Now that some distance had been put between him and the pair, Niko began to wag his tail again, seemingly forgetting that the meeting had ever taken place. Misty had read or heard somewhere—she couldn't remember which—that dogs had very selective memories. At that moment she envied Niko for his ability to romp forward while she still had to replay the last few minutes over and over in her mind.

They were right about one thing, though: there was something in these woods, but Misty had the feeling that whatever they were presented little threat. In fact, they had been terrified of her. What was it that they called her again, a Fomorian? She couldn't remember why, but that word sounded very familiar to her.

Promising herself that she would make use of a dictionary as soon as she got home, and that she would do her best to forget the Greens, she worked towards finding a way out of the ravine.

"Come on, Niko, you got me into this mess. Get your big nose here and sniff us a way out of here before Mom calls America's Most Wanted.

"Burf!"

***

Christina was less than happy when Misty described her encounter.

"I'll call the police," she said decisively.

Misty groaned. "He's a cop, Mom," she reminded her. Clearly, her mother was upset about something beyond a couple of rude neighbors, and she had a sneaking suspicion that it had to do with the huge box that Christina had brought home and that was now taking up a good portion of the kitchen table.

"Still, how rude. If you see either of those two on our property again, let me know."

"I will," promised Misty. It would be an easy promise to keep, she realized; why would she want to fall down that pintsized cliff again?

But if she didn't how was she going to find out more about those...people?

Then she remembered. "I gotta go look something up," she said, rushing from the kitchen and heading into one of the spare bedrooms now being used as an office.

"Fomorian," she muttered, rifling through the massive dictionary her mother had kept from her college days. "Oh, here it is. Fomorian: In Irish legend, one of a race of pirates (well, that's not me) or giants. In Scottish legend, a giant. I guess I must have looked really tall to that little fellow after all. That doesn't explain, wait a second..."

She ran her finger further down the entry. "See also: Sidhe. Where have I heard that word before?" She flipped the pages of the large and well-used dictionary until she reached "S." Finding what she was looking for she read: Sidhe: Ir. Mythol. Also sidhe and (sing.) Sidh of Ir. People of the fairy mound. Hence (esp. in the writings of Y.B. Yeats), the fairy folk, fairies, freq. regarded as the mythical gods of ancient Ireland.

"Oh, yeah, I remember now. Elves."

"What about elves, dear?" asked Christina, poking her head into the office. Seeing the opened dictionary, she came in. "What is it you're looking up? Elves, you said?"

Misty looked down, not quite sure how she was going to explain today to her mother. Going with the idea that the best lies are the simplest, she said. "Yeah, I was watching some program on television about ancient Ireland. Discovery Channel, I think." She closed the book and placed it back on the shelf, grunting as she shoved the ponderous volume into place. "I wanted to look up a word I heard. That's all."

Christina shook her head, from amusement more than anything else. "Misty, you've got Ireland on the brain, always have. One of these days I'm going to figure out why." Laughing quietly, she walked out of the room, leaving Misty with her thoughts.

"Yeah, me too." Misty got up, stretching the kinks out of her knees. Her little tumble down the hill was going to leave some very difficult to explain bruises. Well, she would be more careful the next time.

And she realized then that there would be a next time. She hadn't really admitted it to herself until that moment, but something about that little man was calling to her, something familiar. But the

52

harder she was trying to remember his face the harder it was becoming. Maybe it wasn't that person in particular; perhaps it was more of a general quality that he possessed, that they all possessed. Connell and Siobhan, whoever they were, were definitely of the same race (and she doubted that they were the only others) that was pulling at her. There was a melody about the people that moved through her whenever she remembered that moment. It was moving through her right now. It would be moving through her tonight. It would echo in her dreams for all time. She knew this, as clearly as she knew her name.

Instead of frightening her, this strangeness brought with it a certain excitement. It was the first time she could remember not being afraid of the unknown. Instead, and this resolve was coming to her so fast she could hardly believe it, she could hardly wait until the next day, when she would be able to go back once more. Not even the thought of the Greens (*and they had better not be there!*) could keep her away. Nothing could.

"You look better," observed Christina, as Misty started to pile her plate with garlic potatoes. They were Misty's favorite side dish, and Christina had taken special care to prepare them just the way her daughter liked: lots of garlic. Misty's second favorite dish, pot roast, was taking up the rest of her plate, right next to the mountain of spuds. Christina had made them as a kind of apology for Charley's pulling her away. After hearing the story, she was even more furious at her boss's lack of backbone.

To her credit, Misty never mentioned her disappointment at coming home from her ordeal into an empty house.

"I feel better, Mom, thanks," said Misty, through mouthfuls. Taking a long drink of water, she thought about the next day. It would be Monday; she would have only a short time before school started, and she wanted to see if she could find them again before her days were taken up with schoolwork, before the coming fall and winter made it too cold to wander the woods.

***

"Come on, boy, let's go." She couldn't keep the disappointment out of her voice. For the past week she had come every day to this same spot, had crawled down the same slope, had gathered cuts in all kinds of different places on her arms and legs, and then, finding nothing, had made her arduous way back. She had seen nothing new, just the endless murmur of the creek as it bubbled and splashed over the same mossy rock. Now it was Labor Day; school would start tomorrow.

Niko trotted up, ever faithful, and allowed her to hold on to his leash. It was a symbolic gesture at this point; Misty had long ago given up trying to lead the spirited dog, and he always came when he was called. Pretty soon now, she was going to leave off strapping it on altogether. There was no longer any point, and he still made putting it on him a drawn-out game.

Misty had no way of knowing it, but she was never alone during her searches, ever. Green eyes followed her every move, and only left her after she had begun the steep climb back up the slope.

"She is persistent."

"Yes."

"That could be bad."

"Yes."

A pause. "Still, she does not seem bad. She is not like the others, is she?"

"No, she is not."

"We will have to watch this one, I suppose."

"Yes."

"We should not tell anyone, should we?"

"No."

School

Misty arrived at school an hour early so that she could find her classrooms. The last thing she wanted was to be seen as the new kid. Of course that was exactly what she was, but she didn't see any reason to advertise this. She woke up so early that she was actually able to say goodbye to Christina, who as usual was leaving so that she could be at her office at 7:00 am.

"Have a good day, honey," shouted Christina from the open window of her car. She was shoving the box of papers that she brought home every evening to work on in her office (same box, different papers) and her butt was sticking out of the vehicle, so Misty could barely hear her from the kitchen.

However, Christina had said the same thing to her daughter for as long as Misty could remember.

"Okay, mom, I will," yelled Misty, equally sure that there was about a snowball's chance in a blast furnace that she was actually heard. That was okay, though; for as long as Christina had been saying the same thing, Misty had been giving the same reply. Thirteen years now.

After finishing her breakfast, Misty drove to the school and by some miracle was actually able to follow the directions she had pulled up on the internet the night before.

"Looks like a school," she said, walking the still halls. And she was right.

Sandy High School had an expectant air about it, the kind that the sky would get just before a thunderstorm rolled in. The windows looked newly washed, the hall floors shone, the façade lacked any trace of graffiti, and the lockers were shining. The building itself was almost brand new, and she wondered what the old building must have looked like. She was able to pick up her schedule early from the office staff, even though the students were not supposed to receive theirs until 7:30. She had just put on her best little-girl-lost face and acted like she wouldn't be able to find the bathroom without a compass and a guide, much less all of her classes, all in rooms that looked so very much alike.

They had bought it hook, line, and sinker, and five minutes after entering the office she was leaving, schedule in hand, and a faraway look in her eyes.

Ten minutes after that she had managed to walk the entire school and find all of her classrooms, even though it was a pretty big school. But, she thought, what did you expect? So she passed the rest of the time on one of the benches, waiting for the bell to ring, and hoping that the truth of her home state wouldn't get out too soon.

"Hey, California girl!"

Misty groaned. First period hadn't even started yet, and already the gig was up. Looking around to see who had ratted her out, she rested her eyes on the one person she most definitely did not want to see.

Nick Green.

Misty went on the offensive. "How did you know that?" she demanded.

Nick smirked. "My dad told me. Said you couldn't drive worth crap, either." Behind him a trio of girls giggled stupidly. The girl in the center looked familiar.

Oh, for the love of God. Briana! This day was starting off just perfectly. Here she was, not five minutes into class and already her two least favorite Oregonians were sharing a room.

Still, Nick shouldn't have known what he knew. "That's against the law, what your father did," she pointed out. "That kind of stuff is supposed to remain confidential." She actually wasn't too sure of that, but it didn't hurt to try.

Nick shrugged. "Whatever."

Misty thought briefly about escalating the situation. Her mother would be furious, and she might even want to do something about it. Of course, she barely had time to eat dinner with her daughter, much less enter a legal crusade on her behalf. Still, it made a nice picture in her head.

"Misty Montoya." The teacher was calling roll. Apparently she knew a lot of the other students because she completely skipped Nick's name.

Misty perked up. "Here."

"You're new, aren't you," asked the teacher, looking over her horned-rim glasses.

There was really no point in trying to hide it. "Yes. I moved from California."

"Bunch of freaks," commented Briana snidely, managing to let her voice get just to Misty's ears and not to the teacher's.

Misty turned fully around, not willing to let her get away with it. "Well, if you consider NOT having the urge to dance in a line like a bunch of robots while some singer with a fake Texas accent blabbers on about his wife, his dog, and his truck freaky then, yes, there are a bunch of freaks back home." She turned around, looking the teacher in the face. "No offense."

The teacher (Mrs. Swanson, Misty would later come to find out) smiled sweetly, aware that even though she did not hear Briana say anything, she was still behind the outburst. "None taken, dear." It was a minor victory, at least.

And it shut Briana and Nick up for the rest of the period.

Second and third periods were much like the first. Nick and Briana seemed to follow her from class to class. She was beginning to wonder if there really were only 30 seniors in the whole school, despite its size, and if she was going to be doomed to spend her days with those two.

But when fourth period came around, blessedly close to lunch, she found herself surprised in two ways. Nick and Briana went off into a different direction and there, in her Advanced Placement English class, was a gift.

"Hey, California girl!" This time the words, spoken in complete fun and without malice, were like the sun coming out from behind the rain clouds.

"Kelsey, hey!" Misty trotted into the classroom, moving as quickly as she could to sit beside the redhead.

"I was wondering if you were gonna show up. After all, this is pretty much the main high school around here." She leaned forward. "So what do you have first through third?"

Misty rolled her eyes. "Spanish, Physics and Art. I didn't know what elective to take. I guess I chose the wrong one."

"Why?" Kelsey sounded genuinely concerned.

"Because Nick Green and Briana Coles are in all my classes. Except this one."

"Those two?" Kelsey muttered something else under her breath. "Yeah, I don't think they do much outside reading. Still, you should see about changing your Art class. Mr. Garza's too near to retirement to care much anymore, and Nick and Briana know it. It's why they've taken his class every year for the past three years. I just had Drama. You should try that."

Misty gulped. She had always been shy, even around her friends and relatives. Any time the karaoke machine came out, she went in her room and hid. Still, it had to be better than another hour with those two. "I'll look into it. Who do I ask?"

"Try the counselor," suggested Kelsey. "It won't be a problem. We change classes all the time." She clapped her hands. "Ooh, it'll be fun to have someone in my class that's different."

"That would be me," agreed Misty.

"It's all great. You'll fit right in. I mean the rest of the school thinks we're a little off center as it is." Kelsey ran a finger through her red curls. "Of course we are, but that's not really the point?"

"No, I suppose it's not," said Misty. Smiling, she began to think that maybe, just maybe, this school wasn't going to be the nightmare she feared.

***

An hour later, the feeling hadn't gone away. Amanda Mattos, her English teacher, turned out to be not much older than the rest of the class. They had spent the time listening to her talk about the past year's triumphs and disappointments—it seemed that the latter outnumbered the former by a large margin—and her hopes for this year. Misty learned that it was her second year teaching, and that she still felt as if she were learning, and that the students would have to accept the fact that she didn't know everything, but that she would do her best to always point them in the right direction to find the answers.

Misty liked her after five minutes, and even seeing the course syllabus, which contained no less than ten major essays for the year, including one that was due the very next day, failed to dampen her spirit.

"It's a lot of work, isn't it," whispered Kelsey as they were walking to lunch.

Misty shrugged. "I like to read, and English has always been my favorite subject. Ugh! What is this traffic jam all about?" In the space of mere minutes the hallways had become jam packed with students on their way to lunch.

"Little known fact," said Kelsey in a mock-conspiratorial whisper, "the food's actually pretty good here. But sometimes the good stuff runs out."

"Oh, well that's a change." The pair managed to squeeze into the crowd and slowly inch their way outside and towards the lunch line. Once they got out the door it was like a dam breaking, with students scattering in all directions, some being forcefully expelled from the exit. "Not so sure if it's going to be that worth it, though," she added, rubbing a spot where an overly enthusiastic boy (probably a freshman) had nailed her in an effort to escape the mob.

"We'd better hurry," prodded Kelsey. "I'll introduce you to our crew."

"Sounds good. It'll be nice to meet someone else real."

Misty followed Kelsey across the quad and behind one of the buildings, where she saw a number of students playing, of all things, four-square. This version was played with a little more intensity and a lot more trash talking than the elementary school game Misty had grown up with. Moreover, this particular group seemed to defy the logic of high school: all four classes, freshmen through senior, seemed to be represented, and other than the freshmen receiving a greater amount of verbal abuse, it blended seamlessly.

At Misty's old school a group like this would have consisted of misfits, geeks, and social rejects. At least that was what she had believed, as she had never actually seen anything like this in all her high school days. But she counted two members of the football squad (they were wearing their jerseys), some drama students (wearing shirts from last year's musical), and a few definite slackers, along with a bunch of other normal looking teenagers, with a French foreign exchange student (still speaking French, which no one seemed to understand) thrown in.

Misty took it all in. "You have got to be kidding."

"No," answered Kelsey, breaking into her now familiar grin. "The sport has really caught on. We've got rules and everything."

How bad could it be? "Well, all right," Misty gave in, shrugging off her backpack and walking up to stand in the line.

***

"Come here, Niko, we've got to take just a quick walk," called Misty. Obediently trotting over, the large dog nuzzled up to Misty's hand, giving it generous licks with his wet tongue. "Gross! When are you going to stop giving me baths?"

In answer, Niko began circling her legs, shedding a prodigious amount of hair onto her new jeans, and barking with happiness at finally seeing his friend again.

Misty had never considered, as she had rushed off to school, that Niko would be alone for the first time in weeks. Well at least he didn't destroy anything while she was gone, nothing she could see at any rate. Absently, she stroked his fur, trying to put the day in perspective.

"I missed you too, furface," she said, "but we have to go now." It was true; for all of Ms. Mattos's coolness, she had been assigned a two-page essay entitled, "What is Man?" and it was due the next day. If she was going to finish it, she was going to have to forgo her usual trip into the woods.

"No, boy," she shouted after Niko. The Samoyed had automatically begun walking into the field, like he had done for the last several days now, having gotten used to Misty's habit of taking him into the woods that lay just beyond it. On some level the dog seemed to know that she was looking for something, perhaps that strange little

63

person they had run into before, and he had tried to help as best as he could, getting his big nose close to the soft earth, rooting for any unusual smells. He had found nothing, but his loyalty to his new friend never let him quit looking.

Instead, this day they walked down the road. It was a quiet street, and there were only five or six houses before it ended in a cul-de-sac, forcing then to turn back. Of course the distance between each of the houses was so great that it was quite some time before they were required to retrace their steps. On the way, Misty picked the blackberries that grew on the side of the road. Occasionally, Niko would whine softly for a berry, but the first and only time Misty had fed him berries, they had given the dog the runs, and Christina finally ordered Misty to leave him outside that night, just to stop him from constantly whining to go out and poop in the fields. She had learned her lesson after that incident, and steadfastly ignored his increasing attempts to cajole her.

"Fine, we'll go back home," relented Misty, throwing up her arms. This dog was too smart for Misty's own good. Niko had risen to his hind legs, having expended his range of vocal persuasion; he was now utilizing a trick that Misty had taught him, hoping to win the argument by offering her his front paws.

They finished their walk quickly, and Misty strolled resolutely into the house and straight to the office, promising herself no dinner until she had finished this assignment. While the computer was warming up, she pondered the question that she had been assigned. It was a silly one, actually: What is Man? How could she possibly answer that? After all, she was a woman, not a man. The whole assignment was sexist, actually. Briefly, she considered answering her essay from that point of view, but she realized that it was just an excuse to add space to her paper, and Ms. Mattos probably had a really good nonsense detector. No, for this one, she would actually have to think.

Two hours later, surprisingly, she was done. Time for dinner. Removing twenty dollars from a book—she had moved the freezer money into a book, because she had read somewhere that criminals don't read—she picked up her cell and ordered a pizza.

Her mother wouldn't be home in time for dinner anyway.

**

Christina came in at 10:30. She was hating Thomas Keller a little more every day, and hating her job right along with it, and tonight was no exception. Apparently, "Junior Partner" really translated to "Indentured Servant." Strange that she couldn't remember working this hard in the Bay Area. Still, she told herself, it was the price she paid in order to continue supporting her family; living in San Jose was just too expensive and the Portland opportunity offered better pay on top of a lower mortgage.

But it was times like this, watching her daughter brushing her teeth before going to bed, taking care of herself (and doing a good job of it, Christina admitted), that she found herself wondering if it was really worth all this, if the two of them couldn't have made their way just fine in the familiar place that held so many of their memories.

"Going to bed?"

Misty looked up, toothpaste foam oozing out of her mouth, and nodded before resuming a vigorous brushing. Every so often she would spit, and then she would brush even harder than before, never stopping to say anything.

Maybe this just isn't worth it after all. But what was she supposed to do? Misty had just had her first day of school, and to pull her back, to quit her job, well, it offered too many uncertainties. They would just have to make do.

"Goodnight, then," she said, turning to walk down the hall towards her own bedroom.

"Mom," said Misty, calling after her. Christina turned. Misty was wiping the remainder of the toothpaste from her mouth and chin with a towel. "It's alright. I'm alright, so don't worry any more. Okay?"

Misty sounded completely sincere, trying to put her mother's fears fully at rest. But Christina wasn't buying a word of it.

"Okay, honey."

***

The second day of school was much like the first, and the third was like the second, and so on, for an entire week, which thankfully only lasted four days. Misty did manage to get her Art class changed to Drama, and although she felt as if she had little, if any, dramatic ability, the hour spent with Kelsey and her offbeat friends was the moon and stars over her previous Nick-and-Briana heavy schedule.

Each day, she was obliged to walk Niko down the road, and the big dog soon became accustomed to this new routine; Misty's workload had not decreased with the ongoing time, and in fact Ms. Mattos seemed determined to teach them the whole of English literature by the Christmas break. While she found the young teacher's dedication sort of endearing in a silly, puppy dog kind of way, the nights of little

66

sleep were beginning to wear her down. Saturday, she promised herself, would be different; she would sleep in, and they would take a long walk, resuming their search.

***

"You have got to be kidding me," she said to no one in particular; her mother had already left, as was getting to be usual for her. "My first Saturday."

They (never just one person, this "they," but more of a collective voice) had told her that it was going to be rainy in the Northwest, really rainy in fact, but they never said it would be starting so soon. Should she ever find out the identity of "they," Misty promised herself, she would have a few words. It would start with an admission that they were right.

Stubbornly, she began to pull on her hiking boots, determined to go out into the rain anyway. If she was going to stop every time it began to rain, or got cold, it could be a good seven months before she had free time and agreeable weather actually converging.

"Come on, Niko," she said. Used to the new routine, the big Samoyed had started trotting down the driveway and towards the road. Now, seeing Misty moving towards the field, he quickly turned around and ran to catch up, tail wagging happily.

Misty smiled. "Just what I was thinking, fuzzball. Come on, I'll race you there." She broke into a sprint, racing across the muddy ground. Beside her, easily keeping pace, but unwilling to outdistance his best friend, Niko cantered happily, tongue flopping.

Despite the heavy rain, Misty managed to easily find her way through the dense foliage—most of it had already been pretty well flattened by her daily tramps—and only encountered difficulty when she first reached the deep ravine. Normally she would have had little trouble picking her way down the treacherous slope; she had managed the short jaunt several times now and, but for her first unfortunate fall, had made it to the bottom without incident.

The rain was changing all that.

"What do you think?" asked Misty. Niko, who couldn't understand a word she was saying, nevertheless managed to pick up her worried tone, as he was for once silent and still. "I guess we're going to have to try it anyway." She began to slowly make her way down, coming close to sliding on her butt for most of the way.

The rainwater had cut a deep channel into the ground and down the slope and much of the accumulated mud and slush was attracted to this ever-widening gash in the earth. Misty took care to avoid this as much as possible, while still staying near to her familiar route.

The way was treacherous. Branches and leaves that had before provided a measure of safety for the descent were now slippery with moisture and more of a hindrance than a help. Misty found this out when she grabbed for her first handhold, a root that jutted from the ground like a broken bone piercing the skin. Instead of steadying her, the slick root took on a life of its own and slipped out of her grasp. Misty barely had time to jam her hand into the muddy ground before she began an inexorable slide to the bottom of the hill.

Niko, with his four legs, low center of gravity, and absolute lack of fear or common sense had managed to make it to the bottom in his usual time and was now looking up at her, occasionally barking encouragement.

"Show off," muttered Misty, slowing her pace even more. At times it seemed as if she wasn't moving at all, for she was obliged from time to time to move more sideways across the hill than strictly down it. Her progress became something of a zigzag, where she descended by inches. She hadn't even thought of what it was going to take for her to make it back up the hill. As it was her boots were nearly covered with mud and would have to be cleaned off before she could get back into the warmth of the house.

Of course, if she had taken the time to think of that, she would not have begun this crazy journey in the first place.

"Burf!" Niko had been waiting for some time, rooted to the same spot, and he was getting anxious to get moving; there was still a great deal of puppy residing in his big body.

"Hold on, damn it!" shouted Misty, grabbing for another branch, this one appearing a great deal more reliable (less wet, at least, she thought) than the first root.

She was wrong. Before she had time to think twice about it, she had placed all of her weight and momentum, just for an instant, on this one branch. She had done this many times before. Now, with the mud and rain sucking at her, she was obliged to place far more strain on herself and the tree branch, in order to remain upright.

Snap!

The tumble lasted for a much shorter time than before, because she had less distance to go, but ended up making her far more muddy. This time she wasn't so lucky; there were no branches to shield her from the hard ground, just solid earth made slightly less solid by the rain.

Snap! Her landing might have been better this time, she realized through the pain. For whatever reason, she had failed to land on her rear but instead landed on her ankle, which promptly surrendered to the rest of her body and the laws of physics.

It was broken, and the only way out was up.

New Friends

"She is not a Fomorian."

"I can see that, Connell."

"Uncle said she was a Fomorian," said the first voice. It sounded as if it belonged to a young male, maybe a teenager.

"Our uncle has been wrong before," pointed out the other. It was a female voice, though with a pitch unlike any Misty had heard before.

She had been awake for several minutes now, but upon hearing the light footsteps around her she had played at being unconscious, unsure of who or what was approaching. It was a reaction more of fear than of anything rational, but it allowed her to overhear an incredibly interesting conversation, one that was becoming more and more interesting as time went on.

"Shall we heal her?" It was the first one, Connell, who spoke.

"Maybe," answered the female. "I will have to think on it. Eogan will probably be angry with us if we do so."

"Siobhan!" shouted Connell, though if it was a shout it was the quietest one Misty had ever heard in her lifetime. "We cannot just leave her here. Eventually she is going to get up and try to get out and then she is going to shout because she will not be able to climb back up and then someone, maybe that man and his son, will hear and there will be questions and people, a lot of people and…." He stopped abruptly, and even though Misty had her eyes closed she could imagine Siobhan holding up an index finger of warning; Christina used the same technique to get Misty to quiet down when she was getting a head of steam in an argument.

"Connell, you are being a little premature in your worry." There was a pause and the silence was so deafening that it threatened to flush Misty from her pose of unconsciousness. As it was, it didn't really matter. "Besides, she has been awake for some time now, and has likely heard much of what we have said. Is that not right, Misty?"

Screw it, Misty thought, opening her eyes. "Most of it, anyway." With her vision fuzzy from the pain, she couldn't see the speaker or her companion clearly. In any event, something else triggered an alarm. "How did you know my name?"

The figure—Siobhan, Misty supposed—laughed softly, reminding Misty of silver waterfalls, except that Misty had never been close to any waterfalls, much less silver ones. The closest she had come was Cathedral Falls, in Yosemite, and that had been far away indeed. In fact, the only waterfalls that stuck in her memory were the ones that appeared in her dreams.

But Siobhan's laugh, while not sounding a thing like running water, brought the cataracts of Misty's dreams to the waking world.

"We asked your friend, of course," answered Siobhan.

"He is really quite talkative," said the other, Connell. "For a dog."

Misty shook her head, clearing the last remaining cobwebs. Had she heard right? "Niko? Niko told you my name?" She looked over at the hound, who was all this time sitting patiently by her, tail wagging softly. "Did you develop speech while I was knocked out?"

In response, he pawed the ground, growling and tossing mud over his once-white coat.

Misty tried to get up, winced, and gave up. "Okay, okay, let's assume for a minute that I'm not just seeing things. How in the hell can you talk to animals? Has Dr. Doolittle been living in my backyard all this time?" Even to her, the jest sounded forced, but it was one of her bad habits: making stupid remarks whenever she felt out of her element, and there was no situation that qualified more than the one she was in right now.

"Who is Dr. Doolittle?" asked Connell. "Is he some sort of ranger?"

Misty began to explain, thought better of it, then burst out, "Forget it! Forget I said anything." The two little ones jumped back a little. For some reason her eyes hadn't adjusted to the dim light, even though they had been open for several moments. "My dog. How?" In her state of mind, it was a wonder to her that she was even able to get these questions out. Her ankle twinged with every little movement, and dogs aren't supposed to be able to talk.

There was a pause. Then Connell spoke again. "She is not a Fomorian, you know. It is probably safe to tell her."

"Probably," agreed Siobhan, but Misty could tell she was still hesitant.

Misty perked up; so she had heard right the first time. "You said Fomorian. I thought you did. No, I'm certainly not a Fomorian. No giant blood in me." She was rambling again, and forced herself to take a breath. "Does that mean that you two are Sidhe?"

73

The two jumped back, gasping in surprise. "Yes, we are," answered Siobhan, stepping away from the path and dragging Connell with her. Suddenly, Misty could see them perfectly. "You even spoke it correctly." Misty had pronounced it "she," and was glad at that moment for her mother's extensive dictionary.

She sat there, for what felt a long time, staring at the two. Later, she promised herself, she would take the time to accurately remember them, to describe them in her mind with as much detail as possible. For now, the only word she could find was "beautiful."

And they were beautiful, though not in the sense that people normally use. Theirs was the beauty of nature, of the forest, the meadows, the sparkling streams and brooks that crisscrossed this world, always running, always living, heedless of man.

Misty realized the truth of this, even as she was unable to find the words for the feelings that were pulsing through her heart.

"You are a curious one," said Connell at last. "Not at all like what I imagined."

"Do you mean that...."

"No, no," interrupted Siobhan, anticipating Misty's next question. "We are quite familiar with your people. More than familiar." She frowned, as if reliving an unpleasant memory. "But my brother and I have never actually seen a human before. I do not think that the day you frightened our uncle really counts, as we were unable to get a really close look." Siobhan dug her foot in the ground. "I am sorry. Fomorians we have seen. Our people have seen them, I mean. And because they have ever been our enemies, we know as well. I did not know that humans would look so much like them." She paused, then added, "To us, at least."

Misty was confused. "If you've never seen, uh, someone like me before, how can you know what I am?" she asked. "And if you knew people lived here, why would your uncle think that I'm a Fomorian?"

"We are here, and that means they can be too; it is his greatest fear, that they followed. As for humans, the stories are many," piped in Connell, and Misty got the feeling that such was a habit with him. Although he was taller than his sister, it was clear that Siobhan was the eldest of the two, and certainly the least impulsive. "We have heard many kinds of things about what went on in our homeland, but that was before we were born."

"What kinds of things?" asked Misty, immediately knowing after she had uttered the words that she shouldn't have said anything. But she was unable to take them back. Again, a flash of secret pain crossed the faces of her new companions. "Sorry, I didn't mean to pry." The apology didn't seem to help very much, and Misty wasn't entirely sure if the two had even heard it, because they seemed to be living in a different time at that moment, and she doubted that the time was a happy one.

Siobhan was the first to speak. "It is understandable, your question," she admitted. "May I just say 'bad things,' and ask you to understand. Humans and Fomorians have much in common." Misty nodded. "Thank you," she said. "It is why we have come here, you see, and we try not to talk of the reasons for our journey."

"I personally believe they were thinking that this was Tir Na Nog," said Connell with a small chuckle, indicating his return to good humor.

Several things were occurring to Misty at that moment. In no particular order, they were:

1. She actually knew what Tir Na Nog was.
2. She had by now completely gotten over her initial surprise at this meeting and had accepted the fact that tiny magical people were standing in front of her, and that they were having a conversation unlike any she had ever had.
3. Her ankle was still broken; she had not even gotten up.
4. Niko was barking.

Deciding to address the last issue first, she spoke up. "Someone's coming." There was indeed a rustling in the bushes, and the sound of voices. Familiar voices. "I think it's the Greens." Hadn't she told them not to come back? Well, policeman or not, she was going to file a complaint.

Connell cursed in a language Misty didn't understand, but felt she should be familiar with. Whatever it was he said, it didn't sound friendly. "Siobhan, what do we do?"

"I will take care of it," answered his sister calmly. "I think I have had enough of that man. He is too much like the ones in the stories. What shall it be, brother?"

"Something big, potentially harmful, maybe," suggested Connell, sounding hopeful.

Misty silently agreed.

"No, I am afraid not," Siobhan chided them both, reading Misty's eager expression all too easily, "However, I think this will do." She bent her head. Two seconds later, a loud groan of pain came from the bushes, followed by frantic running, and in a direction that led away from the four.

"They will be voiding for quite some time," announced Siobhan triumphantly. "Rather rapidly, actually." She could not quite keep the glee from her voice.

"Voiding?" repeated Misty, confused.

Siobhan arched an eyebrow.

Then it hit Misty. "Diarrhea! You gave them diarrhea?" she asked incredulously, thankful for the moment that she was already on the ground. If she hadn't been, her gales of laughter would have surely brought her down quickly.

"Is that what it is called?" asked Connell. "I have always wondered. It is not the first time we have used that particular trick. With those two it is always a bit more enjoyable." He sighed. "I suppose that now I shall have to give penance of some sort."

"Mine will be worse," pointed out Siobhan. "After all, it was I who caused it."

"Well, you are better at it that I am. That is not my fault."

"Perhaps if you studied more diligently," Siobhan began to argue. Connell's smile brought her up short.

"A lot of good it did you, now," he observed, smirking. "Still, we do not have to inform anyone of what occurred. It would just worry them anyway. And besides," he added, "then we will have to tell them about Misty, and they—,"

"—would only forbid us to see her," Siobhan finished her brother's sentence. "Fine, we will not tell anyone. But I will do a penance anyway. As for you," she shook a finger at her little brother, "try to at least pretend to feel a little bad."

Misty, who had never had a brother or a sister, could only sit and watch. Finally, she pulled out of it, remembering what she was going to say before her thoughts were interrupted by the intrusion of the Greens. "Tir Na Nog," she spoke up. "That's the Summer Country, right?"

They turned towards her once more. "You have an interesting way of moving from subject to subject," noted Connell. "Do you find it difficult to—OW!" Siobhan had slapped the back of his head.

"I apologize. That was rude, Connell," said the older sibling. "Misty, you are quite accurate. It has been called other things. Avalon, for instance."

"Arthur's Avalon?"

"Yes. You do know some things. However, I cannot tell you if they are one and the same, nor if Arthur is at this moment on Avalon." Siobhan allowed a bit of regret to slip into her voice. Then continuing on, she added, "We have never stepped foot on its shores, and if we had, we would never leave."

"Right," answered Misty. She knew this. She actually knew this. "You would never die there, but time passes so slowly, and if anyone leaves all the years just catch up to them, all at once."

"Again, yes," agreed Siobhan. "However, for the Sidhe this is not a real problem; we are not completely mortal. No, it is something different. Connell and I, and others of our age, the ones born here, were

78

told that we were supposed to be leaving our homeland for all time, to abandon this world and its people."

"What happened," asked Misty, so engrossed that she had totally forgotten about the pain that was still throbbing through her ankle.

"It is really quite amusing," said Connell breaking in to the conversation. At a stern glance from his sister, he rambled on, "Well, it is. Tir Na Nog is west of what you call the 'Old World,' so we came west. Apparently we missed and ended up here instead, a little bit ahead of your pilgrims, as it turns out."

"There were people here at that time," said Misty.

"Surely, but they respected us for what we were and they left us alone," countered Connell. "So our people continued going west until we ended up here, at the end of your continent, with nowhere else to go. Still," he added, indicating the trees with a sweep of his arm, "it is not a bad place to call home."

And despite missing her own home, her friends, and familiarity, Misty was beginning to agree. After all, what were the odds of meeting two magical beings back in the Bay Area? Interesting people, sure, but this was something completely different.

All that being true, she was still sitting on the hard, uncomfortable ground, which seemed to be getting harder with each passing minute. And she still had a broken ankle.

Well, if they could give people the runs, couldn't they also take care of her ankle as well? "Excuse me, but I have a problem." She lifted her leg for emphasis, and winced at the pain. Already the area around the break was beginning to swell. For all she knew she it could be bleeding internally, and that would be bad, really bad. What if they couldn't do anything? She would have to find her way out of here, and who knows how long she had been knocked out. She looked closer. Was that a bone sticking out of her leg?! Why hadn't she noticed this until now?

"It is only a stick," said Connell soothingly, reaching down to remove a branch that had tangled itself into her socks. "And I believe I can help you with your other problem. I get my skill from one of my great-aunts, but Siobhan is not so good at fixing things," he said in a conspiratorial whisper. "But her tricks are more amusing."

"I heard that."

Connell laughed, and though she was used to the sound now, it still carried chills through Misty's body.

"So this isn't a problem...oh!" Misty exclaimed, feeling a sudden sensation of warmth that began with her ankle and continued to spread across her body. Connell had finished doing whatever it was he had been doing, although if she were asked, Misty would have admitted that it hadn't looked as if he was doing a thing; he hadn't even touched her. Her ankle, though, was feeling brand new. In fact she could not remember it ever feeling better. "Thank you," she said. "What did you do?"

"It would be difficult to explain," answered Connell. Still, Misty could see that he was trying to search for the proper words.

"Did you just mend it?" she offered helpfully.

"Not really. It is more like a time shift. I can do it sometimes, with small things."

Misty was perplexed. "Do you mean time travel?"

Siobhan came up, offering a hand to Misty, who was still on the ground. Despite her small stature, her grip was strong and she seemed to have little trouble lifting the much larger girl to her feet. "Not really. Connell just brought your ankle back to a time when it was not injured."

"You have been hurt in that place before," said Connell. He was starting to look a little green, and Misty wondered how much energy his help had taken from him.

"Yes, five years ago. I sprained it pretty badly when I was ice skating. It's why I don't really like doing it," Misty admitted. Then a funny thought occurred. "Are you saying that I have my thirteen-year old ankle now?" She wasn't sure how she felt about her adolescence, but doubted that she needed such a potent reminder of that time in her life.

"No, the ankle is yours," said Connell, taking the time to sit on a nearby log. "It is just been wiped clean of its injuries. All of its injuries. I am sorry," he continued. "I have never had to do that with a human before. Uncle is surely going to suspect something." Niko had bounded up to the diminutive elf, and was now licking his face. Connell, instead of pushing him away, took the bath stoically, even reaching out and scratching behind the dog's ears. "That's a good cu," he whispered, leaning against Niko's ponderous bulk.

Siobhan sat next to her brother. Feeling the difference in their heights quite acutely now—the sitting elves barely came past her thighs—Misty lowered herself to the ground again, even though she had spent a good part of her day in that position.

After a moment or two of silence, while Connell tried to regain his strength, Misty spoke up, trying to change the subject. "You called Niko a cu? That means dog, right?"

"Correct," said Siobhan. "Actually the closest translation is 'hound.' It is rare for one of your kind, particularly a child, to possess knowledge of any Celtic words. "

"I'm not a child," said Misty, bristling at the implication. "I'm not any younger than you."

"I apologize then," said Siobhan calmly. "Connell has lived for 116 of your years, I twenty years more than that, and we will likely survive for many thousands more, assuming my brother does not manage to get us all killed."

"Hey!" Apparently, some strength was returning.

Misty blushed. "No, I'm sorry. I didn't know you were actually that old."

Siobhan shook her head. "No, it is I who should be sorry. I spoke in haste. Actually, Connell and I are among the youngest of our people, and we still have much growing to do before we are accepted as adult members of our society. So you are correct in your assumptions, in a way."

Misty changed the subject, anxious to put the issue behind them. These were the two most interesting people she had ever met, and she wasn't going to let her pride get in the way of a continued friendship. There was, however, a problem. "Your family isn't going to find out about me, are they?"

The two elves shook their heads again, this time simultaneously. "Not if we wish to ever leave the village again," quipped Connell.

"Yes, Connell is right," added Siobhan. "And we must ask that you tell no one of us."

Misty thought of Kelsey, and what a kick the flamboyant redhead would have gotten out of meeting these two, and nodded, disappointed. She was uncomfortable with keeping secrets but even she could understand what would happen if word got out that there were elves in Oregon.

This reminded her of something she had been meaning to ask them. "The Greens, they told me that I should keep out of here, that there was something. They were talking about you, about the Sidhe, right?" She shuddered inwardly at the memory of the two, so alike in their posture, their ridiculous Michigan Militia clothes, and the ominous rifles they carried, ready for instant use.

"Most likely," said Siobhan, "but we do not fear those two. They lack the necessary intelligence to find us, let alone dispose of us. As you can see, they have yet to even come near, and our village has much stronger magic to protect it than what I can produce. Only animals can ever find it. It was quite clever of you to have Niko here try to track my uncle, but we have been watching him from a distance. Eventually, I think, he would have been able to find us. It was only a matter of time."

"I wonder why those two never tried using a dog themselves," said Misty.

"They have," stated Connell gravely.

"I don't understand; where is the dog now."

"He is sitting right next to you."

Misty gasped. "Niko?"

**

83

When Christina came home that night she was surprised to see that Misty had not made dinner yet, though it was well past eight. Although she had been working very late hours for the past two weeks, it was usual for Christina to return home and at least find some leftovers in the refrigerator or the oven, waiting for her. Misty's fondness for making single course meals—spaghetti, jambalaya, and anything else that could be mixed together—meant that it was no trouble at all for her to make something extra, and her daughter had, so far, done so.

Cooking, Christina had long ago realized, was Misty's way of dealing with stress; for many weeks after her husband died, she had not had to cook a single meal for herself, as Misty had delved into the kitchen with a grimly focused determination, bent on baking, sautéing, frying, and boiling all of her pain away. Whether she had known it or not, Christina had begun to see this as normal, to expect it, to take it for granted.

Now, it seemed as if her daughter were entering a new phase.

"Honey, are you here?" she called into the emptiness. From the darkened office Niko came padding out to nuzzle his head against her hand. "Where's Misty, boy?"

"In here." The answer came from the office, but it didn't make sense for Misty to be in a dark room, even if she was on the computer.

Christina came down the hallway. "Isn't it a little dark in here? You're going to strain your eyes." She flipped on a light switch.

"Ow," yelped Misty, blinking her eyes several times, trying to get used to the bright light. "Oh, I was just doing some research, and lost track of time. I guess I just didn't notice it getting dark."

84

"It must have been something pretty interesting if you couldn't walk the ten feet to switch on the light," Christina noted. "Something for school?"

"Uh, not really," replied Misty evasively, "just something I wanted to look up. So, hey, how was work? Is that Keller guy making your life hell?"

Christina pulled up a chair, sighing in relief as she sank into it. "If only it was that simple. Sometimes I wonder if I made the right choice, bringing us here."

Misty turned around. Apparently she had finished with whatever it was she had been working on, and had shut the monitor off. "You did what you had to do, Mom. I don't think you could have done any better." It sounded sincere, and yet Misty had shown such a resistance to the move that Christina wondered if her daughter was just trying to placate her.

But these thoughts weren't doing Misty justice; she had to believe that she had raised a better person than that. Besides, there was as much of Carlos as there was of her in their daughter, and Carlos never told a lie, not even to make someone feel better. It was, she remembered, that quality that contributed the most towards getting him into trouble.

So caught up was she in her memories of her husband in his younger, careless days, that she almost didn't notice Misty getting up. "Oh, I'm sorry, dear. I was listening." It sounded lame even to her, and she desperately wanted to find something better to say.

"Mom, you were a million miles away," said Misty, correcting her. "Or a million years, maybe. It's alright." Leaving the office, she added, "I'll make dinner now."

She had not turned off the computer, and Christina wondered if that represented an unspoken permission of sorts. For several long seconds she sat, staring at the powered down monitor, wondering what had so wrapped up Misty's attention that she, always a stickler for schedules, would completely forget about the time. She was tempted to just take a quick peek, and she almost did. She was stopped by two things: the anger Misty would feel at having her privacy violated, and her fear of the thing Misty was apparently hiding from her.

"Oh, get a grip," she chided herself, embarrassed at her own overprotectiveness. "She's probably just IMing a boy." And that wouldn't be such a bad thing, she realized. It would signal a return to normalcy.

So she left the monitor untouched, making the choice to keep her curiosity on a short leash. And speaking of leashes....

"Hey, did you take Niko out today? It was pouring."

There was no answer from the kitchen, but she was sure that Misty had heard. Still, she repeated the question.

Misty came from behind the counter, colander in hand; she had been washing vegetables, but still managed to look guilty. "Yeah, he didn't mind." She went back to the sink.

Christina frowned. There was something fishy about that answer, but it wasn't going to do any good to bring it up now. Misty would say what was on her mind in her own time. She always did.

"Where did you say Niko came from?" asked Misty, coming out from the kitchen. Christina had moved into the great room and had turned on the television. As was usual for a Saturday night, there was nothing on.

She had been flipping through channels when Misty had asked the question, and she had to pause to recollect. "From the pound."

"I know he was abused," said Misty.

"We'd discussed the possibility, but we can't be sure, really. What makes you certain?" Christina asked.

Misty face went blank. After a moments silence she replied, "I don't know. Just intuition, I guess. He seems a little skittish sometimes. Around people."

Christina nodded. Even if the logic was sketchy, she had to agree. "Actually, I think you might be on to something. Have you seen where he sleeps?"

"All over, hasn't he?"

"Not lately," said Christina. "I've noticed that he's sleeping under my makeup counter." Christina and Misty had, since Carlos died, developed the habit of leaving their doors open at night. Christina felt that it made the two of them connected, even late at night, no doors between them. Niko, apparently a night dog, had wandered from room to room, sleeping in a variety of places. Lately he had been absent from Misty's room. Apparently he had found someplace he liked.

"I wonder why that is." Misty did not sound the least put out that Niko had seemingly chosen her mother over her. Perhaps it was because she had more time with him during the day, when they took their walks. Of course, Christina couldn't possibly know that Misty had other things on her mind. "Should we ask a pet psychologist?" she joked.

Christina laughed, the first real laugh that had come from her in a long while. "Actually, I think I have an answer."

"Yeah?"

Niko, perhaps understanding that he was the subject of the conversation, padded up, rubbing his ears against Christina's hand, and whining plaintively for a head rub. Christina obliged, massaging her hands through the thick white fur. "Remind me to wash my hands before dinner," she said. "Anyway, I read somewhere that abused children will sometimes seek a physical shelter, even when they're not threatened. It's some kind of safety valve for them; they just feel more relaxed with something over their heads. It doesn't even have to be anything particularly big."

"That's weird," said Misty, going back into the kitchen, apparently to keep dinner going. "We're having stir-fry, okay?"

"That sounds great," answered Christina. Then, because this was the longest conversation she could remember having with her daughter in a long time, she continued, "As I was saying, it's just a psychological thing, but I don't see why this wouldn't apply to animals as well."

Misty muttered something.

"What's that?" called Christina. "I couldn't hear you."

Misty reappeared, face red. "I said, 'What kind of bastard hurts a dog.' Sorry. About the swearing, that is."

"Don't apologize to me; I feel the same way. Your father would have too." Christina smiled, remembering a funny moment.

***

Later, after dinner, Christina asked "Did I ever tell you how he got his first dog?"

Misty looked up from her dessert. She was eating, as usual, Mint Chocolate Chip Ice Cream, and had added chocolate syrup. "We didn't have a dog," she said, confused.

"Oh, it was a long time before you were born. Before I met him, actually." She pulled out a chair, and tried to recall the story her husband had told her. "He was sixteen years old, had just gotten his license, and was driving down the street, not really paying attention to anything, when all of sudden he hears this yelp.

"He told me that he turned that car around so fast he nearly spun out. And there, not two doors down from where he stopped, there was this little German Shepard puppy running down the street, being chased by a man with a water hose."

Misty pulled up a seat next to her mother, entranced. "What happened then?"

"He got out of that car and knocked that man to the ground faster than you can blink, told him off good, picked that poor little wet puppy up, and drove off. It was the only time I had ever heard of him hitting someone, and I've never heard him raise his voice, not after I met him in college, and certainly not after you were born.

"So, he gets home, carrying that dog like a trophy of war, and tells his mother that he's going to keep him, and that his name is 'King.' And do you know what your grandmother did?"

"Tell him he couldn't keep it?" ventured Misty.

"No. Your grandmother loved animals more than anyone I have ever known. All she did," and Christina stopped herself, memories of her husband bringing forth both laughter and tears, both of which she tried to stifle. Finally, she gained control, and said "All she did was lift up that dog's tail and inform your father that he had better come up with a better name, because 'King' was a girl."

"That was Princess?" said Misty softly. She had known the dog, who was already very old by the time Misty was old enough to remember trips to her Grandma's, but she had never known how she came into the family. She had always assumed that her Grandma or Grandpa had gotten her. It gave her a warm feeling to know something about her father that she didn't before; it made her feel closer to him. "Mom?"

Christina turned towards her. She looked like she was about to cry. "Yes?"

"Daddy was a good man."

A lone tear crawled down Christina's face, eventually crystallizing into a shiny drop dangling from the edge of her chin. She did not bother to wipe it away. "Yes, he was."

***

Later that night, as Misty was trying to fall asleep, she was haunted by the images of Niko's life before being brought to her. She could only imagine the fear and suffering he went through while under the power of the Greens. It didn't surprise her that they had been unable to find a replacement animal yet; she had already begun to realize that in towns the size of Boring, things traveled fast in certain

90

circles. It was probable that the dog breeders in town had seen the signs and were avoiding the two.

These thoughts did little to calm her, or to help her sleep.

Niko padded into the room, his snow-white fur making him easy to spot in the near darkness. He wasn't the quietest of dogs, and Samoyeds weren't the best of trackers, built more for cold weather and affection than for hunting. It was a wonder that the Greens had kept him at all; perhaps they had started searching for Connell and Siobhan's village after they had already gotten him, and they were just trying their luck. Maybe they hurt him because he wasn't a good enough tracker....

"It's not your fault, boy," she whispered, reaching out. Sensing her hand, Niko walked towards her, darting out his pink tongue to lick her palm. After a short time, he trotted out of the room, making his way towards her mother's bedroom and the shelter of the makeup counter.

Misty was just falling asleep when a random thought crept itself into her brain. Niko. Nick.

Of course.

Secrets

"You're hiding something," said Kelsey, looping her arm through Misty's and dragging her to a nearby bench. "Oooh! Let me guess! You've already met a guy? Misty, you dog!" She made a ridiculous show of throwing up her hands in the air, attracting the attention of every student within a twenty yard radius, as well as embarrassing Misty.

Misty blushed scarlet; unlike Kelsey, who didn't seem to care what anyone really thought, she was still too self-conscious to feel totally at ease at her new school. It was only her second week.

She hadn't seen her friend all weekend, partly because of her adventure in the woods and partly because of Kelsey's work schedule, which tended to take up the bulk of her free time. Kelsey had told her on the previous Friday that she could only work weekends now that school had started, but that she needed the money.

"But you can't need that much," Misty had said at the time.

"I'm saving for something," Kelsey had answered.

"What is it?"

Kelsey averted her eyes. "It's for my family," she said softly. "But don't tell anyone, okay? No one knows."

This was the first time Misty had seen her friend as anything less than exuberant, so she didn't pry.

But despite this disclosure on Kelsey's part, Misty still couldn't tell her what happened. "It's a secret," she said, wanting nothing more than to tell her newest friend everything. Somehow, she got the feeling that Kelsey would understand, would not think that she was losing her mind. Perhaps it was because Kelsey's red hair reminded Misty of Ireland, the place she assumed Connell and Siobhan had come from— she was looking up Celtic names online that Saturday when her mother had walked in—or maybe it was just because the girl was genuine, and Misty had known for a long time how rare and special that was.

Kelsey sat back, taking on an exaggeratedly wounded pose. "Oh, well FINE, if that's how you want it." Despite the words there was no anger in her tone.

"I'm sorry, Kelsey. I really can't tell. But it's not a boy, okay?"

Kelsey shrugged. "It's okay," she said. Then, smiling again, she grabbed Misty's hand. "But you have to tell me when it is!"

***

"I have your first research assignment," announced Miss Mattos, writing furiously on the whiteboard. Already the description took up an entire panel, and the second was rapidly being filled. As the class groaned in unison, she continued, apparently unperturbed, "This will be worth 10 percent of your total semester grade, so I do recommend that you start on it right away. The due date is two weeks from today," she concluded. The class grumbled even louder.

Ignoring her classmates, Misty instead looked at the assignment. Written in bold black letters was the following:

Choosing an ethnic group different from your own, you must research the background of its major migration[s] to America, how it was treated upon arrival, and what literary contributions the people of this culture have made to this country. Pay close attention to the myths and legends of the

culture, as these often inform that culture's literature. Choose no less than two authors and their major works to study. In addition, locate an individual of your chosen ethnic group and interview them on their "American" experience. Page length: minimum 5 pp.

This shouldn't be too hard, thought Misty. Finding someone not of her ethnicity should not be a problem. In fact....

"Hey Kelsey," she whispered. "What are you anyway?"

Kelsey rolled her eyes and stared at the ceiling. Finally, she took a deep breath and began counting on her fingers. "German, English, a little French, I think, and Irish, of course."

"Perfect," said Misty. "I'll take the Irish."

"Really?" asked Kelsey. "Why that? I would think," and she began to speak in an outrageous accent straight out of Monty Python and the Holy Grail, "le français would be more, how do you say, apropos, n'est-ce pas?"

"Oui," agreed Misty. "But I want to learn about Ireland, you see?" adding an exaggerated Irish brogue to her speech.

"Oh, fine," relented Kelsey. "It's the part of me I know a little about anyway, even if my last name is Wagner."

Misty smiled. It was meant to be. And she had a feeling she knew where to get some really interesting information to add to her report. "And you can research me."

Kelsey returned the grin. "Deal. That was easy."

The classroom door opened, and at that time Nick and Briana entered the room, carrying what looked suspiciously like transfer slips.

Noticing Misty, they both gave her slightly ugly smirks and handed the sheets to Miss Mattos.

After perusing the papers, Miss Mattos spoke. "It seems that we have two additions to our class. Why don't you two take those empty seats," she said, indicating two chairs that happened to be uncomfortably close to Misty and Kelsey. Right behind them, in fact. Misty heard Kelsey curse under her breath as Nick and Briana sauntered over to sit down. Nick sat behind Misty.

Even without turning around, Misty could feel Nick's eyes bore into the back of her head and, reddening, she kept her eyes on her desk as Miss Mattos went about explaining the assignment in more detail and giving the newcomers a chance to write it down.

***

Every day that week, Misty and Niko made the climb down the hill to see Connell and Siobhan. After two days, the elves started showing up earlier, having figured out the vagaries of Misty's school schedule. They, having never in their lives gone by a schedule of any kind, were making a heroic effort to respect Misty's, and she felt grateful and guilty at the same time.

And every day that week the three talked about all kinds of things, while Niko wandered around looking for squirrels to chase. Misty learned that the elves never really slept, but spent every moment of their lives in a constant renewal with nature. She also learned that they could communicate with all animals (which explained their friendship with Niko), that they seemed to fear change, and that they would live to be thousands of years old.

Yet in all of these conversations she had not found the courage to ask them the questions she really wanted to, the questions that would help her with her report. There was something that closed up inside Connell and Siobhan, Connell especially, when the subject of Ireland had come up. Afraid to lose the most interesting friends she had, she had said nothing, and had relied on her conversations with Kelsey to help her fill in the blanks.

The problem was, other than her personal history, Kelsey was unable to tell Misty anything that Misty, through her individual studies, hadn't already learned. On the other hand, she was able to give Kelsey a great deal of information the other had not known.

"Oops. I gotta go," said Kelsey. It was the Saturday following the assignment, and the two had been talking of the Mexican-American War, and the fact that many Mexicans were already in California before it became part of the USA. The talk had run on, the time had gone quickly by, and now Kelsey was late for work. "I'll see you tomorrow," she called back, running out the door.

Watching her go, Misty realized at the end that she had given Kelsey a lot more than she had received. But there was no way for Kelsey to know that she was feeding Misty old information. Still, despite the disparity, Misty felt good about being able to help. If her mother had been here, and not at work (again), she could have really given some input. If her father was still alive, he could have written the entire report himself; he had been a fountain of information on his culture. But all Kelsey had was Misty.

***

"You're late, Wagner." It was Steve, the new shift manager, and he was already starting to throw his weight around.

"I know, I know," she called back, running to her locker in the staff room. "But it hasn't happened before, and it won't happen again. Promise."

"See that it doesn't," he replied icily, returning to pull the rest of the cash from a closed register.

The day did not improve from there. She was called to clean spills ten times, and was yelled at by an old lady who was still wearing curlers in her hair for being too slow in packing her groceries. After they were packed, she had to take the bags to the woman's car, a 1970s Cadillac that was taking up two spaces, being parked diagonally. After biting back the comments that were buzzing in her mind, she had to hurry back and start packing other people's groceries.

Her fifteen minute break had seemed like five, and during her lunch she ate so slowly that she barely had time to finish the peanut butter and jelly sandwich her mom had made for her before it was time to get back to work.

After lunch, she was training on a register. Her supervisor for this latest adventure in groceries, not Steve, was an equally obnoxious woman named Betty, proudly wearing a nametag proclaiming "Serving You Since 1972" and a thirty-year pin. Between actual instruction Betty took the time to lecture Kelsey on the continuing moral decay of America, and how it could all be traced back to the lack of respect that young people had for their elders today. If it wasn't so painfully sad, Kelsey would have found if funny that someone would try so hard just to make her miserable.

All in all, it was a pretty lousy day, and she still needed to get home so that she could get started on her English project, not to mention her Spanish homework, her Physics homework, and whatever else that came around the bend. Even Drama, her easiest class, wasn't letting up; she was supposed to memorize a soliloquy and recite it Monday.

"What does culture have to do with writing and reading anyway?" complained Kelsey, speaking to no one in particular. She had already launched her word processing program and was typing furiously. Now, I had better start with a good bit of filler. Of course, this was just to cut down on the number of pages she would have to fill with actual information. What a drag.

Still, Misty had given her a good bit to go on, and maybe that would be a nice place to start. Begin with a personal connection and all that. Teachers ate that stuff up. Sometimes they even overlooked lousy writing because they were so into the story.

"Way to go, Wagner," she said, merrily typing in Misty's background, what she had learned of it anyway. "Save all the good stuff for later," she muttered, "Gotta start with fluff." She began punching more keys, timing her work with the growing smell of sausage and mashed potatoes that was slowly wafting its way from the kitchen, across the dining room, down the hall, and into her bedroom.

Finally, it was too much to take any longer. "I'm done for the night!" she shouted, moving her cursor to the save button. "Oh, come on," she said, gritting her teeth. "You are so slow." Hmm. Maybe it's time to start taking off some computer games. Even saving a word file to the hard drive was becoming a big problem for her ancient computer.

Her desire for a machine that actually ran instead of walked, and perhaps even one day being able to afford one, was one reason she kept her job.

I have to ask Misty about Pancho Villa, she reminded herself, as she walked to the kitchen. I wonder why she hasn't asked me about any Irish folk tales. Oh well, she'll probably ask me later.

"Smells good," she said, sniffing appreciatively.

"It's going to taste even better," promised her dad, carrying a big ceramic bowl to the table. "My mom's recipe never fails."

Kelsey was ready to ask how her grandmother was doing when her mother came in. For some reason, Eve Wagner didn't like to talk about her mother-in-law. Kelsey always felt this was because Eve's relationship with her own parents was tense. While Kelsey knew that Eve loved her new mother-in-law and her new family that came with her, she could see that Eve also envied her husband for his good relationship with his parents. It was this feeling that kept Kelsey from talking about what had happened between her mother and her grandparents.

One day, she knew, she was going to have to find out everything about her family back in their homeland, even if knowing the truth left her hurt. She wanted so desperately to know how they were faring. Knowing had to be better than ignorance, right?

Speaking of ignorance, she often wondered when Misty was going to get around to letting her in on the little secret, the one that kept her friend busy every single afternoon. After all, walking a dog wasn't that much of a challenge. It was hard trying to imagine what could be so important that not even a hint could be given. Sure, they had only just met, but already Kelsey felt that Misty could be a best friend, that she had that potential. And that was weird as well; all she knew was that they were connected, and in a way she didn't understand.

***

Misty hadn't asked Kelsey about Irish folk tales because she had a more direct source. But even with this advantage, she was unable to gather any more information from her two new friends. Of course, she hadn't yet gathered the courage to ask, so that might have been part of it. After Kelsey had left, Misty had taken Niko to the forest, returning later that evening, question unasked and unanswered.

Still, she had to wonder, what could they possibly tell her that would be useful in a cultural study? It was doubtful that when Miss Mattos had asked them to research a culture that she was talking of non-human ones. Also, assuming that Connell and Siobhan were willing to assist her, and that was a big "IF," listing them as one of her sources would be a tricky proposition at best. The Modern Language Association didn't exactly have an example for the proper citation of elves.

***

Then, that Monday, Misty received a surprise.

"So, I was wondering if I could get you to help me with my project." The request itself wasn't odd; Misty was one of the few Hispanics at the school and had already received numerous requests for background information, so much so that she had had to limit the number of people she could reasonably help. She wanted to be friendly with everyone, but she was finding her new circle of friends, the Four-Square Club, an easy group to be with, and she didn't want to give up all of her lunch time. So she had come up with a simple system: she typed up a personal history and kept copies in her backpack for whenever anyone asked.

She just hadn't assumed that one of the people asking would be Nick Green.

She hesitated, remembering what Connell and Siobhan had told her, as well as Niko's reaction to Nick and his father that day in the forest. Finally, she gave in. "Here," she said flatly, pulling out another sheet and handing it to him; she didn't want to be the Queen of Mean, because Briana would be angry if someone else took her title. She, at least, was being consistent, taking time from ignoring Misty just often enough to make some scathing remark about what she was wearing.

"Thanks. I appreciate it," said Nick. He actually sounded sincere, and that threw Misty a bit off guard. "I didn't know what I was going to do."

Kelsey snorted; sitting next to Misty, she had heard every word. "Yeah, you might have, I don't know, had to do some work. What a freakin' tragedy that would have been."

Misty ignored her friend, though she silently agreed with her. "Sure, no problem."

The class went by uneventfully. Miss Mattos spent the hour discussing the Canterbury Tales; it seemed that she was focusing a lot on the dirty parts. For whatever reason, maybe because the room was full of teenagers, this strategy seemed to be working. At the end of the period she assigned a story to each student, and Misty was given "The Wife of Bath's Tale." Due to the size of the class, several tales had to be assigned twice, and whether out of sheer coincidence, or whether fate was trying to intervene, Nick received the same story.

"Great," said Nick, animated again. "Maybe we could work together on this. In the library, you know."

Misty blushed. Now that she had taken the time to notice him—it was the first time she had really looked at him alone, away from his father—he was kind of cute. "Sure," she mumbled. "Maybe."

Kelsey snorted again, this time sounding annoyed.

As the two were walking to lunch, Kelsey really let Misty have it. "Why are you even thinking about associating with that, that I don't know what?! The next thing you know Briana's going to come and join your little group, and we all know what a super person she is, don't we?" Misty began walking faster, and Kelsey trotted to keep up. "Don't you know his father is like the meanest guy on the planet? They had a dog once, and he used to kick it all the time."

"I know about the dog," answered Misty. She hadn't told Kelsey what she had found out from Connell and Siobhan. "But that doesn't mean that Nick hurt him, does it?"

"The fruit doesn't fall far from the tree, you know," argued Kelsey. "Officer Green isn't that nice a guy, from what I've heard."

"Well sometimes the fruit does fall far from the tree," replied Misty coldly; she was getting more upset by the minute. She couldn't imagine why she was defending Nick, after all. But the more she thought about it, the more she began to doubt her original feelings about the boy. Sure, he had said some pretty rude things the day they met, but that could have been because he was trying to please his father. Plus, the clothes he was wearing were almost new; maybe

Officer Green was just making his son come out with him. And Niko was growling, sure, but he could have just been growling at the dad, not necessarily the son. "God, I can't believe I'm actually arguing with you about this; it's not worth it."

But why I am trying so hard to find reasons to not hate him?

Kelsey relented. "You're right. I'm sorry about that. I know that it's just worry talking."

"Besides," said Misty, "there is NO way I'm going to help Briana out." She laughed. "But I doubt she'll have the guts to ask."

Kelsey nodded in agreement. "Yeah. Did you see the look on her face when Nick started talking to you? Green. Eyed. Monster. It was kinda worth him doing that just to get her upset," she reflected.

Misty smiled. "Okay, I'll admit that I enjoyed that a little bit as well. It's not like it's going to be any kind of permanent thing, anyway. I don't even know if we'll be meeting in the library at all. Miss Mattos didn't say it was a group project."

Kelsey, who understood a bit more than perhaps anyone gave her credit for, and was reading Misty's voice just right, only nodded. "I know, Misty. I'm sure this will come to nothing, and I have nothing to worry about."

Nothing at all, agreed Misty silently.

Something New

The week passed quickly. Every night, after finishing her other assignments, Misty wrote her paper. After the first bits of research it actually became quite easy, merely a matter of putting down what she already knew and adding whatever quotes happened to fit her descriptions. In the end, it was like all the papers she had learned to write before, and she assumed it would be like all the papers she would ever write after.

Largely due to Misty's assistance, Kelsey also managed to finish her paper in record time. Of course, since her friend had confessed that she normally began and ended an assignment on the day before it was actually due, Misty assumed that any finish time before Sunday night would amount to something of a record. Nevertheless, it made her feel good to be able to help.

The other difference was Nick Green. True to his word, he met with the two in the library. Kelsey had insisted on being there, "just in case," and spent the time with her eyes glued to the tall boy. Any time Nick tried to bring the conversation outside of the project, Kelsey made a bunch of irritated-sounding noises until he gave up trying. Misty didn't know whether to be happy her friend was looking out for her or totally exasperated at Kelsey's behavior.

Despite the tenseness of the situation, lessened somewhat by the fact of Briana's absence, they managed to get a good amount of work done, at least as much work as could be done in thirty minutes. So when Nick asked, quite politely, if they might meet again the next day, Misty could find no reason to object. The three met in the library every day that week.

On Friday, Misty found herself worrying whether Nick was going to ask to study with her over the weekend; study sessions at someone's house, during which studying rarely happened, were such a cliché, and besides, she could never shake the reality that Nick's father was a complete jerk, and Kelsey's warning that "the fruit didn't fall far from the tree" was never far from her thoughts. Fortunately, Nick told them that day that he had enough information, thanking Misty for her help.

Misty kicked Kelsey in the shins before the redhead could fire off a reply.

"Oww! Okay, I get it," complained Kelsey, rubbing the spot where Misty's boot had nailed her. Abruptly switching gears, and totally contrary to what someone might expect given the situation, including the fact that Misty was on the receiving end of many jealous stares lately (apparently, Briana and her clones did not approve,) Kelsey asked, "So are we going to hang out Saturday? I have the day off. I think I can finish this thing tonight. I really want to see your backyard." Misty had told her of her hikes in the woods, but not, of course, anything about the elves. "All I have is a jungle gym. A rusted jungle gym," she added mournfully.

Misty sighed inwardly. If she took Kelsey too far into the woods, Connell and Siobhan were sure to hide, but if she didn't go at all, they might wonder if anything was wrong. She had taken to walking there with Niko every day, and the big dog had quickly resumed the habit of leading the way, running headfirst down the ravine. Often he would be splashing in the water of the creek by the time Misty managed to make it down; sometimes Connell would be joining in his horseplay, splashing Niko and rubbing his belly whenever the canine rolled over. Whenever Misty got there, though, he would stop and the three would talk for at least an hour. Most of the time the conversations would be about Misty's day at school—a formality that the elves still did not fully understand—and occasionally the topic would drift off into discussions of their cultures. The elves found automobiles fascinating, and Misty found it equally interesting that Connell and Siobhan had spent their entire lives in an area not much larger than two miles square, and had no aspirations to go any farther.

Then there was the music: one day Connell had brought a curious instrument that looked like a cross between a flute and the bagpipes, and he played for Misty a song that still haunted her dreams with times she had never lived and places she had never been. Siobhan had told her it was the Lay of Cuchulain, an Irish folk hero. Misty knew of the person, had read about him several times in fact, but the song did not remind her of him. Instead, the plaintive, wailing notes that emanated from Connell's instrument reminded her of home. Not the Bay Area, but a home that was less solid, a place that she had never seen, but a place where she knew her soul would finally find peace.

It was a land she never knew existed until that day, and the knowledge that this truth was in her heart all this time, and that she never knew it, brought tears to her eyes. It was the first time in a year that she had cried for something other than her dad.

After that day, Connell was more careful with what he played, and although every time he brought his pipes Misty would beg him to play it for her again, he also played more rollicking tunes, inserting lyrics so bawdy that Misty had to hold herself to keep from shaking apart with laughter.

She treasured these times and knew, as the days grew shorter, that they too would diminish until the longer days of late spring and summer returned.

If she brought Kelsey the elves would not be there, and she would miss their conversation, as well as a possible chance to hear Connell's music, which was weaving itself more deeply into her spirit with every playing.

She hoped they would understand.

"Sure, Saturday sounds good," she said.

***

"The mall?" asked Kelsey dubiously, in response to a suggestion that Misty had given.

She had arrived at her friend's house early that morning, taking the time to share a Saturday breakfast. Mrs. Montoya was there, a circumstance that Kelsey had learned from Misty was rare. But she was dressed in her work clothes, which meant she wouldn't be staying long. Immediately after eating, Kelsey had wanted to know when they could hike around the woods; she had been looking forward to a nice relaxing walk all week, and knowing that Misty took Niko out every day it seemed only natural that Misty would agree.

Apparently, Misty had other plans. "Yeah, I need to pick up some winter clothes. San Jose can get a little cold, but it doesn't snow there. I thought that I had better pick up a heavy jacket or something like that."

"It doesn't snow that much here, either," said Kelsey. "Unless you go into the mountains. Do you ski or something?"

"Yeah, that's right," said Misty. "I need to get some skiing clothes, for when it starts to snow in the mountains."

Mrs. Montoya started to say, "Misty, you don't…," but was cut off by a sharp look from her daughter.

Kelsey noticed the interplay between the two, and figured it was something personal. Letting it go, she decided to give in. "Fine, we'll go to the stupid mall. But not too long, alright? I don't want to run into Briana and her clones," she said. She flipped her hair and, in a perfect imitation of the Briana's snobbery, said, "I really don't know what business we have there anyway. After all, shopping is serious."

The duplication was so spot on that Misty had to swallow her milk quickly before she laughed so hard it came out of her nose.

"I'll drive," she volunteered.

Kelsey shrugged. It didn't really matter to her. Someday she would get to hike with her friend, though for the life of her she couldn't say why that was so important, and why it had to be in Misty's backyard. Maybe if they hurried they could have a couple of hours before sunset.

"Fine," replied Kelsey. "Then let's get a move on."

***

"Why does this always happen?" asked Misty in despair.

Kelsey walked over to Misty. She had been busy paying for her latest purchase, a huge bag of bulk candy. "How many times have you been here?" is what she meant to ask. But with her mouth completely full of Gummi Bears, it came out as "hw mnzy imes haz you beenz hr?"

108

Misty understood anyway. "Only twice, but I'm beginning to think that this might be a regular occurrence."

Kelsey choked down the last of the candy. "Well, I've heard it on good authority that Briana does live here." She sniffed. "Her dad gives her so much money I don't know what she would do with it if it weren't for this place."

"Still shopping at Abercrombie, I see," said Misty. "Tends to follow the trends, doesn't she?"

"Yeah," agreed Kelsey. "But if you ask her, she'll tell you that she's setting them. Her entire family's like that. I heard that her older brother practically bought the entire Banana Republic store one time. Of course, that was when BR was like a safari place, with lions and tigers and jeeps all over the store."

Misty allowed her friend to ramble on, grabbing her by the hand and moving towards the sporting goods store. If she was going to stick to the skiing story, she might as well buy some actual skiing equipment. Christina, whether out of guilt for never being home more often, a larger paycheck, an actual desire to see her daughter in snow, or a combination of the three, had given her a large amount of cash.

It was time to go spend it.

* * *

"Well, if you're planning a trip to Everest any time soon, I think you're pretty well prepared," quipped Kelsey. It was several hours later, and with Kelsey making a great show of tiredness, the two finished dragging the last of the bags from the car and into the house.

Misty put her own packages down and glanced at the clock. Although she had managed to stretch out her search to three hours and four different stores, "looking for the right color," not nearly enough time had passed for her to put off Kelsey's desire to hike in the woods. Praying for rain on the way home hadn't worked either. She was going to have to come up with something new, or hope that Kelsey had forgotten about the whole thing. Considering her friend's single-mindedness at times, it was doubtful that this would happen.

Sure enough, "Hey, we still have time to take that walk." Kelsey stared hard at Misty, eyes artificially wide, daring her to try and find another excuse.

Misty almost attempted one; she could have shown Kelsey the website she had found on Celtic culture, the same one she had been looking at when her mother had come in on her a week ago, but Kelsey had emphatically stated that she didn't want to deal with anything remotely related to their project this day. She could have suggested a blackberry picking walk down the lane, but even though she never thought this would happen, she was actually starting to get sick of blackberries.

She had pretty much run out of excuses.

"Okay," she relented. "But let's eat first. We might be out there for a while." With luck, a long lunch, and a really roundabout route, maybe she could avoid taking her friend down the ravine and into her secret place.

As usual, Niko had other ideas. The minute Misty and Kelsey emerged from the house, he began spinning in frantic circles. In fact, he had been waiting outside for the past hour, and Misty knew he was anxious to go play with his new friends. Well, play around them was probably a more accurate term. Sure enough, he started bolting for the fields within seconds, and Misty and Kelsey had to run to keep up.

"Thanks, furball," gasped Misty between breaths.

"Oh, man, this is going to be so cool," chattered Kelsey happily, seemingly unaffected by the sprint Niko was forcing them to keep up. "I've never really known anyone with their own private woods, you know. Every time I go hiking there's always these different people there, and this time I know that we're going to be totally alone. That must be awesome."

Not totally alone, Misty thought.

"So how do you keep up your strength?" Misty asked. They were perched on the edge of the ravine. Niko had led them all the way there, at a breakneck speed, and was already down the slope, barking loudly. For some reason, he seemed more anxious than usual to make it to their spot. Misty had let him go, and spent her time catching her breath from the sprint. The colder air that was coming with autumn was not being kind to her lungs. Despite all this, Kelsey had never broken a sweat, and had managed to talk animatedly all the way. Granted, it wasn't much more than a quarter of a mile, but it was a dead run and over broken ground.

"Dancing," answered Kelsey, waiting patiently by the side of the ravine. "What's gotten into him?" she asked. "Found a squirrel or something."

"Something," said Misty. She moved back to her original question. "What, like dancing in your room or something. I do that sometimes," she admitted.

"No, ballet."

111

Misty was flabbergasted. "Really? I mean, I never thought, uh, never mind," she finished lamely.

Kelsey turned around; she had been looking down the slope, apparently trying to find out how far down it really was. "What's that supposed to mean?" she asked. When Misty didn't answer, but instead turned bright red, she continued. "Oh, come on. I'm just giving you a hard time. No one ever thinks that I can dance. But look at this," she said. Closing her eyes, she brought her right foot slowly up, angling it so much that she was able to grab it with her right hand, with room to spare. Then, lifting her left hand languorously above her head, she performed a neat little twirl, turning a complete 360 degrees (slightly hopping) and returning to the same position.

Misty was impressed, even more than normal considering that her friend had managed to do it not on the smooth surface of a dance studio but the gritty dirt of the outdoors. "That is so cool," she gushed. "How long have you been dancing?"

"Twelve years now," said Kelsey. "I'm not really sure why my mom signed me up anyway. I think it was just to keep me from tearing up the house. I was a rambunctious kid," she admitted.

Misty smiled. "Really?" she drawled. "I just can't see it."

"Oh shut up!" shouted Kelsey, playfully pushing her friend. "Anyway, I can see that you're all caught up." It was true; Misty had indeed caught her breath, but was hoping that the conversation would last a little longer. She found herself truly interested in finding out new things about her friend, and it also just so happened to be a really good way to waste time.

But she relented. "I'll go first," she offered, picking her way down the slope. After so many trips, the descent was almost second nature to her, but remembering her earlier falls, and knowing that Kelsey, despite any risk, would try to keep up, she slowed her pace, noticing with some worry the broken branches that showed where she had taken her tumbles. "We're almost there," she finally said, after ten minutes of careful picking down the hill.

"Niko got there fast enough, didn't he?" said Kelsey.

"Well, he knows the way, and," she added, before Kelsey could point out that Misty also was very familiar with the path, "he's got four legs, and a lower center of gravity."

Behind her, Kelsey said nothing.

***

"We've gone over this before, Mr. Keller," said Christina, pointing out the obvious, and rapidly losing her patience. "You'd have every environmental group all over you."

"Don't care," said Keller, nonchalantly taking another puff on his cigar. "That's what I pay your firm for, to keep those tree-huggers off my back." He leaned back, looked over at Charley, who was beginning to sweat, and winked.

Christina gritted her teeth. Ever since she had come to Oregon, Thomas Keller and his needs had taken up every minute of her professional time and a lot of her personal time as well; she couldn't remember when she had last had a good night's sleep or had a real conversation with her daughter, one that didn't involve some superficial happenings at school, or whatever assignments Misty was working on. She supposed that if she was working on something meaningful, it might have made up a bit for this loss, but fighting for this man's right to destroy a virgin forest, one of the habitats of the endangered spotted owl, so that the tenants of his new luxury estate could have two golf courses instead of just the one was lacking in any kind of meaning whatsoever.

She tried another tack. "This forest provides a vista for hundreds of homes, homes owned by rich people." She hated using this argument, but an appeal to money was the only thing Keller apparently understood. "They're going to fight you, and they could tie this project up in the courts for years," she pointed out, hoping that the stubborn man would see that a lengthy court battle would cost him too much.

Mr. Keller just sat there, leaning back and puffing on his cigar. Christina found herself making a silent prayer for his odious smoke to trip the alarm and thence the sprinkler that was right above his head. But he had been smoking since he had gotten there, and thus far there were no waterworks.

There was just no justice.

***

"All right, we're here," announced Misty.

Kelsey took a look around. She looked unimpressed. "This is your secret place, huh?"

"Yeah, it's where we go," said Misty, indicating Niko, who was splashing in the creek, an activity he did often, and had been doing the moment he had arrived. He never found anything, but that never stopped him from sticking his nose into the wet crevices formed by the many rocks that lined the creek bed. "Sometimes, it's just good to be alone."

"Ain't that the truth," said Kelsey. Taking a seat on a log, the very log that Misty had sat on the first time she had talked with Connell and Siobhan, she closed her eyes and took a deep breath, as if she were storing some of the place in her soul for later use. "So what do you do when you get here?" she asked.

Misty swallowed, racking her mind for a believable answer. "Not much," she finally said. "I found this place by accident." No truer words than that for sure, she thought, grateful that she could add some truth to what would inevitably be a cover-up for her true reasons for coming. "Niko seems to like it here," she continued, pointing to the Samoyed, who had his entire nose buried in the running creek and was extricating his head every so often, just long enough to take a breath, and give a loud bark or two before sniffing after whatever it was that got his attention.

Misty ignored him for the moment (he never caught anything anyway) and rambled on, including details of her first fall and how landing on her butt had probably saved her life, hoping that the sound of her own voice would inspire her to come up with some better story. "Anyway, he keeps leading me here," she said, again including as much of the truth as she could, "but I just sit here and wait until he's ready to go home." Suddenly she stopped, aware that Kelsey had clearly lost interest, and was just being polite now.

"I can see that he likes it here," noted Kelsey. Niko had since moved on, and was now barking at a bush.

Praying that it wasn't Connell and Siobhan that had so attracted him, she called "Niko!" and he immediately came trotting over.

"I wonder what it is he's found," said Kelsey, moving towards the bushes.

Misty practically had to stop herself from tackling her friend. "No! Don't." Seeing Kelsey's bewildered look, she continued talking, making it up as she went along. "There are skunks and raccoons around here. You don't want to startle one. I just took a bath."

Kelsey turned around, suspicion in her eyes. "What's gotten into you, Misty? You've been all jumpy ever since we got down here. Are you meeting your secret man soon? Is that him in the bushes?" she asked, playfully, moving towards the greenery again. "Come on out, you big stud. It's about time Misty introduced you to me."

Niko whined.

"I told you I don't have some secret boyfriend!" shouted Misty, hoping to distract Kelsey enough so that she would forget about the bushes.

It worked. "Jesus, I was just joking around. Of course I don't want to scare some skunk. Do you think I'm a halfwit or something?" When Misty didn't answer, only shaking her head silently, Kelsey said, in an angrier tone, "Well I think it's pretty obvious something has you upset. When are you planning on sharing it with me?"

Misty stood up, trying to remain calm. "I don't know what you're talking about. Maybe it's just Nick and how weird he's been acting lately."

"That's a good story, but I'm not buying it," said Kelsey, growing visibly angry. Then, after reaching down and tightening her shoelaces, she abruptly started climbing up the slope. "Friends don't keep secrets, Misty. Sorry, that's just how I work." Grabbing a tree root for support she pulled herself up the first few feet, grunting with the effort. "Maybe you don't trust me enough. I don't blame you. We've only known each other for a couple of weeks." She had already made it up a great deal, and was speaking louder so that Misty could hear. "Still, I thought that we had a connection. Guess I was wrong."

And then she was gone, clambering out of sight. Misty stood there, uncertain, and watched her leave.

"That's not fair, Kelsey," she finally said, but her friend was already gone.

***

"Of all the nerve," muttered Kelsey, revving up her car, a used station wagon her mom had given her as a birthday present. The car's engine complained at first, and then finally gave in with a sputter that sounded like it was giving her a raspberry. Shifting into first, she continued her litany. "I would tell her if something was up. I know I would."

Ignoring the scenery offered by the bucolic country road, Kelsey let her mood darken even more. Appropriately, as if the weather were reading her thoughts, the skies above began to darken and soon, before she had even reached the main part of town, a steady rain was pelting her windshield. She waited for several minutes before activating the wipers, and when they finally began to clear some of the water from the glass, she sped up to an almost dangerous speed.

The rain continued to hammer down, making insistent tapocketa-tapocketa sounds on the roof of the car, and eventually Kelsey slowed down, common sense beginning to regain control of her emotions. Absently, she turned on the radio. It was permanently set to

Portland's only real alternative station, and she allowed the music of the Smashing Pumpkins to rattle around in her head for a while. In front of her, a minute tongue of lightning flicked the ground, and several seconds later thunder reverberated around her, blending with the music to create a new type of symphony. It matched Kelsey's mood perfectly.

"I don't know why I'm so worked up," said Kelsey, again talking to herself. "What could she really be hiding in the woods anyway?"

As another song played, followed by the obnoxious afternoon deejay rattling off his latest opinions on Nirvana clones, Kelsey began to tune out and focus more on her latest question. After a while of calm thought she began to realize that she may have acted a bit rashly, perhaps immaturely.

"And wouldn't that be a first," she muttered, getting angrier with herself by the minute. "Well, it's coming down hard anyway; I hope Misty got home before it started pouring."

***

Misty let the rain dribble down her face. The thick tangle of trees above her protected her somewhat from the full fury of the downpour, but enough was still penetrating so that her clothing was entirely soaked. Niko had ceased his playing in the water, and was now sitting next to her, whining mournfully and looking as miserable as, well, a wet dog.

It looked like they weren't coming.

"Fine, we'll go." She slowly got up and began to slog through the mud. She didn't even want to think about how she was going to get up that hill.

"I do not think you'll make it."

Misty turned around, catching her breath. Why was it always so easy for those two to sneak up on her? Sure enough, Connell and Siobhan were standing not more than three feet away.

Misty noticed that their clothing appeared to be completely dry, even though the rain was managing to really burst through the trees now. She also saw that they were frowning deeply.

"I know, I know," she said, putting up her hands to ward off any words of theirs. "She was really bugging me to come here, so I had to do it. Besides," she added, grappling for an argument that would make some sense, "I knew that you'd see her and just stay out of sight."

"That is true enough," admitted Connell, "but of all the people that you might have brought with you, why did it have to be that one?"

Misty stepped back, offended. "What's that supposed to mean? I know that I've only known Kelsey for a little while, but she's harmless."

"She is NOT harmless!" shouted Siobhan, on the verge of tears. "And if you knew anything at all, I would think that you should at least know that!"

"Well I don't!" Misty shouted back, getting more and more upset, especially at what was clearly, to her, an unwarranted condemnation of her friend. "And I don't see how you should expect me to."

Connell placed a calming hand on his sister's shoulder, and she seemed to relax somewhat. "Siobhan, how can she know?"

"She knew that she was Irish, right?" asked Siobhan, her glare daring Misty to try and deny it.

119

"Of course I did," retorted Misty. "I used her for my report, after all." She moved towards Siobhan then, kneeling down, affected by how much this was all upsetting the elf. "Siobhan, what's wrong?"

For a time, Siobhan said nothing. The Sidhe was clearly trying to regain control of her emotions. Her shoulders, which had been shaking violently, were starting to slow down in their heaving, and her breathing was less ragged than it was a minute before. Still, Misty could see that the elf was struggling with a deep issue, and she didn't want to press any further. Just as Misty was about to reassure her, to tell her that she really didn't need to know anything, Siobhan spoke.

"Connell is too young to remember our grandfather," she began, taking her brother's hand gratefully, "so he does not know the stories. I think that I will tell you what I have learned, from his mouth, in his words, and in his time.

"Elves are very much a part of the land," she explained, again lapsing into that singsong tone she took whenever she was regaling Misty with other tales of the Sidhe. This time, though, a sadness was woven into nearly every word, and Misty knew that this story would be different. "It has always been this way, and this bond with the earth is what feeds us, and what binds us.

"Once, things were different, the ties were stronger, and each of the Sidhe, from the time they first come alive to the time they lay down the burden for all time, had a special place in the land. It is not like today, not exactly like today. Do you understand?"

"Not really," said Misty, now totally ignoring the rain that pitter-pattered on her soaked hair. Even Niko was sitting quietly. "Tell me more."

120

Siobhan shook her head. "No. I will have to do more than that. I will show you." She took Misty's hand, and took up her narrative again.

And suddenly, Misty was there.

***

Eogan loved his tree, but it was not the typical love that elves had for the trees that were given to them to watch over, nor was it the love that the dryads had for the trees—outside of the borders of elvendom—that fell to them to safeguard. No, the love that Eogan had was purer, he liked to think.

This tree was special, for he had made it his own. From the roots that dug deep into the dark, nourishing soil, pulling all manner of nutrition and sustenance from the rich earth, to the tips of every branch and every leaf that clung tightly to those branches, drinking in the sunlight all the year long, this tree was as much Eogan as it was a tree.

It had existed long before he had come into the world, was already quite mature by the time he had been chosen as its new guardian, his grandfather, the previous guardian, having departed to the Summer Country. And though it was strong it still needed him, in more ways than Eogan at the time could have truly imagined.

So he had begun the slow, patient process of molding his tree into a shape that fit their spirits, their souls becoming more intertwined with each passing year. Unlike his grandfather, Eogan spent countless hours within a close distance, sometimes even sleeping in the cradle of the strong boughs that reached out into the night sky, and sometimes resting his head against the solid trunk that had fixed itself into the ground. He would light his pipe and the ashes would burn amber as the sun began its inevitable westward fall.

These are special days, he would often muse, taking contentment in the simplest of acts, from the gentle flutter of butterfly wings on a spring day to the crackle of golden brown grass on a cool autumn evening. These days would come only once, and that was a truth.

For already he could see the signs. The coming of man, not so very long ago, as the earth measures time, had begun to take effect. The quiet, brooding farmer who sprang up to wrest a livelihood from the green hills of Erin, was changing. No longer content with his lot, he was starting to branch outward, at the same time creating walls of stone to surround that which he had already acquired. And though they were pitiful things, these early boundaries, with each subsequent year the division of the land became more prominent.

Eogan looked over the fields that bordered the ancient forest, at the hillocks in which his people lived. For a time, the humans had seen fit to model their own dwellings after the fairy mounds of the Sidhe. But that was changing, too, and soon enough they would turn their eyes to the forest and see it not as a place of mystery and a picture of the divine but as a source of that all important resource: lumber.

He took a deep draw, allowing the smoke to escape by inches from the corners of his downturned mouth. Indeed, things were changing, and as with the great majority of change, he saw little good coming with this one. Even the young ones could sense it; the play in the woods, the fields, the silent shadowed valleys cut by little brooks, was diminishing, and it was a rare thing now to hear the laughter, once so common it was part of the wind itself, of an elven child.

It had started with the Fomorians, or more accurately because of them. For generations untold, the Sidhe and the giantkin had been in constant conflict, brute strength against fey magic, and it had not been going well. Thus, when man first made landfall on Erin, the Sidhe, who had never before welcomed anything or anyone, called upon the newcomers to aid in their struggle, promising friendship and eternal thankfulness in return.

The men had done their job well. Hundreds of years later, to see one of the great lumbering giants was a near impossibility. The Sidhe had thought themselves fortunate.

They could not have been more mistaken.

Things started out innocently enough. The humans, fresh from assisting their new friends, had not asked for much, just a little land to get started, to make a life. Grateful, the elven kingdom had willingly granted all that they asked for, and more.

So the humans asked for a little more. And after a time they stopped asking.

And now it was too late. Eogan frowned deeper, and his tree, feeling his distress, rustled mightily.

"Be calm," whispered Eogan, forcing his bitterness to recede. "It is not time yet. Not yet. We have a moment more." Above him, the branches ceased to rustle. Eogan, though, could find no surcease from the ache in his heart. "It will come, though, and sooner than I would have wished." He sighed, a heavy thing. "We cannot stop the passage of things." He sank deeper into his connection with the living breathing being that towered over his head and tunneled deep channels under his booted feet.

He found himself thinking of his daughter and her newborn son, also named Eogan. For a long time he had known they were leaving, would have no other choice, and this child would never have the honor of watching over his own tree. He could not say how he knew this. He was one of the few gifted with The Sight, and the receiving of this blessing, or curse, remained a mystery even to the elves. He knew it, though, as sure as he knew the sun would rise in the morning.

And he knew that tomorrow it would rise on a different world.

Someone was running through the tall grass. He could hear the person gasping for breath with each step. He knew what was happening but hoped, as he had always hoped, that he was mistaken.

"Eogan, you must come!" It was Diahan, the headmistress of his clan. Her dress, woven from the fibers of discarded caterpillar cocoons, was beaded with her sweat and her face was damp with the exertion.

Eogan got to his feet quickly, moving fast for one of his age. "I know, my dear," he said. "It is happening."

"All this time we had hoped you would be wrong," she said.

Eogan looked at her, pityingly. At five hundred years of age, she was young to be the headmistress, but her husband, who had guided the tribe with wisdom for many long years, had perished on the tusks of a wild boar, so mad with frenzy it had failed to respect the connection that it, as a beast of the forest, had with the Sidhe. So it had fallen upon her to lead the clan, and she had done the best she could.

"I know. Myself as well," he answered. "But the preparations have been made, so we are not caught unawares."

"All is in readiness," confirmed Diahan. In the presence of Eogan, a respected elder of the clan, she had calmed down considerably

124

and was now moving with her customary purpose. "I decided to fetch you myself. I knew that you would be here, that you would want to say goodbye." She looked at Eogan, then, with a cry of regret at the realization of what this separation would mean to her friend, she looked back at his tree, already falling into the distance.

Eogan took her hand. "I know, young one. But you must not be sad for me. I have seen this day coming for many years now, and I have already said farewell to my oldest friend." Despite his reassurances, uttered mainly to comfort the distraught Diahan, the thought of parting from the tree, his tree, and the knowledge of the fate that awaited it in the hands of the humans, hit him like a blow to the chest. He tried to hide it. In an artificially merry tone of voice, he continued, "It is time for a new place, for stranger skies after all. We have been on Erin for so long."

Diahan looked at him questioningly, "Tir Na Nog is not so different from this place," she said.

Eogan smiled. "Of course, you are correct." He said nothing more.

For he knew, even as the others could not, that they would not reach Tir Na Nog.

An hour later, the sun completely gone, the last of the Sidhe left Erin, never to return.

Eogan spent his days at the rail of the white-sailed vessel, staring at the endless sea. After a time, when all that could be done for the voyage had been done, Diahan joined him.

"What do you see, elder?" she asked.

Eogan smiled. He had decided long ago not to tell her what awaited them at the end of their journey; somehow, it would take the adventure out of it. Instead, he spoke of what was to come in the land they had left behind.

"Hundreds of years from now, there will be tales of the little people. The humans will tell their children that if they catch one, they can get a pot of gold. They will never find any. Our homes will crumble to mere curiosities in a land full of them. The fairy mounds will lose their magic. Soon enough, the people will find their own explanations, or they will create them. Our history will be wiped away, to be replaced with murky legend, and no one living will have seen or heard of the Sidhe. That is how they do things.

"For it is their curse that they forget."

He waited, gathering his strength for the final prophecy, understanding the sacrifice it would require. "And we will forget as well. We will teach our children to fear all that is not of the Sidhe. We will tell them of the Fomorians, who are now gone, and we will forget the humans, as best as we can.

"For how else are we to survive?"

***

"Your friend is one of them," said Siobhan. "The blood of the men who stole our land, who burned our forests, and who forced us here, runs through her veins."

Misty could say nothing. She was horrified, and utterly, utterly, sad at the same time. Beside her, Niko, who had sat patiently as his master seemed to go somewhere else, whined in concern.

"Siobhan, it was a long time ago," said Connell quietly. Despite his attempt to comfort his sister, he sounded upset himself.

Misty found her voice. "I thought Eogan said that you would only learn of Fomorians, but you knew I was human, the day you found me."

"Our uncle is named Eogan. His grandfather is the one whose eyes you saw through. And what he said did come to pass," Siobhan explained. "The tales are still told of the Fomorians. However," she continued, "I have a gift, much like our great-great-uncle did. He was able to see the future; I am able to see the past."

"So that was how you managed to send me there," said Misty. "It was so real. I could feel his heart breaking." The memory of the event stopped her breath for a moment, and she took some time to bring herself back together.

"Yes," said Siobhan. "And what I learned I have shared with my brother. We two are the only elves our age who know of the humans, or so we believe, and we have always managed to keep that hidden until now. Only Diahan remembers Erin as it was. Our home is lost to us."

Overwhelmed by the reality of it all, Misty sank to her knees, and spoke the only words she could think to say. "I am so sorry."

They didn't seem nearly enough.

Still. "I have to tell her something," said Misty. "I can't just pretend that nothing's going on."

"I do not expect that you could, Misty," answered Siobhan, all serenity again. "But you seem to be quite resourceful; surely you will think of something."

And with that she took Connell by the shoulder and guided him back into the brambles from which they had emerged. Soon enough, they were gone from sight, and the sound of their footsteps faded away.

"One of these days, I'm going to have to figure out how they do that."

***

The next two months seemed to pass in an eyeblink, and Christmas vacation was looming ever larger on the horizon. After collecting the research papers, Miss Mattos started assigning extensive reading assignments to the class. This work in English was added to by Misty's other teachers, though, as the school year started to get rolling.

If Miss Mattos's expected reading wasn't so interesting in the first place, she might have seen that as a burden. It still kept her up for hours after she had expected to go to bed. However, that wasn't her teachers' fault. For at least two hours after school, even in the rain, she would visit with Connell and Siobhan, and find herself drawn more and more into their world. With each day she spent with the elves, her own life seemed less and less interesting, and her schoolwork had started to drop off. She had even forgotten to turn in an essay, and that had been a first for her. She wasn't sure what her grades were, but she had the feeling they were steadily dropping. And the real problem for Misty was that she was finding it difficult to care.

Her only hope during this time lay in the fact that she was not the only one slacking off in their senior year, and that perhaps she wouldn't register on the radar. Briana made it an almost daily ritual to complain about the amount of literature they were expected to go over.

Misty, who had noticed the old Cliffs Notes peeking out from the spoiled girl's backpack on several occasions, saw this as a ploy to gain attention and sympathy. Nick Green seemed to be Briana's preferred target.

Nick. Well, he was another issue altogether. Not so much a problem, really, as a puzzle. In the days since Misty had reluctantly helped him, he had been nothing but nice to her. But he didn't seem to be playing the games that teenage boys play when they are trying for a new conquest. Misty, nobody's fool, always knew when a boy was being insincere, which seemed to be pretty much when any one of them opened his mouth.

He hadn't offered to carry her books, hadn't waited by her car, hadn't been "just around," or "what a coincidence finding you here." Instead, he was acting like a normal human being, and that was strange in itself.

Kelsey, though, was behaving just as Misty feared she would.

"Hey there," she had called to her. It had been the Monday after their hike.

Kelsey had not turned around, had pretended not to notice her. She had kept on walking, and gradually Misty lost sight of the red curls among the tangle of heads that bobbed in front of her, the students attached to them on their way to lunch.

And that had been that.

***

"Charley, are you really asking me to do this?" said Christina, flinging down the manila folder in disgust. This, she fumed, is taking it too far.

Charley looked away, unwilling to meet her gaze, instead pretending to notice a speck of lint that had somehow settled on the normally immaculate business wear that was his Monday to Friday uniform. The act he gave of working to get it off was nearly Oscar-worthy, but Christina wasn't buying it. Still, she let the awkward silence drag on for a while, taking some pleasure in her boss's discomfiture.

When she felt that enough time had passed, and saw that Charley was beginning to fidget, she repeated the question in a slightly louder tone.

Since arriving at the Portland office, Christina had learned to play a new game. The first two moves had just been executed, in the same manner in which they always were. Charley would pretend not to hear, so Christina would speak up. So familiar was she with the pattern that she barely registered the next words that came out of his mouth.

"How's Misty?" Innocent enough, on its own terms. There were, she had come to learn, hidden connotations to every sentence the man, bought and paid for by clients rich enough to not have any scruples, uttered. In this case, "How's Misty?" translated to, "Do you like your job? Do you know how hard it is for a single mother to make ends meet? Do you know how lucky you are to be in your position?"

She almost felt sorry for the man. He might have been something when he was younger, vibrant, full of vigor and the challenge of making the world a better place. A lot of lawyers are that way, when they first begin, she had realized. Somehow, she had always managed to avoid selling out. Maybe it was the San Francisco Bay Area, with its counterculture reputation and focus on redrawing boundaries, complete with opportunities to stick it to the system. It might have been

130

Misty, who had managed to hold on to her innocence for so long, until her father had died.

And that was the real answer: Carlos Montoya was no longer in her life, and he had been the anchor, for her and for Misty. Now, Christina saw herself heading down the same path as this hollow man in front of her, reaching the same empty place, filled with big houses, fast cars, and insignificant lives. And where was Misty's road taking her?

Thinking of her daughter brought her abruptly back to the present. Charley had made his move a long time ago, a familiar question. It was her turn to counter.

"Fine, she's fine," she answered flatly. And damned if that didn't have a whole bunch of translations as well. Let's start with, "I never get to see her, so I can't really tell you if she's 'fine' or not." How about, "Well, I can't quite figure out if that far-off look in her eyes is because of school, because of some boy, or the onset of some previously undiscovered illness."

"Good. I'm glad to hear that." This, of course, meant "Then if you would like to have her remain fine, and with a roof over her head, I suggest you do what the nice man Mr. Keller asks and not rock the boat." That was just Charley's way. This little farce would be concluded with him walking out of her office, whistling off key, leaving Christina to ponder her options, of which there were few.

This time, though, she had one final volley. "So, how's Mary?" she asked sweetly. Mary was Charley's wife.

Charley stopped, caught off guard; this was not how the game was supposed to be played. Still, he recovered admirably. "She's doing well. Thank you for asking." He wasn't looking at her when he said it.

Christina, who was learning quickly to keep one ear on all of the office gossip, knew that Mary was filing for a divorce.

Charley made a really good manager, but was not the best of trial lawyers. It was always so easy to tell when he was lying. Christina's friends in the home office had told her this before she had moved, had informed her that the only reason he was a part of this firm, and now the senior partner, was because he happened to share the same last name with the founder. Christina hadn't believed it until this day, but today he had knuckled under to Thomas Keller too many times.

She let him walk out, his embarrassment so thick she could breathe it.

Savoring her victory lasted all of five minutes. Then the reality of her situation came to confront her. She was being asked to lie.

Although "liars" and "lawyers" sound a lot alike, Christina had always seen herself as being above the pettiness and greed that seemed to infect so many of her colleagues. Sure, she had lied before, but it had always been for what she viewed as a good cause, when she had confronted people who would not change their stance no matter what the arguments were because they saw everything in shades of green. At that time, she had felt a certain moral good in deceiving these types of people.

Now she worked for one of them, and the lie she was being asked to give was only going to benefit him. Sighing, she opened the folder and glanced at its contents. After ten minutes, despite her best intentions, she was impressed, but just from a purely legal standpoint. The simplicity of Keller's idea, what he was essentially ordering Christina to tell the enviro-groups, was elegant.

Unfortunately, it was also really, really evil.

Wintertime Blues

To Misty, it seemed as if the year had passed without her being aware of it. One day piled on top of the other, and before she knew it snow had started to touch the lower mountains, and occasionally some would sprinkle down onto the roof of the house, the grass, the driveway.

It took about two days for the magic to wear off. The stuff was inconvenient, she decided the first time her car merrily slipped and slid its way down the road. However, she had managed to learn her lesson before taking out any trees or mailboxes, and was now driving at a slower, more controlled speed.

With one week to go before Christmas break, Misty, by this time a pro, was making her way to school. She had gotten into the habit of leaving a half an hour early; it always seemed like some idiot was getting into an accident these days.

The windshield was still slightly fogged, though the defroster made a heroic effort to combat the dropping temperature. The outlines of now familiar trees whipped past as Misty leaned forward, straining to see through the haze. In the background, the radio deejay, using an outrageously fake surfer/skier accent, was reading out the latest ski reports. It was all just noise anyway, but it somehow kept Misty from becoming too focused on the road.

A long time ago, her father had told her that it was just as bad to pay too much attention to a thing as it was to pay none at all.

Lately, though, that hadn't been a problem. A few weeks earlier she had brought home some bad news.

"Two Ds?" The occasion of this outburst was her mid-semester progress report. Misty had to give her mother credit for doing a bang up job of mixing just the right amount of disappointment, disbelief, and anger in her voice. It was precisely this command over her own voice which made her such a good attorney. Still, it sounded really sincere, which made Misty sincerely doubt that pointing out that it was just a progress report, and not a final grade, would do any good.

Misty examined her options. Play Dumb: That worked pretty well in junior high, when she had her seventh-grade slump, but her mom had gotten a lot better at sniffing that out. *She knows I'm smart, now.* No go. Outrage: the old "my teacher hates me" bit? A bit stale, sure, but why not? *Oh, yeah. Two bad grades.* It might work for one, but only Briana's parents were gonna fall for that one. Meek acquiescence to future demands: *Only if you want her to laugh so hard she forgets why she's pissed in the first place. Okay, how about The Truth?* Misty imagined the speech would go something like this: Mother, the reason why I am doing so poorly in school, especially English, which I know should be my strongest subject, is elves. Yes, that's right. I have been visiting elves for two hours a day, every day, and Niko, who all this time has been pretending to go on walks with me, has merely become my accomplice. In fact, he hardly walks at all, just splashes around that damned creek looking for fish that aren't there, have never been there, and will never be there. Oh, yeah, the elves. Well the reason why I space out so much in class—English class—is that we've only really done early literature, a lot of which is mythology, if you don't count *Jane Eyre*, and all this time I'm thinking that all these writers, most of whose names have been lost to us, really didn't know what the hell they were talking about. And the reason I know this is because I hear the real stuff right from the source. Those elves have, or had, connections, Mom. They knew the real deal, and that's what Connell and Siobhan—the elves, Mom, try to stay with me on this—have been teaching me. I've learned more from them in three months, more about art, music, culture, than eleven years of school have managed to hammer into my head.

Misty broke her thought—Christina was looking worried, like she was wondering if her only child was having a "teen" moment—and tried to figure out if she was missing something. *Oh right: Pre-calculus is boring, and I don't like it. Let's add that in there.* There, that ought to hold her mom for a while.

She shook her head. Who was she kidding, anyway? There was only one card left to play, and it was a good one, tried and tested by high school students since the first cave man grabbed his first stick (no rulers back then) and told a random group of cave teens to sit down, shut up, and copy the scrawlings on the cave wall: Ignorance.

"I thought I was doing better," she said, attempting to inject a bit of innocence in her voice. The trick was not to overdo it, because then parents will just think you're being a smartass. Which she was.

Christina arched an eyebrow. "You know me better than that. Let me tell you why senior year is important." She then began The Lecture.

Misty had heard this one before, had even memorized parts of it. So she just tuned her mother out and remembered the previous year's version, this time inserting "Senior Year," in the place where

"Junior Year" used to be. It was all the same recycled stuff about colleges looking at a student's overall GPA, through all four years, and being alarmed at drop-offs and blah, blah, blah.

The funny thing was that Misty had kept up good grades all through high school, even the grueling junior year, the year colleges looked at really hard. Why was this year different? Managing to stop herself before beginning (or rebeginning. *Is that a word?*) her internal narrative about the elves, Misty instead listed the other things that were keeping her mind occupied, and it was quite a long list: *Kelsey's still upset at me, so I gotta figure that one out; Nick Green's been acting like not a jerk, and that's just weird, considering who his father is and the fact that he still tolerates sitting next to Briana; speaking of Briana, oh forget that issue. She's not worth the trouble. Where was I? Oh, right. To top it all off, my mother is never around.*

Just as she was finishing this last bitter thought, Christina was wrapping up her opening statement. "Honey, I just want the best for you."

Misty came awake. Unwittingly, her mother had just given her the perfect ammunition for staving off any punishment that might have been forthcoming. It was so easy, she felt almost bad using it, but there it was right in front of her in all of its majesty: Guilt.

"How am I supposed to know that? It's not like you're ever around anyway," she muttered, making it just loud enough for Christina to hear.

It worked, a little too well, and the instant Misty saw her mother's face go slack she wished she could take back those words, said not in haste or emotion or idleness, but in a calculated move intended to draw attention away from her own failings. It was a lousy trick.

She saw that it had struck at her mother's heart, saw all the layers of sorrow that were weaving themselves over her mother's face. She saw that she had totally disarmed her mother, the one person who in Misty's life had never been at a loss for words.

She could never take them back, and that was the worst part.

Instead, she tried to undo the damage. "Mom," she began, reaching out for her. It was too late; Christina was walking towards her bedroom, shoulders slumped, totally defeated by her seventeen year old daughter. Misty jumped up, following her down the hall.

"You're right, Misty. I have no right to question you," said Christina, in a dead tone, closing her bedroom door. They were the perfect words to incite someone to pack their bags for a guilt trip, a brilliant countermove to Misty's stinging accusation. Except it wasn't a move, Misty knew. This was genuine hurt, with no attachments to it. And it had just put another wall—in this case a closed bedroom door—between her and her mother.

Creeping slowly down the hall, she managed to get close enough to press her ear against the light wood. Holding her breath, and trying not to make any sounds, she listened for a tortuous minute, trying to discover what Christina was doing. What she heard and what she knew shattered her: her mother was crying. This was not so rare a thing to hear in the Montoya household, especially this past year. What made it like a knife point was knowing that, for the first time, Misty could not make it better.

She had lost her friend, she was losing her mother, and soon enough, if she continued to not care about her school, her future, she would lose herself. Could the elves really be worth all this?

Before it was too late, she would have to decide.

She was brought back from her reverie by the line of cars waiting to pull into the school parking lot. Misty let her car idle, allowing the warmth of the defroster to infuse itself into her body before facing the cold day. By the time she got out of the car, she had made a decision.

She had to get her friend back.

***

What hurt the most, Christina decided, was that Misty was right. The last thing she had been in the past months was a mother to her daughter, and at a time when Misty clearly needed one. Work, as always, seemed to be taking up all of her time. The larger paychecks and Oregon's lower cost of living had allowed her to take care of her daughter without any other support, true. What wasn't apparent was the hidden cost that came with her higher earning power. What was the use of being able to afford dinner at the most expensive restaurants if the only thing you had time to eat was takeout delivered to your office?

But that wasn't the worst of it, for more and more Christina was finding herself believing that the less she saw her daughter the better it was for the both of them. She was changing, making compromises in her personal and professional life that Carlos, for one, would never have allowed. If Misty were to catch on, Christina doubted that her daughter would tolerate her choices either.

So it was that on the same misty, foggy, frosty morning Misty was driving to school and trying to solve her life at the same time, that Christina, in the luxury car that came as part of the package, was taking the longer commute time to recall one of her less proud moments. With each day, she had a few more to choose from. As was usual, this one involved Thomas Keller.

"The tract of land in question isn't a very large one." The speaker, the counsel for the alliance of environmental groups currently trying to make Mr. Keller's life a little harder, looked as if he had stepped right out of a Brooks Brothers catalog. He was so polished he almost glowed, and his tone of voice, eminently reasonable, contained layers of meaning, and Christina could tell that her client was incapable of grasping any of them other than those that went counter to his interests.

But when something did present an obstacle the man had an uncanny knack for subversive thinking. And the man was thinking right now. Also, rather uncharacteristically, he was being quiet, allowing Christina to do the talking.

Probably just wants to let me do the dirty work.

Christina stared at her opposite number, trying to gauge his reaction against that of Keller's. The firm he worked for was formidable, with an impressive record of settling a large number of cases before they went to trial, nearly all leaning in the favor of their clients; it was strange the amount of money that could materialize from these environmental groups when they were provoked. It didn't necessarily mean that this particular person was going to be a challenge. He obviously knew the trade, or at least read the books, but he was very young, and books, of course, meant very little in a situation like this.

It had been two hours of careful maneuvering in order to get to this point, and it was getting rather tiresome.

Sipping gingerly from her mug of steaming tea, more to stall than anything else, Christina reviewed what the young lawyer's next move would be. It was actually rather easy to guess. Ten years ago these little gambits were her bread and butter.

First, he would try to offer a compromise. Well that had already been done. It was, naturally, weighted heavily in favor of preservation of the forest in question.

Not for the first time that day, she found herself wondering what chain of events had led up to her sitting across the table in direct opposition to a cause she couldn't agree with more. Each time she thought of it her stomach soured a little, but it was a hard question to simply put out of her mind. She tried to distract herself by continuing to read her opponent's mind.

After the first attempt to "be reasonable" the implied threats would start to come out. This is where things sometimes became ugly. It was entirely possible that this case, with its numerous appeals, could remain tied up in the courts for years. Not to mention, the publicized proceedings, complete with protesters, would do a lot of damage to the reputation of Keller's firm. All of this combined could be enough for Mr. Keller's investors to lose interest and become skittish. Generally the only winners in this were the law firms that collected the heavy fees.

While the thought of Keller parting with a great deal of his not entirely honestly gained money gave Christina a thrill, Charley had

141

informed her in no uncertain terms that it was not to come to that. He wanted Keller as a long term client; the man attracted so much attention and controversy he represented the proverbial cash cow to any firm ruthless enough to hold onto him. To put it bluntly (and because Charley could never be blunt, she had been forced to read between the lines of his little daily reminders) Christina's job was tied to Keller's continued patronage.

So Christina couldn't let it get to the courts.

"You're right, actually," said Christina, shocking the other lawyer into a state of attention. She scanned the surveyor's map, pretending to look interested while hiding the fact that she was making this up as she went along. The choice land, with a view of the river and Mt. Hood in the far distance, would be strictly off limits if the enviro-groups had their way. Thomas Keller would be a fool to let this happen.

So Christina, per his instructions, had to do it for him. "We'll have to look over this," she said, trying to make it look at least like she was putting up some resistance. "But I think that this is something that Mr. Keller and his firm can work with." *That's your cue, Thomas, so let's get this over with. Maybe I can actually have dinner with my daughter.*

Keller jumped to his feet, a look of outrage on his face so phony. Christina almost lost her composure, and her job along with it. Hiding her mirth with another sip of hot tea, she decided to let him get a head of steam before she jumped in to slow him down.

He wasted little time. "Ms. Montoya, you're taking quite the liberty with the future of my company," he thundered.

If only I could, you windbag, but don't let me stop you. You're doing so well.

142

"I think that I'll decide whether or not...", he stammered, seeming to realize that he was on the wrong tack here if his plan was to make Christina do the dirty work. He fumbled ahead, apparently sensing that his attorney wasn't quite ready to rescue him. "Shouldn't we be discussing this in private before you go off making any promises?"

Well that's enough of that. "I think that when you have seen what I have seen, you will agree with me. Mr. Newsome, you may tell your client that we'll be happy to accept his proposal." She took another drink, and watched the other man leave the room. *I'm sure you think I'm just another dumb broad.* Seeing Keller allow himself a smile after the lawyer had left, she added, *I guess you're not the only one.*

Now they were alone.

"Bet you thought that was funny, letting me dangle," muttered Keller.

Christina shrugged. "Seemed more real that way. Why am I here anyway? It seems like anyone else, or you for that matter, could have just lied."

Thomas chuckled, not sounding at all mirthful. "Plausible deniability. Once we start construction, which we will, seeing as it's my goddamned land, I'm going to throw you under the bus. Just some rogue lawyer who wouldn't let me get a word in edgewise. So they'll withdraw the suit, we'll give them some time, and then start building. By the time they get their act together, the land will be torn to pieces, not worth fighting over anymore, all the little owls gone." He grinned maliciously. "They'll move on to other causes. We'll get hit with a fine, eventually, but our profit will more than cover it.

"Of course," he added, heaving himself from his padded leather chair and sauntering out the door, "your firm will be well rewarded. I'm sure that'll cover any damage to your reputation." He closed the door, leaving Christina to fume. That was two months ago, time which Keller's corporation used to get all in readiness for development. Now, the "agreement" was going to be presented today, and she still hadn't decided what to do. If there was anything she actually could do.

***

"We need to talk."

Connell left off whittling his branch. Through his patient work, the cast off from a pine tree was slowly becoming a rather good statue of Niko. Being that the dog could never sit still long enough for a picture, much less a sculpture, this made the elf's work even more impressive.

It was the afternoon after Misty had made her decision. Now she had to tell her other friends what she had told Kelsey that morning.

"I don't know if you understand what it's like to be new to a place," she began nervously, "but it's been really hard for me. The new school, not knowing anybody, my mom never being around. It's just been a really hard time for me.

"Anyway," she continued, "I have a friend."

"Kelsey, correct?" said Siobhan, peering up at Misty from her seat on the fallen log that Misty, wanting to be closer to her wandering dog, had dragged next to the river a month ago. "You brought her here once. I remember," the elf said. She crinkled her eyebrows together, but whether it was from reminiscence or frustration or just plain anger Misty could not tell. "Is she well?"

Misty released a huge breath, watching the air mist up in front of her open mouth, and looked over at Connell, who was playing in the water with Niko and pretending not to listen to the conversation. Apparently, he had decided to let his older sister handle this. He didn't seem to be the least bit uncomfortable in the chilly stream, and Misty allowed her mind to drift for a second, wondering whether it was another gift of the magical folk or whether Connell was just trying not to be rude by expressing his discomfort. Niko, being nothing more than a walking bundle of fur, wasn't having very many problems either. Still, Christina, assuming she was going to be home (and that was a very large "if"), would insist that he be dry before entering the house. This meant Misty would spend an uncomfortably cold ten or fifteen minutes toweling the Samoyed off, all with the inviting warmth of the house so near.

Still, she was a long way from that particular duty. Somehow, whenever she was near Connell and Siobhan she never really felt the cold of the winter days. It was only as she mounted the slope to begin the upward trek that had become so familiar to her that the wetness and chill began to seep through her clothes and penetrate.

It must be magic, she thought, breaking herself out of her reverie. Magic, like so much else that surrounded the Sidhe.

She reopened the topic, unaware that she had been staring off for some time now and that Siobhan, ever polite, had been waiting for her to say something. "We're having a problem. A problem of trust," she clarified. "Ever since that day when I brought her here."

"Which we rather you would not have done," said Siobhan, reminding her. More sternness was creeping into her voice.

145

"I know, I know, but she insisted, and there's no way I could have just said no. Anyway, it's too late." She wasn't going to regret the past. "You might have done that thing that you did with the Greens. You know, make them want to go," she argued, feeling a little guilty at the same time. Somehow, the thought of Nick Green in discomfort didn't make her laugh inside anymore. It had to be that father of his that was pushing him to search for Connell and Siobhan's clan.

"No, we couldn't," answered Siobhan matter-of-factly. "The two of you are connected. So she is connected to us."

This wasn't the first time that Misty had heard this, but she could never get anything more out of the elf. So this "connection" had been filed away in Misty's mind as just another mystery.

But it gave her an idea.

"That's what I wanted to talk to you about," she blurted.

Siobhan quirked an eyebrow. "Really," she said. "Why?"

Misty searched for the words to tell her friend, who had never known loneliness, surrounded as she was by her clan for as long as she could remember, what it was like to feel disconnected from the world and every person in it. She wanted so badly for Siobhan to understand that Kelsey had been her first real friend in a world new and strange, and that through the first disconcerting days of school it was Kelsey who had steered Misty towards a place of acceptance.

She owed her friend that much at least. And if Siobhan didn't understand—it was clear by now that Connell, who was still affecting blissful ignorance (and a total lack of hearing) was definitely going to leave this up to his sister—Misty would be forced to make another choice.

Like it or not, she was of this world, and Kelsey was the one who would accept any and all as her friends. Could she in good conscience choose an insular folk over her? She didn't think so.

Siobhan must have sensed this as well, and as Misty watched her, breath held, the female Sidhe seemed to make an internal decision. Connell came over, and Misty knew that he, again betraying that strange connection, felt an answer was coming.

Finally, Siobhan spoke. "You do not really have a choice in this, do you?"

Misty shook her head. "No."

"If our clan knew of our meetings with you, there would be severe consequences, but still we are here, every day," Siobhan said.

"As am I," answered Misty.

"This friend is to be trusted?"

Although Misty had only known Kelsey for four months now, she gave the answer she knew was right. "I would trust her with anything."

Connell dug his toes into the muddy ground. "Siobhan, Misty's friend is, well, one of them. You do understand what would happen if they found out."

"I think I do, little brother," snapped Siobhan. Then calming, she added. "Still, it is not for us to decide who in this world has the potential for good and who does not. We must have faith that each person is more than the parts that make them up. Is that not right, Misty?"

Misty thought of Nick Green, and who his father was. "It is," she said, gratitude in her voice. She would be able to keep all of her friends now. Looking at the elves, she saw happiness in their faces as well, despite Connell's warning. "What will your clan do if they find out about us?" she asked. She certainly didn't want to get them in trouble.

Connell shook his head. "Ah, they are too occupied right now to be chasing after we young ones. Too much going on."

Misty was curious. "What's happening?"

"They will not tell me," admitted Connell.

"Nor I," added Siobhan, "but there is something amiss lately. I do not think it involves our clan. Perhaps one of the others."

This was the first that Misty had heard of there being other clans; she had always assumed that Siobhan and Connell's group was alone in Oregon. Maybe they weren't supposed to talk about other clans.

Of course, they weren't supposed to do a lot of things.

"I'll bring her by this weekend," said Misty. At their puzzled glances, Misty added, "In two days." She had forgotten in her excitement that the elves had no concept of a weekend, as one day flowed into the next, and Misty's attempts to explain the concept to them had proven fruitless.

At the elves' nod, she scrambled back up the hill, Niko in wet pursuit. She couldn't wait to tell Kelsey in person.

***

"Group, I was a little disappointed with your short papers," said Miss Mattos, scanning the group of tired faces in front of her. "The great majority read like they had been written the night before." Of course, they had been. Procrastination was nothing new.

Kelsey stared at the back of Misty's head, wondering about the change that had come over her today. She had walked in bubbling with

148

excitement, but Miss Mattos had shushed them before she had had a chance to say anything. Of course, with the way she was acting, she could very well have been waiting to talk to Nick. She had been awfully friendly with him lately.

But you're not supposed to care, are you?

Then why was she?

"Hey, Kelsey." The redhead was startled out of her reverie by Misty's urgent whisper. Looking up, she saw that the students, including Nick and Briana, had already begun filing out of the room. Apparently the bell had rung and she hadn't noticed.

Great, now you're losing your hearing. Or your mind. "Yeah, what is it," she asked, remembering that she was supposed to be irritated.

Misty plowed on, unfazed, "I need to talk to you. How about the library for lunch?"

Kelsey's stubborn streak woke up. "What do you have to say that's so important that you can't say it here?" This close to the end of the semester, the gossipers and their kind avoided the library like the Black Plague, because it had a nasty habit of becoming infested with students who were actually, contrary to every impulse of teenage behavior, studying. In other words, it was the perfect place to talk with someone about something you didn't want blabbed all over the school; no one was going to pay attention to you anyway.

Kelsey, with that one question, managed to convey to Misty both her indignation at what she felt to be shoddy treatment (which was definitely not on par with how a person treats New Best Friends) a comprehensive understanding of the intricacies of seasonal library

149

etiquette, and a curiosity about what really was so bloody important that it involved entry into a territory that even Drama geeks tended to let well enough alone.

"Come with me and I'll tell you," persisted Misty. It was obvious that she wasn't going to let anything slip, especially not with Miss Mattos sitting there pretending to grade papers.

"All right," relented Kelsey, trying to conceal her happiness at once again speaking to Misty, and having her willing to share secrets.

Because that's what friends do best.

***

"Get out!" It was the loudest whisper Misty had ever heard, and it was no surprise that it came from her friend's mouth. She wavered between joy at her renewed bond with this ludicrously unique girl and terror that people in the library had heard more than they should have.

"Shh!!" Apparently they had.

"Listen," she continued. "We'll go tomorrow, okay, and I'll show you."

Any other person, except with the onetime exception of her father, would have laughed out loud or expressed disgust that Misty would stoop so low as to deceive them with such a pathetic story. It spoke volumes for her friend that she was willing to take Misty at her word, no questions asked. Volumes of what was of course an entirely different matter. When it came right down to it, hearing herself telling the story out loud for the first time, she was hard pressed not to send for the men in white jackets.

"Right after school?" Kelsey could hardly contain her excitement, and was visibly twitching. She seemed about to fly out the window, with the chair still attached to her butt.

"Right after school," promised Misty. She took a long breath. It had felt good, really good, to be able to get it out. But there was something else Connell had made her promise to do. She wondered if her friend would be able to take it, or if she would lose Kelsey so quickly after she had given up so much just to regain her trust and loyalty. "There's something else, something you don't know. Actually, it's the reason you weren't able to see Connell and Siobhan." It was easier to think and speak of the elves by their names; if anyone was actually eavesdropping, it wouldn't sound so freaky, "It's something they asked me to tell you before you came. It's important."

Kelsey leaned forward. "Okay. Sure."

Misty dreaded what she had to do, and before she started she wanted to be certain. After all, it had been a long time. "Kelsey, remember when we talked about your background?"

"For Mattos's class, that first project, right?"

"Right," said Misty. "Do you know anything about your Irish side? Any stories or anything like that? Anything your family used to do, you know, for a living, or anything like that," she finished lamely.

Kelsey furrowed her brow. "This can't be a coincidence. I was just asking my mom about her side of the family. You know, her maiden name was McMollen, with an 'o' not a 'u'. I never knew that before. Anyway, I can tell you what is going on now.

"My family's never had it good, at least as far back as they can remember. They still aren't doing well back in Ireland, and the Potato

151

Famine was ages ago. Crappy luck is why my mom's branch of the family left the country, finally. The others are still there. Funny, they get through the famine, and it's just a great big streak of bad luck that finally drives them away. I'm pretty glad they came here, for sure. Maybe those back there are wishing that they had come along.

"The thing is, according to my mom, no one in the family can remember when times were good. As far back in our history as we can go, the McMollens have always been poor, have always had bad fortune, and have never been able to get any further along. Some of the stories I've heard are just plain weird. You'd think that at least once in a thousand years something would go their way. But it never has. Really, I think the only reason we are doing alright here is because of my dad. He must have brought some good old fashioned German luck along with him."

Misty was intrigued. "What stories exactly?"

Kelsey plowed ahead. Misty had learned that once her friend had gotten a head of steam it was an easy thing for her to talk until the end of time (or lunch, at least). "Well, ever since as long as my family can remember, we have never been able to grow anything. Not enough to make any kind of profit. They used to be farmers, or tried to be. Actually," she continued, scratching her head, "I'm not really sure why it never occurred to any of them to try to do something different. I guess when people get used to doing something they stick with it.

"One time, when my great-grandfather was running the farm, he actually thought the crop was going to make enough to actually, I don't know, pay off some of the mortgage. The river flooded over. In the late summer. Another time, they had cleared a bunch of stones

152

from one of their fields, because they were supposed to plow it the next day. The next morning they wake up, bright and early, and all the stones are back, except this time they were put in all these different places. That happened three or four different times. All the holes pretty much ruined any chance of planting anything regular."

"It sounds like agriculture isn't your family's forte," said Misty sympathetically.

"That isn't the half of it. The list of calamity stretches back forever. Sick oxen, rusted plows, a tree that smacked right into the roof during a storm. Geez, it made me depressed just looking all this up. I don't know why my mother insisted on writing down all of that stuff anyway. Reminder of a worse time, I guess."

Suddenly, Misty didn't feel so bad about her own situation. "It sounds like the whole world is against your family."

"The whole of Ireland, at least," said Kelsey, not succeeding very well in keeping the bitterness from her voice. "I don't know why they even stay there."

"Maybe they're waiting for a miracle." Or forgiveness, Misty thought to herself. She was pretty sure what, or who, was behind the misfortunes of Kelsey's family.

And remembering the images of the elves' flight from Erin, Misty had a hard time convincing herself that Kelsey's family hadn't deserved what they had gotten. Still, so much time had passed. Maybe it was time to let bygones be bygones.

Somehow, she doubted that Connell and Siobhan were going to be able to convince their clan to ease up on the McMollens. Assuming they would even want to try. That was something that Kelsey would

153

have to discuss with them. She only hoped that her friend would understand.

It had now become more important than anything that Kelsey see what the elves had shown Misty. No matter how much it might hurt.

"Listen, I've changed my mind. We're going to go today."

"Are you sure?" asked Kelsey. Misty could tell she was just asking in order to be polite; she was practically busting.

"Yeah, I am. And," she went on, "I'm glad I told you. I just hope no one heard anything."

Kelsey snorted. "In here? Not very likely."

But someone had. Stuffing her notebook, from which no studying had been done, into her bag, Briana smirked evilly, throwing it jauntily over her shoulder.

She knew just who she was going to tell.

Settling

"They're going to take it," Christina said, feeling the guilt slowly crawling up from her feet to stab her in the heart.

Thomas Keller leaned back in his swivel chair, tossing Charley a smug smile. "See, what did I tell you? Stupid tree-huggers. I'll let my boys know."

Christina looked around the office. The bright Christmas decorations didn't seem to fit in at all with the totally un-Christmaslike atmosphere of greed that now seemed to have made a permanent home in the office of the senior partner. Behind his desk, Charley threw a sick smile at his employee, and Christina felt her respect for the man to drop a few more notches.

Not that it had much further down to go.

Of course, her self-respect was also managing to plummet quite nicely, matching the pace of Charley's drop for drop. There was just something about Keller that made her feel less than totally human. And the more she thought of it, the more she realized that this was close to the truth.

She hadn't been able to defend her own ideals since arriving here and was in fact actively working against her own better nature. She was receiving a ridiculous paycheck, an equally ridiculous car, a nice office, and all it was costing her was her own sense of right and wrong, along with a good dose of self-worth.

And her daughter.

So she was the only one in the room who wasn't smiling. "Glad you're happy," she said quickly, turning to leave. "Now perhaps I can get on with some other projects."

"Oh, I don't think so, sweetheart," Thomas corrected her, managing to sound even more oily than usual. "This here development is just the beginning. We've got some nice beach property to look at pretty soon. Damned hippies are starting to make waves about the seals." He chuckled at his own joke.

"Of course," he continued, "once this current thorn in my side is proven ineffectual, and thank you very much for a stellar performance, by the way, I don't think these new ones are gonna give me any more trouble. None at all."

His laughter followed Christina out as she left Charley's office, fists clenched. It was only with a supreme force of will that she had managed to keep in check her desire to turn around and spit in the man's arrogant, condescending face.

Something had to give.

***

Misty held her breath as Connell and Siobhan emerged from the bushes. Everything was the same: she was sitting on her log, Niko was splashing in the water, still searching for invisible fish, and the elves came right up to her, never hesitating.

But everything wasn't the same.

"She has some of the blood, diluted though it is," said Siobhan by way of introduction.

"That is a rather interesting way to start a conversation," chided Connell. "I apologize. Kelsey, is it? My name is Connell, and this is my

156

older sister Siobhan. She is normally more polite, but we have never met one of those responsible for what happened, distant though the events may be. It has shaken her."

Now that it had been pointed out, Misty did notice the extra amount of tension on the face of the female Sidhe. Trying to ease the pressure, she broke in. "Kelsey has a lot of German in her, really. She's never even been to Ireland."

"That's right," offered Kelsey meekly. In the five months she had known the redhead, Misty had never seen her so subdued.

She probably didn't think I was telling the truth, Misty realized. She looked over at her friend, who had not moved from where she was standing, staring in awe at the diminutive creatures. "Kelsey, it's okay to come sit down by me."

As if awoken from a trance, Kelsey shot forward and hastily sat down, crimson with embarrassment. "Oh right, sorry. I'm sorry. It's just that I never, uh…." she trailed off.

"You have never seen anything like us, have you," said Connell, "but I think you have always known we existed. Some part of you, at least," he insisted. It all struck Misty as surprisingly perceptive of the younger elf, and seeing Kelsey nodding her head, eyes misting with unborn tears, she knew that Connell had hit the mark. It was just that she had been expecting Siobhan to be doing most of the talking, the reasoning. Connell was bright enough, and he had a gift for music that his sister did not possess, but as often as not he would spend their daily meetings frolicking with Niko in the stream, even riding the large canine on occasions.

Now he seemed to be speaking for both of them. Misty wanted to find out why, but it was a question that would have to wait. "I know she was not supposed to come until tomorrow, but there are some things she told me, about her family that is. I think you should know." She reached for her friend's hand, grasping it impulsively. "Kelsey, tell them."

At first the stories came out haltingly. Then, as her friend gained more confidence, perhaps forgetting to whom she was telling the tales to, her voice increased in volume and settled into a practiced rhythm.

A gift of the stage, Misty knew.

Eventually, it was over, and the pair of friends waited for the Sidhe's reaction. It came as a disappointment.

"So?" It was Siobhan who finally spoke. Beside his sister, Connell didn't say a word.

Misty was horrified at the callousness. "Is that all?" she stammered, rising to her feet. "Her family is suffering, and they haven't done a thing to you!"

Siobhan turned dead eyes (and Misty had never seen that) towards her. "You act as if we have any power to change what has occurred. The curse was laid down long ago by our greatest ancestors, and we are, after all, young elves. Even if we wanted to, we would not have the power. The entire council—."

"Then tell them!" pleaded Misty. Even after seeing what had happened to the Sidhe, she couldn't find the justice in bringing punishment down upon the McMollens, as well as the descendants of the other guilty families, for the sins of their forefathers.

Looking at Siobhan, though, she knew that it was a hopeless cause. Well, they owed Kelsey at least one thing. "You should tell her, at least."

Even though Misty thought it impossible, Siobhan's face hardened even more. "You are asking me to share our history with her, with a McMollen. You do not know what you ask."

All this time, Kelsey had remained silent, though Misty could see she was suffering. Of course she was feeling rejected. Who wouldn't?

"No. I am asking you to share your history with your friend. Because whether you know it or not, sitting right there," she said, pointing at Kelsey, "is a beautiful person, who accepted me without any questions, who didn't care who my parents were, or my grandparents, or my great-great-great, whatever!

"And," she continued stubbornly, "this girl has such a big heart that any friend of mine is a friend of hers. She can't live any other way but with an open mind. I'm asking you to give the same gift to her that she has offered by coming here to you. At least let her understand." Finishing that, she sat down again, pulling Kelsey, who had begun to cry now, gently closer.

Connell nudged his sister. "Siobhan," he whispered.

"I know, brother. I know," said Siobhan. "Does she know what she will see?"

"I'll tell her," insisted Misty, grabbing her friend by the shoulders. "Kelsey, Siobhan is going to show you exactly what happened to her clan, so that you can understand. It's so you won't have this anger, okay?"

Kelsey nodded once. "What's it going to be like?" she asked.

"It's going to be just like you are there. It's going to be beautiful, so beautiful that it breaks your heart. And it's going to be scary, really scary. And sad, but that will come in the end, and maybe you'll be used to it by then. Are you okay with doing this?"

"I need to know," answered Kelsey.

That was good enough.

Siobhan began to speak in the rhythmic cadence she used with Misty, but this time Misty was not taken away from her seat. Instead, she watched Kelsey's eyes glaze over as the story started taking over the girl's perceptions.

It was interesting for Misty to just hear the words. Now that she was still here, she was actually able to hear the entire story from Siobhan's lips and not from the perspective of Eogan. It amazed her when the Sidhe's voice altered itself to perfectly mimic that of her long ago ancestors; Misty had thought that the story had just been to sort of get her started and after that the past took over. Instead, Siobhan was acting out the actual parts, taking her "lines" from the collective consciousness of her people.

It did little to spoil the beauty of Erin in the past, for Misty was still able to close her eyes and remember, and she did.

"Misty, wake up." It was Connell, and he sounded worried.

"Wha-what is it?" Misty looked around. The forest had darkened considerably, yet she couldn't remember falling asleep. But glancing at her watch, she saw that it read 5:03, so she must have. Already it was so dark that she doubted she would be able to make it home without trouble, even though she practically knew the way by heart.

160

She had forgotten all about Kelsey. "Where is—"

"Your friend is there," said Siobhan, coming to stand beside her brother. "You fell asleep while I was speaking. Are you well?"

"I'm rested, at least," replied Misty, feeling guilty at leaving her friend alone for so long. "How long was I asleep?"

"Until I finished the story," said Siobhan. "Connell woke you just after I was done."

Misty was shocked. "It took that long to tell? I don't remember it taking two hours the time you told me."

"Of course not. You were there. The time is going to seem different. However, I did not think that it would darken so soon. While Connell and I will have no problem finding our way home, it appears that the two of you might."

"Yeah, we're not cats," said Misty.

"That would be useful," replied Connell. "But I think there is a larger issue than that at the moment." He pointed towards Kelsey, who had not moved since Misty had woken. "You might want to go to her. Talk to her. We will find a way to get you home."

"Connell, should we be doing this?" asked Siobhan.

Misty saw a rare resolve come across the younger elf's face, and for once he seemed to be the more mature of the two. "We should. I know that some in our clan think that I am feckless at times, irresponsible, casual with my duties. I will admit that I sometimes prefer the company of the creatures of the forest. And Niko," he added, scratching the big dog's head vigorously, "while you and Misty talk. Still, she is my friend, and I am hers. Even you must admit that is more important than old traditions and rules that stopped making sense a thousand years ago. So I will call them, and they will guide Misty and Kelsey home.

"But first, Misty, you must give what comfort you can. She has seen much, I know, and she is in need of you right now. Do not worry about the darkness." Connell walked off deeper into the woods, and began singing softly, leaving Misty alone with Siobhan and Kelsey, who had now started to move, but only to rock slowly back and forth.

Siobhan looked at her brother, and Misty could see respect growing in the female's eyes. Giving a short nod, she followed Connell.

Misty walked over to Kelsey and sat down, not really sure what was the matter. Of course she knew the story, had been there, and had been affected by the events on a deep and personal level. But this was different: Kelsey seemed paralyzed. "Kels, what's the matter?" she asked, putting a comforting arm around her friend's shoulder.

Kelsey came awake abruptly. "Nothing. Nothing at all," she stammered, reaching her arm up to wipe her eyes.

Misty smiled sadly; she had cried as well, when it had been her turn to see the past. "It's tragic, but it happened to them a long time ago. Connell and Siobhan have gotten over it. Well, as much as they are able to. You will too. I promise."

"It's not that, Misty," moaned Kelsey, shaking her head.

"Then what is it?" asked Misty, turning to look at her friend, face to face. "Oh." She recognized that look now. It was the same one she had seen in the mirror for months after her father's death.

Guilt.

Misty took her broken friend into her arms as Kelsey's body shook with sobbing. "Oh, Kelsey, no."

162

Thirty minutes later, the two walked up the slope and through the woods. Ahead of them, will-o-wisps twinkled, danced, and swirled in front of them, lighting their way and guiding them home.

***

Christina saw the lights at the edge of the forest as she looked out the window. She had just been contemplating whether to go into the woods after her daughter herself. Sighing with relief as she watched Misty and her friend emerge from the darkness, she couldn't decide whether to be grateful that they were safe or angry that they had been gone long past dark without telling her where they were.

Well, at least they were getting along again. Christina had hated the sight of Misty moping around the house these past weeks, especially as it was almost Christmas, and it would be their first without Carlos. But she would have to get used to that, she supposed.

Seeing Misty and Kelsey climb up the porch steps, exhausted but clearly friends again, Christina felt a warmth surge through her, an affection for her daughter that had always been there but had lately hidden itself behind the compromises she had had to make at work. So she made herself a silent promise, one she most definitely intended to keep.

Misty would not spend Christmas alone.

***

Kelsey cried all the way home.

She couldn't blame Misty for this, no matter how easy it would have been. No, it had been Kelsey all along who had insisted that she be let in on the mystery, without thinking of the consequences, so sure that Misty was just being secretive in order to keep something

163

interesting all to herself. But the truth ended up being a lot more difficult to swallow.

Her friend had been trying to protect her, and she had repaid Misty's caring and concern with an attitude that would make a first grader proud. Of course, it hadn't helped that Kelsey had put all of her years of theater into the performance of "HURT FRIEND."

Now she got to reap the rewards.

She couldn't tell her parents, that was certain. How do you begin that conversation? "Hey mom, guess what? I found out what's been behind the family misfortune all this time. Elves! Yeah, they cursed us, you see, because a long time ago, we stole their land and destroyed their trees and chased them off of Ireland." She could just picture how her mom would take that.

Then there would be the lecture about not mocking the family, whom she had never met in the first place. At this point, her dad would probably join in, as he was himself very proud of his own heritage, and very aware of the sins of his own fathers. He was even uncomfortable talking about the Holocaust, and that was historical fact.

Of course, so was what happened to the Sidhe, but there would be no way she could convince anyone of that.

"And it's supposed to be a secret, idiot!"she scolded herself, clenching the wheel in frustration, "so why are you even having this conversation?" She hated to think about the look that would be on Misty's face if Kelsey ever broke her promise to her friend.

It sucks, Kelsey decided, having to choose between family and friends. If she hadn't made a solemn promise, it might have made it difficult. But she had, and as far as her family was concerned, they couldn't do anything about it anyway. Connell and Siobhan had assured her of that. The actions of the past are not so easily washed away. Besides, the two elves were still children in the eyes of their clan. And just imagining two beings older than her grandparents as children was something else entirely.

So by the time she had reached her house, Kelsey had fully rationalized the problem away, deciding to keep it to herself.

It just wouldn't do to upset her new friends, all three of them; who knew what kind of curse they would cast on her. The thought of Connell and Siobhan casting a curse on her was laughable, of course.

But you never knew.

Christmas Time

"What are you going to be doing this Christmas?" asked Nick Green. He had come from around the corner, and Misty, digging through her locker for her Pre-calculus book, had not seen him approaching.

"Um, I don't know," she replied, off guard. Looking around, she saw that Kelsey was involved in a conversation with one of her Drama friends and hadn't noticed to whom Misty was now talking. While she herself was starting to warm up to Nick, Misty doubted that Kelsey, who would naturally attach the good-looking boy to Briana the Antichrist, would be so willing to make a fresh start.

But Nick had been nothing but polite ever since that first awkward encounter, and the first day of school, and how many months ago was that, anyway? Five? It was really time to give the guy a chance, she thought, repeating the same argument that had been running in her head for at least two months now. It was just that with Kelsey acting on her worst behavior the last thing Misty needed to introduce into her life was another complication. Things were different.

And he was cute.

Misty wasn't sure how long she had been spacing out, but it was probably long enough for Nick to interpret her silence as rudeness or stupidity, so she decided to say something before the situation got any weirder. "Nothing. I don't think I'm doing anything," she blurted. And that could have gone better.

Nick looked down at his feet, making himself seem even more adorable. How could this guy be related to his father? Maybe he was adopted, Misty reasoned. *And just what has gotten into you, anyway? Not a week ago this guy was the furthest thing from your mind, and now you're falling to pieces. Get a grip, girl.*

Maybe it was because she didn't have to worry about Kelsey anymore, or it could be the season—Christmas always did bring out the romantic in her—or maybe she just felt normal for the first time in a long time, and chasing boys was what normal girls did. And vice-versa. Maybe she was in a good mood; her mother had told her that she would have a special Christmas surprise for her, which meant that she would actually have to be home to give it, which meant that she would actually be home.

It was turning out to be an okay holiday after all. And here was Nick, who was patiently waiting for her to stop smiling stupidly as she stared into space. "I'm sorry, Nick. I was somewhere else. What were you saying again?"

Nick cleared his throat. "I was just thinking that maybe we could hang out sometime over the vacation. I mean, if that's okay with you."

Misty weighed Kelsey's probable reaction, decided that a true friend would support her in her decisions, figured that her mother was never home anyway, so there was little point in asking her, and did all of these things in two seconds. "That would be great. Sure!" She took out a piece of paper from her overloaded backpack, scribbled out her phone number, and was about to add her address as well, but…. "I guess you already know where I live," she said.

Nick laughed, dispelling the tension, as he folded up the paper and put it into his pocket. "Yeah, I guess I do," he admitted. "I never really apologized to you for what my dad did that day. I should have stuck up for you, but all I did was follow his lead. He's not too easy to live with sometimes. I guess he thought that 'hunting' for whatever it was we were looking for would bring me and him closer together. I probably thought so too. Anyway, I'm sorry about that. We haven't been down there since. At least I haven't."

Misty frowned. That last part was a lie. He and his father had come down at least one more time, and the elves had given them the runs. Of course, she rationalized, not many people would want to admit to that in the first place; he was probably embarrassed. And Connell and Siobhan had never sensed them after that one time, so he was mostly right.

Though she would never have done so even three or four weeks ago, she told Nick it was okay for him to call her, and they could meet up. He promised to call, slung his bag over his shoulder and went bouncing down the hall. Smiling, Misty watched him go.

"What was that all about!?" If Misty had been a cat, she would have left claw marks on the ceiling. As it was, she only jumped and gave a little squeak. By the time she landed, she realized that Kelsey of course would have come to find her, and was wondering just how much of the conversation the redhead had managed to eavesdrop on.

Misty got defensive, seeing no reason to lie. "Nick just asked if I wanted to hang out sometime this holiday is all."

Kelsey turned a bright red, her face matching her curls. Misty could see all the possibilities running through the girl's mind, and headed her off at the pass. "Relax, it's not like we're going to be going on some date or anything."

"A date is exactly what that is," her friend pointed out. Sticking her hands out in front of her for emphasis, she slowly brought them together. "When two people agree to go from their homes, and meet each other somewhere else," she said, touching her fingertips together, "that is defined as a date. You have a date with Nick Green," she said accusingly. "What's next, shopping with Briana?"

"I just knew you were going to go there," snapped Misty. "Not everything and everybody in this school is connected to that spoiled brat. Just what is your problem with her anyway? I thought that I was the one she loathed."

"Do you really want to know?"

"Yes, really."

"Then, c'mon, let's take a walk," said Kelsey, storming down the hall.

Kelsey started talking before they reached the door leading outside. "Look, Boring ain't exactly the biggest place around, so a lot of us have been going to the same schools ever since we could walk. It's been my misfortune to follow Briana for all of my school career, or more rightly, to have her follow me.

"Try and remember all the bad things you can about middle school, those wonderful years of puberty. For me that would take about the rest of my life. Junior high sucked, and most of the sucking has to do with that twit and her little clones. At first it was the curly hair. I got 'brillo pad' a lot, but I guess that got old. Before that I was Raggedy Ann, but that was in elementary so they had to start getting a little less

169

childlike. After the hair bit they would generally start in on my clothes; I used to be something of a tomboy. I still am, actually," she said, pausing to glance significantly at her wardrobe.

Misty couldn't see what was so bad with it, but she could understand why a mindless fashion follower like Briana would bare her claws at the sight of the sensible clothing Kelsey chose to wear.

"Anyway," continued Kelsey, "it was something of their lunchtime sport to harass me, call me names, stupid stuff like that, but it made it real hard to make friends. Hardly anyone at that age has a mind of their own, so most of the kids were too afraid to be nice to me, because they figured that witch would target them next."

Misty grabbed Kelsey's shoulder, slowing her friend down before she smashed nose first into the back of one of the football players, easily recognizable by their jackets. "Kels, that was a long time ago. Junior high kids are vicious and cruel. I don't think anyone gets out of that age totally unscarred, but most of them end up changing."

"I know," agreed Kelsey; she was letting some of her frustration get past her gritted teeth and into her voice, "I have scads of friends now, and most people here are too wrapped up in their own things to really care what anyone one else is thinking. That's the reason why high school movies and TV shows are so silly nowadays; if all that stuff actually happened in that short a time span, we would all be in therapy.

"But you're getting me off topic, Misty, probably on purpose." Kelsey appeared calmer now, even to the point of being able to sit down. The two had walked the length of the campus, not an incredibly difficult task, and had reached some out of the way benches, rarely used by students. "You need to know that I'm a big girl and that I do understand that this is sort of what happens at that age. But Briana is still like that! Don't you see it, those stupid comments she keeps making about California, and about illegal immigrants, and strawberry picking, all that racist crap that some people never seem to let go. She's picked a new target, and you've been too wrapped up in your," Kelsey's voice dropped to a shadow of a whisper, "other friends to really notice. It's like junior high for me all over again, except that I get to watch this time."

"That and the fact that no one outside of her fan club is paying any attention to her," Misty pointed out, "including me."

"But you should. No one should be able to get away with what she's saying."

Misty brushed her friend's argument aside. "What does this have to do with Nick? You still haven't told me."

"I guess it doesn't really matter now, but Nick was like a male Briana a few years back. He just mimicked whatever she said. They even went together for a while."

While it didn't shock Misty that Nick had been easily led in the past—he had admitted his occasional inability to forge his own way to her just ten minutes ago—it made her a little uneasy that he had held any sort of feelings, even the artificial and superficial emotional attachment of a twelve year old, for the bratty and stuck-up girl.

Kelsey had not noticed the look on Misty's face and went on talking. "I know that it was a long time ago, and he's been okay these past two or three years, although I can see why his dad could creep you out. I suppose I'm not as good as I think I am when letting go of the past. And he still hangs around Briana, doesn't he?"

171

"He sits next to her, but I think he just tolerates her is all."

"Oh, I never noticed."

"In fact," continued Misty, "I'm not sure if he even talks to her at all anymore. Not that I really care," she said quickly.

Kelsey laughed. "Sure. Whatever you say."

***

Christmas vacation came soon after, and the cold kept Kelsey indoors a lot more than it used to. Except for her shifts at the store, she was spending more and more time online. What she was looking for she couldn't say, and she repeatedly rebuffed her mother's questions.

Now, seven days into the break, she sat staring at the screen, only occasionally glancing down at a legal pad, on which she had written a string of words. She had crossed out the ones that led nowhere, gave too many possible sources, contained information which she had already received from her new "friends," or, because of this association, which she knew to be entirely false.

McMollen

McMullen (She had gotten a whole bunch of movie references with this one.)

Sidhe

Fomorian

Irish Folklore

Celtic Folklore

Leprechauns

Pot o' Gold (It was at about this time that she had gotten silly.)

Connell (A Celtic name meaning "friend." She was going to have to share this one with Misty.)

Siobhan (The Celtic version of "Joan." Or was it the other way around? Not much help there.)

Elves (Anything from mythology to Orlando Bloom with this one. Maybe she should have tried something more specific.)

Grumbling with frustration, she began typing in a new search.

Tir Na Nog/Tir Nan Og

The search results that came up with this one were interesting, and Kelsey spent the greater part of the next hour looking through them. If she hadn't previously studied the Great American Migration (this was her capitalization; it had looked better on her notes,) this wouldn't have even registered. As it was, she found herself devouring the data. Something about the supposed placement of this paradise was starting to work on Kelsey's mind, but she couldn't say what it was, or why it was so important. But she knew that if she made it make sense, a mystery of sorts would be solved.

All through dinner she was quiet, chewing her food thoughtfully, sucking at every bite. Her parents were obviously concerned, as normally a lively conversation was the norm around the Wagner dinner table, but were too polite to mention anything. Instead, they focused on their own meals, only glancing at each other when they thought that Kelsey wasn't looking.

It wouldn't have mattered if she had seen anyway, because her mind was most definitely elsewhere. She certainly didn't want her dinner to be over so soon, because that would mean she was out of mental ammunition and would have to scrounge up some dessert, possibly losing the tenuous thread she had in the process. Of course, she had no idea why this should be so important, but her inability to finish the connection had awoken an unusual tenacity.

Outside, the rain pitter-pattered against the dining room windows, providing a steady rhythm to her musings, though she was barely conscious of the weather. Long after her parents had gotten up, clearing their dishes and retreating from their crazy daughter to the sanity of the living room television in order to watch made-up people's made-up kids, Kelsey sat stock still, only occasionally darting her fork at her mashed potatoes or an uneaten carrot. She had vowed to no one in particular that she wasn't going to get up until she had figured this one out. This could potentially be bad news for her rear end, which was slowly growing numb from overexposure to the unyielding wood of her chair. Plus, assuming she stayed there the sun would be rising and shining right into her eyes the next morning.

The sun rising….

"Damn it!" she screamed, frightening the wits out of her parents, who now came scampering back. The sun rising, that was a connection. *And where does the sun rise from?* Ugh, this was getting to be like a cheesy Monty Python skit (*And what else floats on water?*). *Gee, let me think. . .the east. And that means?*

"Is everything alright? You sound as if you've seen a ghost." This was her mother's favorite expression.

"Fine," said Kelsey, not really meaning it.

"Well, as long as it's nothing," said her father amiably, moving away from his clearly disturbed daughter.

"Okay, that's good, dad. Go back to your show." He was watching reruns of The West Wing.

The West Wing. That was the connection! Okay, not entirely. Still, she had to tell Misty. She ran to her room and picked up the phone.

Several seconds later. "Hello."

"I've got it, I've got it!"

"Kelsey, I'm glad that you have it." Misty was sounding extraordinarily calm. "What exactly is 'it.'"

Kelsey took a breath. "I know why the elves are in Oregon."

***

"It has to do with the West," said Kelsey.

The two were in Misty's bedroom. Kelsey had come that night, driving over in record time, although Misty couldn't be sure why. After hearing her friend, she still wasn't sure.

"Yeah, you already lost me. You're going to have to be more specific," she prompted.

"I'm not entirely sure where to start," said Kelsey, digging around the pile of papers she had brought with her. "I'm going to have to use my notes."

Misty was amused. "You actually took notes? I guess you were taking this a little more seriously than I thought."

"Actually, a lot of this is left over from that stuff I found for you when Mattos assigned us that first project. Then, well, this happened, so I started doing some research of my own. But don't get too impressed; I ended up printing a lot of this straight from the internet."

"Kind of like how Briana 'writes' her essays, but it's not the same thing, you know." said Misty, taking a moment to relish the time when Briana had her entire essay read aloud by Miss Mattos, because it

175

was so good, only to be told that the "A" would have to go to the professor from the University of Washington who actually wrote it. She hadn't thought it was possible to achieve that shade of red.

"There," announced Kelsey triumphantly, "I think I've got all of this organized. I think when I'm done I'll see if I can make something of an extra credit report out of it. Maybe Mattos will like it."

"I'm sure she'll find it interesting," said Misty, "I know I will."

"Okay," said Kelsey, taking a breath, "I'll have to start with the general idea."

"Wow, Kels, you sound just like a teacher."

"Shut up."

"Yep, just like a teacher."

"Do you want to hear this or not?"

"Sorry."

Kelsey plunged ahead. "It all starts with the West, the West as an idea, not any sort of geographical designation. When I was looking up your elves online—and what a chore that was—I found something interesting about Tir Nan Og. The only real direction anyone can come up with is that it's to the West, beyond the sight of Ireland, England, or Europe. That's assuming that people have said it's in any direction at all, and a lot of people don't.

"Okay, so Tir Nan Og is associated with Avalon, which is where King Arthur went when he died, to come back when he was needed, to be reborn in a sense."

Misty remembered all of this from her conversation with Connell and Siobhan, but she let her friend continue.

"The Welsh have called this place the Summer Country, the Greeks called it the Elysian Fields, and a bunch of other peoples have similar ideas of places of paradise that are reached either after death or as a place where death does not touch you. Almost every culture has something like this."

"What does this have to do with elves and Oregon?" asked Misty. While all of this was interesting, she was waiting for Kelsey to make her point.

"Just give me a second, okay. I want to lay the groundwork. Plus, I put all this time into looking this stuff up. The least you can do is listen."

"Right. Sorry."

"It's fine," continued Kelsey, unperturbed. "Okay, this preoccupation with the West is not just limited to a few cultures, but the weird thing about it is that it makes no astronomical sense."

Misty's brain reeled with the sudden change of direction. "I'm afraid you lost me again. Did you say 'astronomical?'"

"I did. Go with me on this. Where does the sun set?"

"Is this some kind of trick question?"

"Just answer," said Kelsey, impatience creeping through her voice. "I want to get to the good stuff here."

"Okay, fine. The west," said Misty.

"Right, and that isn't necessarily a good thing. The coming of night in general, especially in the countryside with its wolves and whatnot, was a thing to be feared. It signals the end of something, the end of light."

"The end of life," interjected Misty.

"Right, and I don't think that was, or is, something that people, including your elves, were searching for."

"It could just be a metaphorical end," said Misty, trying out a new term that Miss Mattos had taught the class.

"I've thought of that. Maybe the end of an era or something. It's a possibility," admitted Kelsey. "But if that were the case, it doesn't explain why the elves ended up in Oregon."

"Why are they here, then?"

"Sorry, I'm getting ahead of myself. I need to get back to this concept of the West. You see, it's not just a fairy tale kind of thing. Think about the history of America, even of European exploration."

"You mean the 'New World'?"

"Right. It doesn't make any sense. North and South America weren't any more new than the rest of the world, but people today still refer to the Western Hemisphere as the New World. Even the concept of a Western Hemisphere is ludicrous. The division is totally made up, and I don't think we can just put it down to Columbus sailing west when he tried to get rich.

"Plus, after the white settlers arrived it was only a matter of time before they looked to the West. It was like a new beginning, for everyone. This idea is probably something that runs in the blood of everyone, apparently even your new friends. What's funny is that you would think that if someone was looking for a paradise, a place of renewal, it would be towards the East, where the sun rises."

"The Garden of Eden was supposed to be in the East, wasn't it."

Kelsey shrugged. "I don't remember. I think so. But that was closed off, if you believe the story. Plus it has more to do with the beginning of things, not continuations."

On the outside of Misty's window, the chill of the night had formed frosty spider webs. Misty shivered with just thinking of the dropping temperature, though the heat from the vents was steadily flowing into her room. The thought of the cold, along with the new ideas that Kelsey was bringing compelled her to say something.

"Kels, we have a choice. Either we need to wrap this up, or you can spend the night. I'd prefer that you stay."

Kelsey grinned, reaching into her knapsack and pulling out a pair of well-worn pajamas. "I knew that you were going to find me fascinating. I already asked my parents."

Misty smiled back. "Great. I do want to hear about what your research has to do with Tir Nan Og, but take your time."

Kelsey ran into the bathroom to change into her pajamas, giving Misty time to think. Trust Kelsey to take things into waters she herself would never have even considered entering. It was enough for her to know that the Sidhe were driven away, and that they came to Oregon, eventually. Anything further than that wasn't really necessary; they were here now.

But what did this have to do with Misty? Other than the fact that the elves had chosen to take up residence, hundreds and hundreds of years before she was born, in what would become her backyard.

For Kelsey, with her familial connection, it must have been different. Probably it was her guilt that led her friend to seek answers in places Misty did not, but all of this had to come out of something more.

179

The elves had said that she and Kelsey were connected in some way, but were unable to say more than that. Of course the connection that Kelsey had with the elves was tied to her heritage.

She wasn't allowed to think on this further, as Kelsey had bounced into the room, hair tangled, ready to renew their conversation.

"Okay, now do you remember your vision, the one that Siobhan gave you?"

"I do," said Misty, her voice catching as she recalled the infinite sadness in Eogan's eyes as he bid a final farewell to his home and his tree.

Kelsey either didn't notice or was being polite, for she added, "I'm not sure if your vision was the same as mine, but mine had an old man, sorry, old elf in it."

It had been the first time that Kelsey had mentioned her experience to Misty, and Misty was anxious to see what she was willing to share. "Mine did too. His name was Eogan."

"Good, that's good. We shared the same sights. It'll make this next part easier. When he was on the boat, he said something to that other elf."

"Diahan. Actually he never said it. He was just thinking it."

"Yes, Diahan. Anyway, when he was thinking about the journey, he knew that they were never going to reach Tir Nan Og." Kesley scratched her head. "I'm still not real clear on how we were able to know what the fellow was thinking."

"Magic," supplied Misty.

180

"Yeah, magic. Duh. Back to my point. It doesn't matter that he knew their future, because I'm just suspending my disbelief on that. Of course, if you had said elves exist I would've—"

"Kelsey," Misty jumped in, "what is your point."

"Right. Well I started thinking, and I couldn't get one question out of my head."

"What is it?"

Kelsey leaned forward, dropping her voice to a whisper, as if the walls themselves threatened to overhear, "What if the reason Eogan knew they were never going to reach Tir Nan Og is that there is no Tir Nan Og?"

***

By the time Christina had pulled into the driveway it was already midnight. Unfortunately, the deeper she became involved with her client, the more these extremely late nights were becoming the norm. The firm had been informed that the alliance of eco-groups, through their attorney, would have a decision by Monday, three days from now.

Two, actually, Christina thought, seeing from her watch that Saturday had officially begun. It was Christmas.

So it was with some surprise that she found Kelsey's car parked in front of the garage, behind Misty's space. She should have realized by now that her daughter would turn to other sources if she wasn't able to find support with her mother. It just seemed odd that anyone would be staying over Christmas Eve; none of Misty's friends had before.

"We already opened our presents at home," explained Kelsey, when Christina came into the room. She and Misty were drinking hot cocoa, their pajama bottoms clashing with the somber leather of the Montoyas' new couch, purchased, as everything else seemed to be, with Thomas Keller's money. "It's something of a family tradition. But this year we did it even earlier because I had to get back to some research."

Christina laughed, feeling happy to be in the same room with her daughter, to be sharing her friend. "Your teachers must be bears to be giving you research projects over the break," she said.

Kelsey took a loud gulp of cocoa. "Yeah, they are. But I actually think it's important that I learn this stuff."

"See, Misty," said Christina, "I'm not the only one who happens to think that knowledge is important." She gave Kelsey an approving stare.

"I know, mom," said Misty automatically.

This kind of back and forth about studying and grades had been going on as long as either of them could remember. The positive effect of this was that Misty's grades always hovered among those of the top-ranked students in her class. Another effect, sometimes hard to ignore, was that it occasionally threatened to drive both of them nuts.

"But," added Misty, "I also happen to think that the thing Kelsey is working on has some value beyond a grade. A whole lot of value, actually. I'm looking forward to seeing what else she comes up with. We were just talking about it before you came in."

Christina brightened, realizing how much she had missed being a part of Misty's world, even the duller aspects of school and homework. Maybe by sharing with her friend, she could find some reattachment to daughter. "What are you working on, then?"

"It's research into cultural background, mostly. Different legends and stuff like that. I'm part Irish, so I'm focusing on Celtic myths, like leprechauns and giants."

Christina dove in. "Are you researching just the myths themselves or the mythopoeia of the culture?" she asked.

Kelsey swallowed. "What was that word again?"

"Oh, mom," groaned Misty. "Sorry, Kels, she's just showing off her big vocabulary again. Why don't you tell her what it means."

"It means how the myths were created, how they came to be," explained Christina. She wrote the word out on a piece of scratch paper, then slid it over to Kelsey. "If nothing else, you should find a reason to slap that word in there and surprise your teacher. It's amazing how many points get added for using big words, and using them correctly.

"But I'm sorry, I was rambling," she continued. "What again is your research about?" she asked, giving Kelsey an opening.

"Well, I guess it would be the mytho. . .poeic thing," said Kelsey, testing out the new word. "Actually, that is exactly what I'm researching," she added, throwing Misty a significant look that Christina would have had to be blind to miss. "I'm thinking of expanding the ideas of particular myths, and applying the same research to different cultures, to see if there are similarities."

Christina could tell by the way Kelsey was warming up to the subject that she had already begun, or perhaps even finished, her investigation. She could also tell by Misty's stricken expression that her daughter was getting more and more uncomfortable.

She decided to quit while she was ahead, and take the time she had had with Misty as a gain. "Well, it certainly sounds interesting," she

183

said, letting her daughter off the hook, "but I'm going to bed. We'll open our presents tomorrow. Misty always was impatient, so it continues to be good practice for her to wait until Christmas morning."

"I got you something, so you can stay," said Misty, speaking to Kelsey.

Kelsey smiled. "Sounds great. As it turns out, I have a little something for you too."

"Well that's settled, and I'm off to bed. Good night, girls," said Christina, leaving the living room.

The last thing she heard before she closed her bedroom door was Misty's urgent whisper, "Be careful what you say, Kels. She'll pick up clues. She is a lawyer, after all." This was a favorite expression of Misty's, used when she was particularly upset at some rule or particularly imaginative punishment. She had said it most often to her father, who learned early on to turn a deaf ear to this particular complaint.

Perhaps she was just wishing, but for the first time it sounded like her daughter spoke those words with a hint of pride. It was a start.

Before finally falling asleep, Christina made a promise: starting now, she would do everything she could to keep her daughter from losing that pride. No matter the cost.

***

"What do you mean there may not be a Tir Nan Og?" asked Misty. The two girls had returned to her room shortly after Christina left and Misty was anxious to continue their conversation and perhaps find some answers.

"I know it sounds a little weird," admitted Kelsey, "but come on, this whole thing left the realm of reality some time ago. Hang on a sec." She reached around behind her and Misty could see that she had pulled out her English notebook. Kelsey must have been using it to write down all of her ideas. That way if anyone got curious, she could just say she was doing research. "I know I'm going out on a limb here, but the more research I did the more I was able to make one assumption."

"And that is?"

"Well, for all the legends of a paradise here on Earth, no one has ever found it, or any version of it, not anywhere. So I got to thinking that maybe it doesn't exist in this world. Maybe it's just an idea that people have been keeping in their heads. Or maybe it's like the idea of Heaven in that you can only reach it after you die."

"The Sidhe aren't exactly people," said Misty, pointing out the obvious. "There's no reason they would believe the things we would."

"And why not?" persisted Kelsey. "We know that Connell and Siobhan are younger elves, so we do know that they age. A lot slower than us, sure, but they age just the same. Otherwise that Eogan fellow we both saw would still be alive and he's not."

Misty allowed what Kelsey was saying, though it was alarming. The more she thought about it the more it made a scary kind of sense, and she knew that she was going to have a new topic of conversation for Connell and Siobhan the next time they met. And since they met every day, she was going to have to put the facts together pretty fast.

She began working it out. "So, if there is no Tir Nan Og, not one that anyone, even elves, can reach that means that every one of them that left Ireland, uh, Erin, never made it. They all ended up here." This

185

wasn't making sense. "There's no way that they could all fit in my back yard." Even as she said it she realized how ridiculous it sounded.

"I think that goes without saying," agreed Kelsey, laughing softly so as not to wake Christina. "But it's a good bet they're all over the place. Maybe close by." She hesitated, and it was clear to see that she was thinking along a different line than Misty.

"What do you mean?"

"Well, it's kind of a long story, but I have a really weird mother."

"So that's where you get it from," said Misty.

"Hush. For a few years she got on this kick about road trips."

"Road trips?"

"Yeah, road trips. You get on a road and you take a trip. So from the time I was ten to when I was thirteen or fourteen, I've traveled to every state west of the Mississippi. We hit all the major parks, all the attractions. It's funny how much of America is still really wide open. I don't think we can quite understand."

"Kelsey, what does this have to do with our friends?"

"I was getting to that," said Kelsey patiently. "You lived near Yosemite, right?"

"Sort of," said Misty. "We only went a few times."

"When you went, did you get any weird feelings?"

Misty thought back, remembering the time her father took her and Christina up, along that precarious road and into the crowded parking lot. He cracked jokes during the entire trip. Fighting back the urge to cry, she forced herself to remember the long hike the three of them took after setting up camp, far away from the tourists and into the wilder part of the park. There was something.

186

"It watched me," she said at last, her voice breaking.

"Excuse me."

Misty cleared her throat. "The land. It watched me. It felt like…it felt like my backyard feels now, especially right before Connell and Siobhan come out."

Kelsey nodded. "Yeah, I got the same feeling. I got it at Yellowstone, at the Grand Canyon, when we rode down on donkeys and camped at the bottom, and a whole lot of other places." She finished and was silent for a long while. The only sound was her and Misty's breathing.

"I think that's why I got so upset that first day," said Kelsey, "I knew that something was going on, something I couldn't explain. I was mad at you for not making me feel better, for not telling me."

"I'm sorry."

"I'm over it now. No, now I'm a little worried about something else."

"What is it?"

"I'm thinking about Eogan and his tree. I'm thinking that when his tree died a part of him died as well. I'm thinking that America has had a lot of trees cut down, and it's a good chance that some of those belonged to the elves. And I'm wondering just how that must make them feel." She turned silent again, lost in emotion.

Misty was the first to speak. "I would be mad."

"Yeah. Me too."

Dates to Keep

The next morning Kelsey left after opening presents. She knew that Misty would want to talk to the elves about their conversation, and she knew that Connell and Siobhan weren't totally comfortable with her yet. She hoped that would change soon.

And she knew that in the evening Misty had a date with Nick Green.

The furthest thing from Misty's mind one hour later, as she sat with the elves, was Nick Green and their "meeting." She had refused to call it a date even after Kelsey spent an hour trying to convince her otherwise. Somehow she knew that if she started thinking of things in those terms that she would lose track of the important things her friend had had to say the night before, that she would lose the focus she realized she needed in order to guide Connell and Siobhan to the same conclusion that she and Kelsey had reached: the Sidhe, every one of them, were in America.

"Are you okay?" she asked. Her friends had listened in polite silence while Misty spun her narrative, filling in what had previously been gaps in knowledge with her own best guesses. Now Connell sat in what could only be called a stunned silence while Siobhan assumed the quiet meditation that, so Misty had learned, accompanied her whenever she entered one of her trances. She was most likely at that time running backwards through her people's collective memory.

Figuring that the female couldn't hear her anyway, she had directed the question at Connell.

"Hmm. Oh, yes I am, Misty. Thank you for asking, and for your concern," said Connell. "I am just trying to digest the information you have given me."

"And?"

"I find it difficult to reconcile what I have learned with what you are telling me. There are of course other clans."

Misty had guessed this by now. She was disappointed that she had apparently not earned enough of the elves' trust up until this time. Connell had obviously decided that she knew enough by now to be told.

"So there are other clans," said Misty, looking at Connell, trying to penetrate his sky-blue eyes, but Connell flinched slightly and looked away.

"I'm done," announced Siobhan.

Thrusting her emotions aside, Misty turned her attention to Siobhan. To think that they had a chance to solve a mystery that had plagued the Sidhe for an age, and that she would be a part of it. She and Kelsey. It was quite exciting, actually. Of course, they would never be able to tell anyone else, but it was enough that they would know.

Kelsey should be here.

But her friend had left, not wanting to interfere, or so she had said. In truth, she still felt awkward about Misty and Nick, and was trying to hide it. Misty knew how she had felt; she'd been there.

"What did you find?" she asked. There was no time for regrets.

Siobhan scratched her head. "Who is Theodore Roosevelt?"

Misty was perplexed, mimicking the elf's motion with one of her own. "What is this, Jeopardy? He was one of our Presidents. People called him Teddy. What does this have to do with anything?"

Siobhan ignored her question. "And what exactly does a President do?"

"He's the one who runs the country. Well, sort of. There are three separate branches of government and each one is responsible for a different…Hey! When did this become a civics lesson? School isn't until next Monday."

Siobhan nodded. "So he is like the leader of a clan."

"A very large clan, yes. Except our clan never really gets along."

"How can you be a member of a clan always in conflict?" interrupted Connell.

While Misty was deciding how to answer Connell's question, which she wasn't sure she was qualified to do, or whether to demand an answer to one of her own, Siobhan rescued her. "I think I can tell you about your national parks now."

Misty was getting dizzy with the abrupt changes in direction this conversation was taking but tried her best to ride it out. "You mean our national park system? Is that why you asked about Teddy Roosevelt?"

"Yes."

"But why?"

"It is a long story."

"I've got time."

For the next hour Misty and Siobhan spoke, while Connell listened attentively, with the first part taken up by Misty filling in historical gaps outside of the Sidhe's knowledge.

Then, things got interesting.

". . .so in 1884, his wife and mother died, and Roosevelt began spending a lot of time on his ranch," Misty said. She had been giving a brief history of his life, answering Siobhan's questions as best as she could. She felt lucky that her government teacher had, in the second month of school, assigned a President for each student to research and that Misty had wound up with Roosevelt. Of course, such coincidences were now pointing to a larger design. The more time she spent with the elves, the less she was seeing things as being up to mere chance. She was meant to have this conversation.

"I think I can, as you say, fill in the gaps now," said Siobhan, "but first let me ask you a question. Does it not seem strange to you that a man born of wealth in a very large city, as this Mr. Roosevelt was, would become one of your nation's supreme champions of the wilderness?"

"I suppose that it does seem weird, but he really wasn't an environmentalist." Misty said. "He was good for the national parks, though. A lot of people just assumed he wanted a bigger place to hunt. I just think that the experience of losing his wife and the time he spent outdoors right afterwards had something to do with it."

Siobhan nodded once, and looked upward through the leafy canopy. It seemed as if the elf were trying to find just the right way to go about saying what she had to say. Recognizing the importance of her friend's concentration, Misty sat waited patiently, barely stirring. Even Niko had stopped splashing in the stream and had trotted up to where Connell was sitting. Now he sat on his haunches, head tilted quizzically.

Finally, Siobhan spoke. "I know that you have felt a sense of your own uniqueness when you were allowed to find us. It must have

191

been very similar to the way that my brother and I felt as well. You are the first person of your generation to look upon the Sidhe, and to do so with our blessing, which counts for much more than one might think."

Misty, sharp-eared, had caught the qualifier, and jumped in, "You said that I was the first of my generation, right. But that means that…."

"You are not the first. Not the first American, by any means. In the latter part of your nineteenth century, Mr. Roosevelt met someone very special. Let me show you."

Siobhan began speaking, and this time Misty was prepared for the leap, the same type that she had taken before, that she had encouraged Kelsey to take as well, with mixed results. Somewhere in the dimness of her consciousness, Siobhan's foreign words began to make sense, just as the world began to blur.

"In 1885, Mr. Roosevelt met Eogan…."

***

Eogan was dying. This was not a new revelation; he had been slowly fading away for centuries, ever since greedy Irishmen had put axes to his beloved tree, ripping it from the earth only to set it ablaze in a dozen fireplaces, meant to keep a dozen houses warm. Houses that had long since returned to the earth from which they had been forcibly sprung.

But the old elf, the eldest of the Sidhe, was still around. For a little while. But he was no longer the creature he was. With the loss of his connection to the Earth, his gift of foresight had begun to fade, his hair began to turn from silver to gray, and his bones began to ache with mortality. Soon enough, he too would warm the earth while his spirit scattered to the four winds, to see what was left in the world that still contained wonder.

He would be free.

"Ach, I am not dead yet," he said with a huff. Although he was a solitary figure in the Badlands of the Dakotas at that time, he was rarely alone these days. Diahan, in particular, seemed always to be fussing over him. "It's not as if I am to be keeling over just yet," he was fond of saying when her ministrations became overbearing.

Most of the other elves of his clan had continued West, how many centuries ago was it? It didn't matter, really. Only he, Diahan, and a few other stalwarts were left, having decided that they had had just enough of moving, thank you very much. Well, perhaps it was only just him. The others stayed out of loyalty. When he was gone they would go as well, continuing their endless journey.

It had been a difficult time. After the landing on the eastern coast of this land (and what a disaster that was) the various clans of the Sidhe, all of them, had branched out, each elf convinced that the land of Tir Nan Og was over the next mountain, across the next river. Each of them but one.

Of course, none of them bothered to remember that Tir Nan Og was an island, and thus very unlikely to be located on a continent. People have to have hope. Elves, too. So Eogan just shut his mouth and went along, and once they crossed the widest river any of them had ever seen, he decided that he had gone far enough.

He was still here.

"You're a little one."

Under any normal circumstance, it was impossible for a human to sneak up on an elf. But Eogan was preoccupied, wrapped up in memories of other times, happier and sadder, easier and harder. Also, over the past two hundred years he had started to lose his hearing, although he would never admit to it. Diahan and the others just smiled when they thought he wasn't looking, and talked a little louder with each passing year. Three years ago they had dropped the whole game and just shouted at him, but always in the nicest way. Also, without his tree he wasn't nearly so tuned in to the comings and goings of the creatures upon the Earth.

So Eogan could forgive himself for being caught off guard, and managing to do that in an instant, he sprang to his feet with (relative) speed. Straightened out once again, he looked the tall stranger in the eye and was surprised to find the man staring back at him with an unflinching gaze. Eogan found himself looking straight into the man's heart.

"Hmph. I would say you have aged a little bit more than your years would let on."

The man smiled, even if it was a bit of a sad one, squatting down so as better to look at the Sidhe on an even level. It was a small act of courtesy, but it was enough of one that Eogan liked him immediately.

"You would guess rightly, my friend, but my worry at this time is more for you. They do not call this area the Badlands for nothing."

Now that the man was lower to the ground, Eogan was able to get a better look at him. He was powerfully built, but it was a power added on in his later years. Even with his dulled senses, he could tell that this man had at one time been gravely ill, and had triumphed over his affliction. The victory was still in the man's eyes, but coupled with a more recent sorrow.

"Hmph. Young man, I would say you have more cause to worry than myself. I have spent more years than you can count wandering this place," said Eogan gruffly.

He wasn't quite sure why he was having this conversation. His general rule of thumb in dealing with humans is that you didn't, if you could help it. After all, the whole leprechaun legend had sprung up from all the times the Sidhe had encountered humans only to promptly take off running in the other direction. Now the clans were raising their young in a way that Eogan couldn't quite agree with. Instead of commonsense guidelines about how to deal with humans, who were encroaching more and more upon the unspoiled land, the Sidhe resurrected stories of the Fomorians, their ancient enemies, and lumped the humans right along with them, so much so as to keep any younger elf (and some older ones as well) from knowing the difference. It just didn't make a great deal of sense.

But it wasn't up to him, now was it?

Of course, in the big picture, what the human tribes had ended up doing was far worse than the Fomorians, nothing more than lumbering, dull-witted giants when compared to the Sidhe (or so a Sidhe would always maintain), had managed to do in the centuries of their supposed warfare.

What all of this history did was make Eogan's choice not to run an interesting one. If he had been asked why he had stayed at the time he wouldn't have been able to give an upright answer. When it came down to it, he sensed something good about the man. Plus, he was old, and really didn't care what anyone one else thought about him.

So it was that Theodore Roosevelt, the man who would be President, and Eogan, leader of the Sidhe (technically speaking) sat in the hot noonday sun, in one of the most inhospitable places in the country, and had themselves a little talk.

Eogan learned of Roosevelt's great loss and, having seen the loss of an entire culture and all that he had known, felt sorrow for him. Thus the two had a connection before the first real words were spoken, and that connection meant something to both of them.

"Something about this place speaks to me," said Roosevelt, digging his knife point into the ground and rooting out a rock. Checking it over he grunted, unsatisfied, and lobbed it towards the nearest hill, watching it skip over the rough ground. "I can't say I know why."

"It is still pure," answered Eogan. "Your people have not truly come here. Oh, I have seen the digging, though I cannot say I understand the importance of what they are looking for. But other than these few, this place is untouched, and that is what makes it beautiful." While he spoke, his mind wandered back to Erin, and he lamented the loss of a land that contained only shadows and ghosts of what once was. Still, these fragments would enchant people until the end of time, he knew, precisely because they were tiny reminders of a magical past.

Maybe something of Eogan's melancholy found its way into his voice. Maybe Roosevelt—Teddy—was thinking about his own irrecoverable loss. Whatever the cause, something happened to the man that day. He looked around the battered land, the Badlands, and saw them for what they were: innocence. He knew something else, too.

196

This person next to him was offering him a great gift, one of the greatest, without even comprehending it.

"You're not just a little man, are you?" asked Roosevelt. Taking Eogan's silence for agreement he continued. "I thought there was something different about you. It's in your voice. It's weirdish. When you were talking just then, just for a few seconds I was thinking of green hills, tall trees. Was that your home I was seeing?"

"My home has not had trees like those you saw for a long time," replied Eogan sadly, his heartbreak plain in his voice. "And I do not think it will have them again."

Teddy leaned forward, wonder in his eyes. "Just how old are you?"

Eogan didn't care at that moment who knew the truth, and this young man was more honest than most. "The world has taken its course around the sun 3,929 times since I was born." There, the man would think him crazy, or he would not. It didn't matter.

"That is a long time," said Roosevelt with no surprise, "but your people have always been long-lived, have they not?"

"What do you mean, my people?" asked Eogan, alarmed.

"You know of what I speak. You're a leprechaun, right? What are you doing in America?"

Eogan let his pride overcome his better judgment. "A leprechaun," he repeated disdainfully. "We prefer 'Sidhe,' if that suits you. If it doesn't, then think of me as an elf. A leprechaun! Why, I never."

Roosevelt bowed his head in apology. "A Sidhe, then. Why are you not in Ireland?"

197

"Ireland is lost to us."

"As this place is not," reasoned Roosevelt. "I see that now." He reached into his knapsack, pulling out a sandwich wrapped in wax paper. He offered half to Eogan, and when the elf shook his head in refusal, he shrugged and took a monstrous bite. Taking a mighty swallow, he said, "You know, America is not a half bad place to live. I can see why you came."

"We didn't come. We crashed," corrected Eogan.

"Oh, well lucky for you then. This is a land that's wide open. A man can breathe here. I reckon an elf can as well." He took another bite, this time chewing thoughtfully. "Of course, I don't know how long it's going to last."

"More people arrive each year," said Eogan. "The land will run out. Always it is this way with humans. You reach out for more."

"That we do," agreed Roosevelt. "I shall be sorry to see it go. I've got money, you know, and I've seen a lot of this country. More than I'll remember at any rate. Why, just a few hundred miles that way," he pointed west, "there's hills that brush the sky, geysers of hot steam shooting from the ground, and, God, rivers so blue it makes you cry."

"They will be gone soon enough," said Eogan. At that moment he felt an ache in his side. Yes, it wasn't going to be long now. How strange that it should be happening here, at this time, in the company of this man.

Roosevelt, not noticing the stricken look on Eogan's face, went on. "Maybe. Though they don't have to be."

Eogan looked up, the pain momentarily forgotten. "What do you mean?"

"Our government's a funny thing. Imagine how wonderful it would be if someone would just set the land aside for everyone to enjoy. What an accomplishment for a lifetime," said Roosevelt. He was getting a faraway look in his eye as he said these words. "What a way to make amends for things one had to do."

Eogan noticed. "For your lifetime, perhaps," he said slyly.

Roosevelt guffawed. "No, oh no! Politics isn't the game for me, sir. They'd have to drag me in kicking and screaming."

The pain came back, and with it a final burst of clarity. "I have made a good choice in coming here, on this day. You are a good man, underneath it all, and it is not for me to tell you your destiny. But I am content to have spent my final moments by your side." Eogan lay down as he spoke, his last words coming as a whisper.

"Say there, chap!" shouted Roosevelt, "don't be leaving on me. I've just met you, for God's sakes!"

"Theodore, my time has come. It has been counting down for many centuries," said Eogan weakly. "I understand now why I have been tied to this place for so long. I can go now. There are other places out there. This one is done with me."

"I don't understand what you mean! Tell me what you mean!" pleaded Roosevelt desperately. But it was too late. Eogan's eyes had closed, a little smile was on his face, and he looked utterly content.

No one in the clan ever found Eogan's body, never even knew where to look. Instead, it was Teddy Roosevelt who buried him, not understanding at that moment how much the few hours he spent with the elf had affected him.

Some people say that Roosevelt came out the Badlands a changed man. They were right.

**

"Wait," said Siobhan quietly, "there is something else."

**

Thomas hated Yosemite. He always had.

But his father, being determined to raise his son to appreciate as much of the world as he could, insisted on taking him there every year, as a sort of final farewell to the summer before the school year started. Every summer was the same: a month-long trip to some new and interesting place in the world followed by the same long Labor-Day weekend at Yosemite. They wouldn't even stay at the Ahwahnee, which his father could have easily afforded to buy, if it came to that. No, they had to "rough it," staying in the same crappy canvas tent they had owned for all of Thomas's life.

Thomas had long ago ceased staring out the car window at the scenery that the park possessed in abundance. It was always the same. Same trees, same mountains, same rocks, same El Capitan, same Half Dome, same everything. Accordingly, David Keller had long ago ceased pointing out anything to his son, and the trips were now spent in silence.

Thomas was fifteen years old.

"Same spot again, right," said Thomas, boredom seeping through his voice.

David nodded, gritting his teeth in an attempt to maintain his patience. Thomas could hear the molars grinding against each other.

200

"As always, son. Perhaps one day you will appreciate it more. It really does have quite a tremendous view."

Thomas had to agree. It was a tremendous view, always the same. It wasn't that he hated nature; as a matter of fact, he found it to be quite soothing, to be surrounded by it, far away from the crowds. But the crowds always seemed to find this place, and others like it, the great unwashed tide of people that descended each and every year to gawk at the sights he took for granted. Now, when he looked at the famous valley, crowned with true mountains, he saw only waste.

"How many people come here, anyway?" he muttered, not really intending for his father to hear.

David had heard, though, and perhaps out of some wishful hope that Thomas was finally becoming curious about the place, attempted to answer. "Oh, I can't say. Seems like almost a million a year. Maybe more. A lot of people."

"Too many people," complained Thomas.

"Maybe you're right," said David, "but everyone has a right to see this. It's one of the great things about this land of ours: it's free for all to roam."

Thomas tucked his chin into his shirt. "It shouldn't be."

David misunderstood. "Well, they do charge a fee. This place has to be kept up, to be maintained so that your children, and theirs, can continue to enjoy it."

Thomas ignored his father, was already looking into the valley. In his mind's eye, he envisioned a paradise of stately homes, manicured gardens, swimming pools, an enclave where the privileged could enjoy the fruits of their wealth amid natural beauty, unspoiled by the lower classes.

He could not have been more different from his father. Although David had also been born to wealth, with every need catered to, he had gained an early determination to be his own man. When World War II came, he had refused the easy posting offered by his family's friends in Congress and instead enlisted as a private in a combat unit. He was not alone among the young and rich who had done this; it was a different time. During the war he had befriended boys from as wildly disparate backgrounds as could have existed, most of these poor. After the conflict, and at the beginning of his years of nightmares, he gave many of these men jobs with his father's company, a favor which they repaid with dedication and hard work. Every Christmas, one or more of these men, along with their own broods, occupied the family manor, sharing the holidays with the Kellers.

And, Thomas felt, acting as if they were his equals.

He was determined that, when he came into his inheritance, he was going to get as far away from them as possible. What better way to do that than to pluck a piece of desirable real estate and shut it off from all but those he knew to be worthy?

"I'm going for a walk," he said to his father, who was still unloading the truck.

"Be back in an hour, then," called David after his retreating son. Maybe he was happy that Thomas was attempting to feel the call of this place. Thomas didn't care. He just wanted to get away from the man.

His ramble took him across familiar streams and through well-worn fields, and always he tried to avoid the RVs, the flimsy tents, the screaming, dirty children and their slack-jawed, mouth-breathing parents. It wasn't easy to do this.

Finally, though, he put enough distance between him and anyone else and felt that he could at last breathe. Again, his mind filled with plans, plans that would never come to fruition, not in this place, protected as it was by damnable federal laws. Still, there were other places, other realms to carve out for himself and for those he chose.

Why did this place make him so uncomfortable?

He would never come to find the reason, would never understand that he was being watched, just as he was watched every year of his life, every time he took off into the countryside. He would never know that he was uncomfortable because he was made to be so by creatures older than mankind's memory.

The Sidhe knew that there was something broken in Thomas Keller, and that he could not be fixed. Some people are just born that way. And though they may have felt pity for the poor child, they could not tolerate his presence. So they made him feel unwelcome whenever he ventured out, no matter how many times he came, and he was never able to stay long.

They could not have known that Thomas came to a decision that day, after so many years of discomfort. If he could not have this place he would seek out others, and any time he felt the way he was feeling right now, he would rip and tear that place away and shape it into something his own.

At fifteen years old, Thomas Keller declared a secret war against the elves, an enemy he didn't even know existed.

***

"Why did you show me that?" asked Misty.

"I do not know. It came to me as something important. Do you know this man?"

"No, but maybe my mother does. I can tell that something at work's bothering her. It could have something to do with him. I saw that last name on some files she was carrying into our house."

"You are connected, that is sure. It is probable that your mother is the connection."

Misty looked at her watch and groaned. "Oh, God, my mother. I don't even have time to ask her." She got up and called Niko over.

"Do you have somewhere you must be?"

"I have a date. Sort of," said Misty, already climbing up the hill.

"What is a 'date?'" asked Connell.

"I'll explain later."

Dates and Decisions

"So, are you having a good time?"

Misty sat down on the hard bench, breathless and ankles aching from going around the rink. Around and around and around, and always in the same direction. Now, as the zamboni was resurfacing the ice, she and Nick had a chance to actually talk. She couldn't believe that she was ice skating, which she had told herself she would never do again. For good reason.

"Yeah, I am. Sorry I'm such a klutz. We never used to go ice skating that much," she said.

"Not much skating going on in California, huh?" asked Nick. He bent down to retie his skate—he had brought his own hockey skates—but it was clear that he was still listening.

"Not really. They do an outdoor rink every Christmas, at Embarcadero Center. That's on the bay side of San Francisco. I only saw it once. I think I've only skated two or three times in my life." She blushed at having to explain herself, thinking that Nick could not have been interested. His patience over the past hour with her surely must have reached the breaking point by now.

"Well, I'm glad that this place is open tonight. I wasn't sure it would be, being Christmas. And, just so you don't think I'm some kind of pro or anything, I didn't start skating until I was about thirteen or fourteen. My dad wanted me to play football, but my mom said hockey had more pads, so hockey it was. They're both rough sports, but I've seen some guys get majorly hurt playing football. Every game it seems."

Misty smiled. "Or maybe hockey players are just tougher," she said, punching his shoulder.

"Yeah," Nick grinned, "maybe. Come on, the ice is done." He grabbed her hand, surprising Misty. "It's a little slippery for the first few minutes, so be careful until it's carved up a bit, okay."

"Okay." And they were off.

The next thirty minutes went by in a blur, albeit a never-ended circular blur. Misty never thought she could have so much fun doing the same thing over and over. It was weird, but Nick was nothing like she had first imagined him to be. She had had the picture in her head of a younger version of his father, and for the first few months she had allowed that illusion to rule her decisions regarding the handsome boy.

It wouldn't be the first time she was wrong about something. It was just rare that her instincts were so completely off.

"Whenever you're ready, we can get some dinner, if you like," said Nick. The endless monotony that is public skating seemed to be wearing on him.

"Okay." *Make a mental note*, she thought to herself, *to stop using the word "okay" so much.* She almost cringed as she thought a silent *"okay,"* again.

"Let's get out of here and find someplace not infested with our classmates; though I'm not sure what's going to be open." Sure enough, as soon as the words came out of his mouth, a loud "Oooh!" came from above. Looking over, Misty saw Briana and one of her clones, white figure skates in their gloved hands, leering over at her and Nick, who either hadn't heard (not likely) or was doing a good job at ignoring the spiteful girls. In fact, was that a bit of jealousy hidden beneath Briana's baleful glare? Misty briefly pondered whether or not it would be better to ignore the girls or to really give them a dig and wave back.

"Come on, they're just being stupid." Nick took her hand again, making a show of it, and helped her walk out of the changing area, allowing her feet to regain their balance now that they weren't perched on two thin steel blades.

***

Christina tapped her fingernails on the polished wood table, yet another item newly bought with some of the money Thomas Keller regularly infused into her firm, and watched the clock. Misty had left three hours before, and was supposed to be back by midnight.

So, midnight was her deadline. She was going to have a decision made by then, and she was going to share it with her daughter. Everything. She doubted that Misty would care about the loss of the income; losing her father had taught her just how little money means. Still, if Christina's choice meant a move back to California, just as Misty was starting to adjust and make new friends, that could be trouble. There was something really special about that Kelsey girl, the type of friendship that comes along once in a lifetime. Strange that she knew this having only met the girl once. Perhaps it was just having her over on Christmas Eve that made Christina automatically catalog the girl in her mind as one of the family.

And she could tell that her daughter was starting to bond. Why, tonight she even had a date. What right had she to take Misty from this now, in the middle of the year?

About as much right as she had to bring her to Oregon in the first place.

She tapped her fingers again, a nervous habit that Carlos had never been able to break her of. The clock read 8:02.

Four hours to go. Four hours and a choice.

***

Kelsey lay on her bed, hands behind her head, thinking.

Her parents had always said their daughter was psychic. They had been referring to her ability to duck chores, but she always took it seriously. It meant something to be special, so in her heart's most secret place she believed it.

So when she found herself unable to shake the uneasy feelings she kept having about Misty and Nick, it wasn't so easy to dismiss these as just envy or jealousy on her part. There was just something that didn't feel right about the whole situation. What made it worse was that, except for the first few weeks of school when he was still talking to Briana, Nick had done nothing at all to earn her distrust. And even if he had, Misty had not, and she certainly didn't need Kelsey to watch over her.

Besides, she thought, *you have bigger things to think about.* Like the enormous amount of faith Misty had shown by allowing Kelsey to know the elves, and Kelsey's knowledge that she had as yet been unable to return the favor other than with a suggestion that they were in America, all of them. A fat lot of good that did anybody, and it certainly didn't change things. Not the problems of her mother's side of the family, not the fact that she really couldn't talk to anybody about this.

There was a knock on her door. "Are you okay, honey? You've been in there a while, and dinner's getting cold." It was her mother.

She got up, rolling off the side and landing on the floor. It wasn't going to do any good hiding in here; her parents weren't ones to just leave her alone if they thought she was upset over something. "I'm fine, mom. I just dozed off."

Dinner first, problems later. An old Wagner saying, that.

***

Nick pulled carefully up to Misty's driveway, taking care not to spray gravel all over the place. Misty, who had long before been assigned the chore of sweeping up any of the rocks that ended up on the street or the porch and depositing them back where they belonged, appreciated the gesture. It was one more act in a night of small acts of consideration, and it all added up to Nick Green not being nearly as bad a guy as she thought he was the first day they had met.

Still, there were rules. "I had a good time, tonight," she said, getting out of the car before things got awkward. Her father had always said that the longer a person spent in someone else's car without actually going anywhere the more dangerous things could get. And, he had maintained, if the driver ended up shutting off the engine, you were in the red zone!

Carlos had always been an overprotective dad, which used to drive Misty crazy. Now, on her first date since his death, she found herself missing it.

But he had taught her well, and her rear was quickly out of the passenger seat of Nick's truck. "Thanks a lot!" she called, waving goodbye.

Nick, to his credit, seemed to take it well. Waving back, he called, "I'll see you in school, then."

That was a nice touch, Misty thought, not asking the cliché question: Uh, so when can I see you again? And he even waited until she was inside before driving off.

Christina, who had the eyes of a hawk and the hearing of a bat, and had been peeking from behind the kitchen blinds, noticed as well. Misty knew that she would be there. It used to be her dad's accustomed spot, and now it was her mom's.

When Misty came in the front door, Christina was waiting for her. She noticed that her mother looked nervous and, because that was rare, it made Misty nervous as well.

She opened first. "Hey, mom. Is there something you wanted to talk about?" It was pretty obvious that there was; she could practically see the wear marks in the carpet where Christina had been pacing.

"Actually, there was. Could you come with me into the dining room? I've been doing some work in there, and I wanted to share something with you." Without waiting for an answer Christina practically ran into the adjacent room.

Misty, confused by the alarming behavior, followed after, not quite as fast. She doubted that anything could have happened in the short time that she had been gone. No, it seemed more likely that Christina had been agonizing over something for a while (probably at the office, for she surely hadn't been at home that often) and had come to a decision.

It was suspiciously similar to what happened before they moved to Oregon.

Misty groaned inwardly. "Not again," she whispered. "I'm not done yet." She spoke the words before realizing what she was saying, or what they meant.

Christina had heard them. "Not done with what?" She was already seated at the table, a mound of papers spread out before her, threatening to overcome her.

"Nothing, just some school project," said Misty, thinking quickly. She changed the subject. "What's going on?"

"Sit down, Misty."

Misty sat before she could think to do anything else; her mother still had a measure of power over her. "All right, why don't you tell me what's going on."

Christina took a deep breath. "I know that I haven't been able to spend as much time with you as you would have liked. I wish it had been different these past few months. I really haven't been that good of a mother to you."

It was out now, a simple confession, and Misty, who at times had wanted to shout, to beg, to cry, anything to get Christina to perk up and remember that she still had a daughter, could say nothing.

"It's a hell of a Christmas present, isn't it?" said Christina.

"Yes, yes it is."

"Well, I have another confession to make then."

"What is it?" asked Misty, almost afraid to know what could come after the brutal, honest, and short statement she had just heard pass from her mother's lips.

"There's a reason for why I chose Boring as a place to live."

"Not your own twisted sense of humor, huh," said Misty.

211

Christina smiled. "No, not that. To be honest, I knew that Portland would be a better place for you, at least at first. It's much more like the Bay Area than out here. As much as any place in Oregon can be."

"Then why didn't we live there?" Misty was confused.

"Oh, we could have afforded to, surely. If there was one advantage to selling out, it was the paycheck," Christina said. "No, it's a little more affordable here, and that's what I wanted. I wanted to be able to save some money. I'm making a lot more than I was back home, and Carlos's insurance, well, we have enough money, but I just wanted to save more."

"Why?"

"I thought that it would be nice to take a trip together after you graduated, anywhere in the world you wanted to go."

"Mom, you didn't have to!"

Laughing, Christina said, "Well, I'm glad to hear that, because I don't think we're going to be taking that trip anytime soon."

More work, then. "Oh," said Misty, disappointed, "I understand."

"No, honey, you don't. We have the money, right now. We have more than enough. Enough for college, for vacations, for whatever. It's just that I think we're going to be needing it.

"I've decided to quit."

For a long moment Misty could say nothing. Her mother, quit? Why, she had never quit anything in her life, even when it was making her miserable to continue. Guilt snuck in on her thoughts. Had she seemed so ungrateful? *Oh no.* "Mom, I never meant for you to quit. It hasn't been that bad, really."

"No, it's not you. Oh, I know that I haven't been around, even though I promised you that I would try. Or maybe I just promised myself, and ended up breaking it. I think I realized two things, both at the same time. One, that it wasn't going to be much use going on a vacation, no matter how marvelous, with a daughter that resented me. And two, that the people I was forced to associate myself with in order to get three, maybe four, quality weeks with you were just too unpleasant to be around. You would have spent the time being angry with me and I would have spent the time dreading each passing moment that brought me back to dealing with that fool Charley and Thomas Keller.

"Do you know that I have actually been feeling physically sick every Sunday night? The thought of going back to work distresses me that much!"

"And we really have enough?" asked Misty.

"Yes," Christina went on, "we have enough to live on until the end of the year, enough and more. Long enough to see you off to college and me back to San Jose, where maybe I can find a place with a firm that has its interests closer to my heart. It took me becoming a partner to realize that this one doesn't. I thought I would use the time to get to know you again, if you'll let me."

The tears Misty had been holding back came loose then, and she rushed over to her mother and crushed her in a bear hug, realizing for the first time that Christina, the woman who had brought her forth into the world, had raised her, was now shorter than her. She wondered when that had happened.

"Oh, mom, I am so proud of you. Dad would have been too." Saying this, Misty knew it to be true. But there was something else, something Misty had almost forgotten. It was important, though.

"Mom, did you say 'Thomas Keller'?"

**

"It really is a disgusting plan, isn't it?"

Misty looked at the final draft of the "proposal" Christina was supposed to deliver to the enviro-groups tomorrow. "Yes, it is."

"Um, I'm a little curious about something," said Christina.

"What is it?"

"You had an interesting reaction when I mentioned the name Thomas Keller. Was there some reason for that?"

Great, thought Misty. Trust her mother's lawyer instincts to kick in at the worst possible moment; now, just when the two were truly coming together, she would have to lie. And it would have to be a good one in order to fool Christina.

She came as close to the truth as she dared. "Oh, it's just the last name. There's someone I really don't like who has that name is all." She had come to the precipice of truth without actually toppling over. Now she had to see if it would hold.

"I'd say you don't like this person rather a lot," replied Christina. "Well, how do you think I should handle this?"

Misty had to fight to keep the relief from audibly pouring out of her, trying to focus on the question. For Christina to ask her advice on how to handle a situation that was essentially legal in nature was out of character. Frankly, there were few people who knew the ins and outs of the legal code as well as her mother. But just being asked made her glow inside, and gave her an added sense of responsibility.

Having hovered around Christina's work since she was old enough to stand, Misty felt fairly confident that she could be a sounding board for her, which is what she knew Christina really wanted.

"He made you sign a nondisclosure, right?" asked Misty, feeling just a bit foolish in doing so. She had no right to be doing this.

But her mom was asking her, and that meant something. They were sitting together and talking, and that meant something too. Okay, so it was business, but Christina couldn't possibly know in how many ways this was touching Misty. Sure, there was the time spent. What really piqued Misty's interest, though, was that she was actively working towards something that would help the Sidhe. She was helping her mother fight to preserve their homes.

Christina's answer dampened her spirits a bit. "Of course. Thomas is no fool. Even if I hadn't, I wouldn't be able to assist the environmental groups anyway. I have had access to privileged information, told to me in confidence. I could be blackballed in Oregon and California, and I'd never be able to find a decent job. It's hard enough for a woman in this business even without the stigma of that. No, we're going to have to think of something else."

"So you can't say anything…." began Misty.

"And neither can my daughter, so you can stop that train right there." At Misty's disappointed look, she added gently, "I'm going to be watched. So are you. I wouldn't be surprised if he tries to have our phone lines tapped. He has the connections."

215

Misty became worried. If she was watched, then that could mean trouble for Connell and Siobhan. "How closely will I be watched?"

Christina smiled, easing Misty's anxiety. "Oh, not that closely. Those walks you take in the woods won't be monitored, but you'll have to be careful of what you say on the phone, especially to Kelsey."

In more ways than one, thought Misty grimly. Her mind working at a furious rate, she managed to carry on her conversation with Christina while pondering the possible consequences, positive and negative, to her relationship with the elves. Finally, she let her anxiety go. With all of the high-tech surveying equipment, all the satellites and whatnot, if the elves were going to be found through the use of modern-day surveillance, they would have been discovered already. No, it was likely that the magic that seemed so much a part of the Sidhe, had been used to effectively shut out human intrusion of all kinds.

Mostly.

Misty got back to the subject. "So, when are you going to tell Keller?" Maybe there was some way to thwart his plans without being active about it.

"I've given it a lot of thought, and I believe that the only thing I could do, the best thing, is to resign during the meeting with the groups. It would be a very public act. I wouldn't be able to give any reasons, but if they perceived a weakness in Thomas's little plan, they might be able to do enough digging on their own." Christina shrugged. "It's really the most I could do, and I'm even taking a bit of a chance with that."

Misty got up and hugged her again. "I think that'll be good enough."

And Misty would see what power was in the elves to assist.

216

**

***

"Are you sure this information is accurate?"

Misty sighed. She had gotten up early and walked Niko down the ravine just to have enough time to tell Connell and Siobhan everything; she knew they would sense her presence and come to meet her.

"Yeah, it is. I got it from my mom, and she was in pretty tight with these people. Well she used to be anyway," Misty said. "I'm not really sure what you can do with this, but if that vision you showed me of Keller is for real, there's probably some elves around that area. Another clan, maybe?"

"It is possible," admitted Siobhan, "but my brother and I are still considered children, and we will not be privy to the councils of our clan for a few more centuries."

"Hmm. I don't think I'll be able to wait that long," said Misty. Perhaps there was another way. "Could you tell someone in your clan? What about your uncle Eogan?"

"Our uncle remains convinced that you were a Fomorian," said Connell, reminding her of that first day when she had fallen on top of the older elf. "He has gone a bit barmy before his time, it seems. He cannot keep from mixing up the stories with the facts. Either that or he is putting on a good act for we younger ones."

"Connell, you will not speak of our elders in that manner," said Siobhan sternly. "They have seen and experienced things that you or I can scarcely imagine. Well, you at any rate," she added. "And I sometimes wish that I had not been blessed with the Sight. It is a burden."

217

"How can you say that?!" cried Misty. "If it weren't for your sharing your past, your people's past, with me, I would never have understood you as well as I do. My best friend might still be mad at me for all I know. Seeing your history has changed me!"

"I am sorry for that wish, then, my friend," replied Siobhan, not unkindly.

"Besides," said Misty, grinning, "who knows when I would have actually gotten to use that Roosevelt report for something useful."

Feeling then an irresistible urge to hug Siobhan, Misty acted on it, quickly and without warning. Engulfed in the girl's arms, Siobhan could only gasp, "What is this, and why are you doing it?"

Misty let go. "It's called a hug," she said. "It's what people, what humans do, when they want to let someone know they care. What's the matter? Are you going to tell me now that the Sidhe don't ever hug each other?"

"Actually, no," offered Connell. "I think we consider it crude in a way." Misty reached for him, and he wasn't quick enough to scamper out of the way. After a moment, when the elves stopped struggling and allowed themselves to experience Misty's show of affection, he added, "But I rather think I like it. It's like speaking of love without using words."

Misty let them both go, and leaned back to look at them. For some reason, she was crying. She would figure it out later. "That, my dear friend, is exactly what it is." She got up, stretching out the kinks in her back. She had gotten very little sleep the night before. However, these were thoughts for another time. "I should have done it a long time ago. You two are my friends, and I don't think you realize how important that is to me. I don't know what I would have done if I hadn't found you, if I hadn't taken this fleabag," she scratched Niko's big head, "for a walk, and if he hadn't been so determined to find you."

"Actually, we called him," said Connell. Siobhan poked him in the ribs, but it was too late.

Misty swallowed, considering the implications of his statement. "But your uncle ran from me, that day."

"It was not that day."

"Oh, God," said Misty, putting her hand to her head. "You called Niko the day I fell down. You're the ones who got me knocked out."

"Are you angry with us," asked Connell. He sounded worried.

Misty laughed. "Angry? How can I be? If I hadn't taken that spill I would never have met the two of you. No, I'm not angry. Just curious. Why did you call to him that day?"

Siobhan shrugged innocently. "We knew that he would bring you. My brother and I had wanted to see a human for some time now."

Misty was flattered. "And you chose me?"

"It was your actions of the first day that decided things. You helped our uncle, and you saw him for what he was."

"Yes, I did," said Misty uncertainly. "What does that have to do with anything?"

"The Sidhe are not so difficult to capture, not when we are weak or disoriented. Our uncle was in pain, and for several moments he was vulnerable. You chose not to act on that weakness. You chose to let him go," explained Siobhan patiently.

"I'm not so sure if I was all that aware at that moment either. But I thought that the stories of the pot of gold were just that, stories."

219

"They are. But we still have a power in us. You have seen it, both in my visions and in Connell's music."

"Like I was there," said Misty, remembering the haunting tunes that came from Connell's pipes and the vivid images that were Siobhan's gift.

"Exactly right," said Siobhan. "And what price do you think a person would be willing to pay to go the places you have gone, to hear and see what you have?"

"Anything." Misty's voice caught as she understood. "Oh."

"We have power here, to defend our people, but the farther away from the land we are, the harder it is to maintain ourselves. A Sidhe thus captured would become a shadow, a slave to the desires of any man foolish or greedy enough to chain us.

"No, Misty, you have proven yourself. And because Connell and I are still young, we felt it best to act on our desires, before fear and tradition stamped them out."

A large smile bloomed on Misty's face as she realized the incredible honor her strange friends had bestowed upon her by granting their trust. It was one thing to be a person's friend. It happened all of the time. This was different, special. Closing her eyes, she made a promise right then, under the green darkness of the forest, even as a newborn rain misted down from above to collect on her face and dribble down her nose. She would never betray these two, no matter what should happen in the future. She said these words only to herself, without even a whisper to hint to Connell and Siobhan just what was running through her head and heart. Only the sound of the rain as it struck the leaves and the ground, and the sound of Niko's tongue lolling in and out of his wide mouth could be heard.

Finally, she was done, and she opened her eyes. The elves were looking at her curiously, yet giving her the time not to speak until she felt it was right. Even though she had kept the swearing of the vow to herself, Misty knew that these two were too connected to her now not to understand that something very special was happening.

Niko barked then, bringing her back to her senses. The large Samoyed had gotten more than a bit wet during her lapse, and now he was looking positively miserable, more the wet mop than he usually was in these winter weeks.

"Okay, then, we'll go." It was not an easy thing, she realized, having obligations. "Get on up there. Go on."

Obeying her, Niko sprang up the hill. He would beat her to the top by a far margin and then he would wait faithfully until she arrived. He was just that kind of dog.

"I have to go," said Misty, looking back at her friends. She sighed. "I want you to tell me what you find out, as soon as you can."

Siobhan and Connell nodded simultaneously, betraying that sometimes eerie connection the Sidhe shared. "As soon as we know. We promise," said Siobhan.

"I should be able to learn something," added Connell. "As it is, the people of our clan do not really take me that seriously."

"Really, I must confess I do not see why they do not," replied Siobhan, gently sarcastic. "Of course he is right. Of the two of us I have long been considered the more curious. Connell, with his reputation as something of a layabout, will probably overhear something useful. I will take it upon myself to see that this information reaches the right ears. After that, well, we shall see."

Misty nodded. "Thank you. Anything you can do to help would be great. Great for my mother, I mean."

"No, Misty, it is you and your mother that deserve the thanks in this. We Sidhe are too few now. Every year we fade further into the mists of legend, and soon all trace of us will vanish. Perhaps with your help we can delay the coming of that time. Farewell." With that, the elves disappeared, heading back to where they came, wherever that was.

Misty had a lot of time to think, as Niko was unusually passive, content with walking by her side. This might be the solution to one problem, but what future would Christina face? Certainly not one within Portland's legal circles; her firm and Keller would see to that. Then where? San Francisco?

Strange as it would have seemed five months ago, the last thing Misty wanted was to return to the Bay Area. There was something about this place that was filling the missing piece of her heart, empty since her dad had died. It was Connell and Siobhan. Niko. Kelsey.

Kelsey. Somehow she fit into all of this, and more than just through the mistakes of her ancestors. But this particular puzzle piece was eluding her.

***

Christina tried not to look at Thomas Keller as he walked in the door, smugness exuding from his pores. Across the table were two of the lawyers from the coalition of enviro-groups, looking barely out of law school and clearly out of their element.

She sighed, thinking mournfully that it was only a matter of time before their youthful idealism and belief that they could make a real difference was going to vanish. Soon enough they would be sitting on her side of the table.

Except she wasn't planning on being there.

"I think we're ready to begin." Christina's stomach did a flip-flop when Charley spoke. The recorder was turned on, and all was business. If she wanted to do this it would have to be done now, or she might have trouble down the road.

Well, she thought, *I've set things up as well as they're going to be.* Looking at the two fresh-faced attorneys, she added a silent prayer: *Learn something from this, please.*

"Actually, I'm going to need to leave," said Christina, rising as quickly as she dared from her chair.

Confused, Charley actually moved out of her way before he thought to say anything. "Why are you leaving? We're in the middle of a settlement, for God's sake." He was being remarkably calm, considering the circumstances.

"Do you really want to know?"

"Doesn't matter," said Thomas, sounding extremely put out. This was supposed to be his show, and here was this girl taking center stage.

"Okay, then," agreed Christina, ignoring Thomas's venomous glare.

And she told them.

When it was done, and she had cleaned out her desk, she had never felt more free or more frightened.

Kelsey

Kelsey awoke cold, finding her blankets strewn on the floor by the side of her bed. Sighing, she leaned to pull them back over her. Looking over at the clock she could barely make out the blurry red lines: 3:45. Groaning, she turned over and tried to salvage what was left of the night.

It hadn't been the first time in the week since Christmas that her nights had been sleepless, and likely it wouldn't be the last. It wasn't the thought of having to go back to school. That had usually done it in the past, but now that she was a senior, Kelsey was seeing the end of the road looming. This time something else was on the back of her mind, nibbling relentlessly. Now if she could just figure out what it was.

After an hour more of tossing, she gave it up for a bad job. Who was she kidding anyway? She knew damn well what was going on.

Sliding silently into the kitchen, her frog slippers making the barest whisper on the hardwood floor, Kelsey found her way to the medicine cabinet. There, behind the cold medicine ("and the wet medicine," her dad was fond of saying) were the pills she was looking for. The bottle was half-empty.

That was all right; the prescription had expired anyway. Swallowing quickly, she rehid the bottle. Her mother had gotten them two years ago, after she had received a particularly distressing letter from the family back home. She thought she had thrown them away, but now they were helping her daughter sleep.

***

"My head," she moaned, grabbing her temples and trying to massage the throbbing from them. Taking the pills had seemed like a good idea at the time. She had had the same idea the night before. And the night before that. Making her way to her mirror, she confronted a goblin.

"Ugh, I actually look how I feel."

"Kelsey, breakfast is now or it's cold!" shouted her mother from the kitchen.

She snapped awake. If her mother saw her now she would freak. It was what mothers did best. Grabbing her robe, she threw it hastily over her shoulders and hustled to the bathroom. A little cold water would help and—she breathed out into her hand, scooping the exhalation into her nose—oh, God yes, a generous helping of toothpaste and she should be okay.

For today at least. But the days never seemed to last long in the Oregon winter, and in two nights she would have to face waking up for school.

"Hmm. I wonder if the dress code forbids pajamas," she said idly. It was amusing to consider the principal's reaction to her strolling in with just a robe, fuzzy bottoms, and her slippers. The vision of him growing redder and redder nearly made her spit tartar-control toothpaste all over the mirror and sink.

It kept her mind off of her problems for now.

"So, what are the big plans for tonight?" asked her mother between mouthfuls of fiber-loaded cereal.

Kelsey scratched the last bits of sleep from her eyes. "I thought I would go visit Misty," she said, playing with her own little bowl of oatmeal. "I've only been able to talk to her over the phone because she's been busy, and grandma and grandpa were over too. I wanted to see how things were going with her mother." *And to tell her about the talk I had with the old folks.*

"Oh, I didn't know there was any problem with her mother. Is everything okay?"

Kelsey debated for a moment whether she should tell her mom anything about Misty's mom, finally deciding against it. It had been told to her in confidence, and Kelsey knew her mom. Sometimes telling her a secret was like placing an ad on the front page. Her mom had always blamed it on her Irish blood, but Kelsey had always regarded it as simply a pure inability to keep a secret.

So she said, "Nothing more than what's normal," keeping her voice carefully neutral. "I just wanted to make sure she was okay." *And,* thought Kelsey, *I really need to see those elves again, and I don't think they'd take kindly to me just showing up.* She scraped the last bites from her bowl and into her mouth in almost one motion. "I gotta get ready."

On the way down the hall, she could hear her mother flipping through the newspaper pages again. Good, that meant that the issue was forgotten. Otherwise she would have been shadowed to her room and mercilessly peppered with questions. Her mother was a bloodhound when it came to things like that.

Thirty minutes later, and moving faster than her mom could keep up with, she was out the door and into her, hopefully, not frozen car.

226

***

"Oh, hi Kelsey. Come on in," said Christina, opening the door to admit Kelsey into the house.

"Thanks, Mrs. Montoya."

Christina waved her hand airily. "It's Christina, Kelsey. You're almost an adult now, so you might as well get used to it." She smiled. "It's one of the few perks of growing up, I'm afraid. The responsibility that comes with age isn't so easy."

Kelsey caught on. "How are things with that?"

"Over, for now," Christina answered. Sitting at the dining room table, which was covered with paper, boxes, and paper in boxes, she started sorting again, having obviously been interrupted by Kelsey's visit. "I'm just trying to pick up the pieces of my office at home, seeing what I need to send back to my firm. I think I got it all, but I want to make sure."

"Yeah," said Kelsey, feeling a bit lost. "You've got to make sure. Um, anyway, is Misty around?" She could hear the shower running, but it felt more polite to just ask.

"She is, but she's in the shower." Christina had answered in a monotone, working deeper into her pile. It looked as if she had been going at it for some time now.

Kelsey looked closer. Was that a tear?

Pulling out a chair for herself, Kelsey moved closer. It felt strange to be so near a person, almost a stranger really, who was sad and to try to offer comfort. But all of Kelsey's intuition was telling her that she was doing the right thing. And she was starting to pay more and more attention to that lately.

227

"Is there anything I can do?" she asked softly.

For a moment, she wondered if Christina had heard, and was preparing to ask again. Finally, though, she heard Christina say, "I would love some help, but I don't really know where to start."

"Maybe at the beginning."

Christina nodded. "Okay, but I'll have to talk fast. I'm not sure how Misty would feel about me sharing anything with someone outside the family."

Kelsey thought of Connell and Siobhan, Misty's greatest secret. "You know, I think she'd be all right with it. But you can hurry if you like," she said gently.

"I don't know if Misty told you about her father," began Christina.

"She did."

"Well, that makes this part easier. No mother is perfect, you know, but I thought that if we got away from San Jose, maybe started someplace new, we could find our way past the sadness.

"It didn't work out that way. At first Misty was reacting like any teenager would, myself included when I was that age, but it started getting worse. She started going away, for really long intervals. Sometimes the whole afternoon. I would call and there would be no answer, so I knew she was out walking the dog."

Kelsey grimaced inwardly. There was no way she could possibly assuage Christina's fears on this count, not without betraying the trust of Misty and the elves, so she merely nodded and gave the closest thing to the truth she could. "Yeah, she said she was doing that a lot. Said it helped her from feeling lonely." And wasn't that the case!

Blushing, Christina said, "I guess she had a right, didn't she?"

Kelsey faltered, unsure of where to go. While she had always been willing to take on the adults of her own family over issues, even those barely involving her, this was an entirely different ballgame. It comforted her to know that Christina was capable of chastising herself if she felt that she had done something wrong, but she couldn't exactly find it in herself to do it; her respect for elders was too ingrained. Besides, it was not as if Christina had been given a lot of choice in the matter.

So, instead she said, "I guess it's not too easy being the adult, is it?"

"No," said Christina, shaking her head, "it isn't." A tear did manage to trickle down her face then, but Kelsey pretended not to notice.

Christina continued talking. "Well, I think I did the right thing, for once. The right thing for me and the right thing for Misty. I just wish I hadn't taken so long to get around to it.

"Now," added Christina, "I'm more scared than before. I've never really been out of work before. It's not the money. Not yet. But it doesn't feel right to be here this morning. I mean most Saturdays I'm going to the office, to work on something or to drop off papers. Now, I'm just cutting ties, making sure I have nothing to do. It's weird.

"And do you know what the worst thing is?" Kelsey shook her head. "I actually feel like I've betrayed them. Charley, and even Thomas. The two men who turned me into someone her own daughter doesn't even know. It's pathetic."

"Misty told me some stuff," admitted Kelsey, trying to make this really great woman feel better. "I know that you were saving money. It looks like you were doing the right thing all along, and maybe your head just hadn't known it. That's what I think."

"Do you really think so?"

Kelsey nodded once, with conviction. "I really do. And I think that it's going to work out fine. Most of the time people follow their hearts it ends up working out all right. Sometimes it doesn't, but you're going to feel bad if you don't try anyway, so there's really no risk after all, is there?"

Christina looked up, and Kelsey could see a new respect there. "You know, you're a lot more mature than you look."

Kelsey laughed. "Yeah, I'm getting that a lot lately, but trust me, it's a new development."

Right then, the shower stopped running, and Christina scrambled to the kitchen to grab a tissue. Kelsey moved to the living room and plopped on the couch, making it look as if she were there all the time. It wouldn't do for Misty to think they were talking about her.

Shortly after, when Misty emerged from her bedroom, all she saw was Kelsey sitting on the couch, flipping through the channels, and her mother sitting at the dining room, right where she left her, seemingly lost in papers.

"Oh, hi Kels,"

"Hey yourself. How've you been?" Not waiting for an answer, Kelsey plowed on. "Sorry, but I was barely able to get any work done on our project," she said, referring to her ongoing research into the migration of the elves.

Christina looked up. "Oh, is that your school project, then?"

"Yeah," answered Kelsey quickly.

It was harder than it looked, Kelsey decided, juggling little lies and half-truths. Misty could be upset if she found out that Kelsey and Christina had been talking about what was pretty personal stuff. But even though she had to keep the secret of the elves from Christina, she realized now that perhaps they had been meant to have their conversation, and that it was no accident that had propelled her to the Montoya house at this hour. Plus, she was starting to really like Christina; she reminded her of what an adult should be.

"Going for a walk?" she asked innocently.

Misty caught on. "Yeah, I am, as soon as Niko feels...well never mind, he seems to be ready," she said just as Niko started whining urgently from the back porch. "See you later, Mom," she called, as Kelsey allowed her to lead the way outside.

Niko was sitting there, and Kelsey felt warm all of a sudden. It was as if the connection between all of them had grown stronger in the past hour, and even Niko was starting to feel it.

Misty apparently felt differently. "Gross, Niko!" cried the girl, as the dog started licking her hand vigorously. Tousling his fur, she shoved him playfully out of her way. "Lead on, furball." He barked once and bounded off towards the woods.

"So," said Misty.

"So," said Kelsey.

"Do you want to go first, or should I?"

"You go. It's about Nick Green, right?"

"Yeah, it is. I think I like him."

231

Kelsey sighed. It was looking like it would be a while before she got to tell Misty about her grandparents. "Go ahead, then."

Misty waited until they had walked fully into the woods before beginning. "We had a really nice date last week."

Kelsey rolled her eyes, hiding her face from Misty. This was apparently going to take a little time. "Yeah? I'm glad."

"Are you, really?"

Kelsey debated silently for a moment, and decided she was. "I am, Misty. I'm glad for you, and I'm glad that Nick didn't turn out to be the loser I always thought he was."

Smiling, Misty said, "Well I'm glad to hear that. When the next semester starts I'm curious to see how things go."

"Me too," answered Kelsey. "I hope things work out."

"Thanks."

"Don't mention it."

The two were silent for a while, walking slowly towards the hill and letting Niko get far ahead of them. He would find his way, as he always did, and Kelsey expected to see him frolicking in the stream by the time they reached him, his shaggy coat protecting him from the cold.

This gave them some time. "Look," said Kelsey, breaking the silence, "can we hold up here? I wanted to tell you about my week, and I don't think your friends need to hear it."

"Okay," said Misty, obediently coming to a stop at the top of the ravine. "I guess it must have been pretty interesting."

"That's one way to put it," agreed Kelsey. "But you don't know my grandparents."

232

"Why don't you enlighten me."

Kelsey hesitated. Now that it had come to this, she didn't know if she should be telling Misty this. It wasn't her fault, after all. "My grandparents want us to move back to Ireland, and my mom has already agreed."

Misty gave a little gasp. "When?"

"Now."

"But you can't. You're in the middle of school."

"I know that," snapped Kelsey. Seeing Misty's hurt look, she softened her tone. "I'll really miss you, but that McMollen luck's gotten worse, and my grandmother seems to think it's her fault that things are so hard in Ireland, because she left when they needed people to stick around. She thinks that if we move back we can help the relatives better." Telling this to Misty brought to Kelsey's mind the images of the last conversation her family had. The bitter words were still there, and it was clear, to Kelsey at least, that her grandmother was placing her own guilt on the shoulders of Kelsey's mother, who had only been to Ireland once and, after seeing the dire straits the other branches of her family were in, was reluctant to return, preferring to send money to help out.

Now, it looked like money wasn't enough. Through the week, Kelsey's father had been silent, offering neither agreement nor disagreement. He couldn't know that his wife would interpret his silence as assent, or he would have said something.

As for Kelsey herself, well, she didn't get a vote.

"I don't know what to do," said Kelsey. "I'll have to go." She felt perfectly miserable.

Misty brightened. "We'll talk to Connell and Siobhan."

That was the one thing Kelsey didn't want to do.

"No, Misty, no. We already know that their clan is wrapped up in the problems with your mom's old employer. Your friends said themselves that they've been preoccupied for some months, and now we know why. The last thing they're going to want to talk about is helping the descendants of the people who destroyed their land while they're dealing with the same type of people right now.

"Besides," she added, "if they say anything, the whole clan is going to know that they've been meeting you, and that will be the end of your friendship. God, who knows what they'll do to you and your family. They'll probably think you were trying to corrupt their kids or something."

"What can I do, then?" asked Misty, sounding miserable. "I can't lose you now."

"Right now, we can't do anything, except go meet your friends. But let me handle it, okay? This is my problem?"

"No, Kels, it's not," said Misty, placing an arm around Kelsey. "Connell and Siobhan said we're connected, and I knew it before they told me. That means we're family, and that means it's our problem." She started walking down the hill. "All of ours."

Kelsey felt her insides warming. Seeing Misty like this, full of resolve, it felt like it seemed everything was going to work out in the end.

"Wait up."

***

234

Minutes later, as they sat and waited for the elves, they discussed how they were going to solve this. Niko was nowhere to be seen. He had probably run farther down the river.

"How are we going to ask them?"

Misty shrugged, which only made Kelsey worry the more. "I haven't figured that part out yet. I was thinking that we should probably ask them about the problems the other clan is having. If they wanted to, I'm sure they could find a way to let them know that my mom is inadvertently helping their cause."

"It never hurts to have someone owe you a favor," said Kelsey.

"No, it doesn't. Especially them."

The friends sat in companionable silence for several minutes, enjoying the rare winter sunshine as it sifted through the trees above. In that time, Connell and Siobhan hadn't shown up, but this was far from unusual. Kelsey killed time by starting an impromptu game of Tic Tac Toe, using the toe of her hiking boots to dig into the soft ground. It gave way easily, exposing moist soil underneath. It was a quiet time, and it felt good to just be silent, to play at nothing very serious, and to allow nature to make its own noise.

They played three games, tying each of them, and were about to rub out their markings and draw a fourth grid when they heard a commotion from above them.

"What's that?" whispered Kelsey, getting up quickly.

"You act as if I should know," said Misty, coming to her feet as well.

"We'd better skedaddle before it comes poking around here. I thought this was private property."

"It is."

Suddenly, Kelsey had a thought. "What about Niko?"

"I think he can take care of himself. Come on."

Misty was already scrambling into the brush, the same brush, actually, that Connell and Siobhan normally emerged from. Kelsey followed shortly after. Concealed as well as they could, the pair waited for who or what was making the noise to show up.

After a few minutes, it did.

"Oh, it's Nick," said Misty, nearly rising to her feet.

Kelsey grabbed her jacket, pulling her back down; something about this didn't feel right. "Wait a second," she said softly.

"Misty, are you here?" the boy called into the woods.

"This is stupid, Kels," said Misty, crawling out from the bushes. "I'm here, Nick," she answered. "I just didn't know it was you."

"Your mom told me you were walking your dog," said Nick, by way of explanation. "I wanted to drop off something. Here." Kelsey watched as he handed Misty a large leather-bound book. "It's my father's, but I figured you might be interested."

Kelsey couldn't tell what it was, but by Misty's reaction it was a good thing. Still, she kept hidden, waiting to see how things would play out. Misty, for whatever reason, didn't tell Nick about Kelsey hiding in the bushes. Maybe she was feeling something too.

"This is really sweet, Nick," said Misty. "How did you know I was interested in this stuff? I never told you."

Nick smiled, showing all of his teeth. "How could I not? You were always talking with your friend—she's Irish, right?—I would have had to be blind not to notice. I've gotta admit, though, most of the time the conversation was over my head."

Kelsey gasped. Had they been that obvious?

Misty seemed uncomfortable as well. "I guess we…we talked about it a lot," she stammered.

"Yeah. Well, I thought you might like it. Like I said, it's my dad's. But he doesn't really read, you know."

Kelsey saw Misty open the book, and was burning with curiosity. She would have given a year of her life to see what Misty was seeing right now. But she had to be sneaky. And if she showed herself now it would be like she had been hiding all this time so that she could spy. She would come out of this looking like a wormy little eavesdropper, and Misty wouldn't look much better.

So she waited and waited, her muscles cramping. Just as she was on the verge of squeaking in pain, giving her hiding place away, Niko came bounding up the river, providing just enough of a distraction so that Kelsey could find a more comfortable position.

Now she watched Misty reading. Engrossed as she apparently was, she failed to notice that Niko had drawn back several feet, his ears flat and his teeth bared. Kelsey saw the whole thing.

Right about the that time Niko was backing up, beginning to growl, Misty was realizing what the book actually contained.

"Nick," said Misty, "you haven't actually read this, have you?"

"No, I haven't," answered Nick innocently. "Why?"

"This is a family diary." Kelsey could have sworn she heard horror in her voice. "It goes back a really long time."

"Really?"

Kelsey could barely stand the suspense; she wanted desperately to peek at the pages and see what was upsetting her best friend so much.

Still, she waited.

Misty had apparently forgotten all about her, and was flipping through the pages. Kelsey could see that she was turning a little green around the gills, and again suppressed an impulse to run up and demand just what was going on.

"Your family," asked Misty, her voice shaking, "have they always been hunters?"

Nick nodded. "For as long as we can remember. Among the best, at least that's what my dad says. He hasn't been too successful himself. But he's taught me a lot."

Misty closed the book suddenly. "Such as?"

Nick smiled, and the next words he spoke nearly tore Kelsey's breath from her body, sinking her closer to the muddy earth.

"You see," he began quietly, "when hunting elves, you have to be careful not to let on what you're after. They have a way of telling, you know." Even from her place in the bushes Kelsey could see that his old smirk had returned, and that this one was real. "My dad and I haven't had too much luck, but he was pretty sure that if there were any elves around, they would be here, as far west as they could go, and as far north as they would probably want to be.

"I never used to believe him, just thought it was some stupid dream of his and his family's. He even picked up that thing over there," he said, pointing at Niko, "to help us track them down. Yeah, I recognized the worthless beast from the moment I saw him. He

238

probably recognized me too. I always knew he could do more than he was, but all the beating in the world never seemed to work. Well, at least he seems pretty scared now. It wasn't me who blinded him. That would be my dad. Just a real friend to animals, he is." He laughed cruelly, and Niko whined, hunching down and backing slowly away.

"Of course, that all changed when Briana told me that she overheard you talking about something strange. The girl's as dumb as a doorknob, but she hates you enough to remember everything you've ever said when she was around."

Kelsey frantically tried to think of the conversations she had had with Misty, and could recall none in the presence of Briana. She was truly fighting the urge to reveal herself now; something was telling her that she had an advantage, being hidden as she was. Maybe she could do something. *But what?*

Wait and be patient.

Kelsey looked around, wondering where that thought had come from.

Nick, oblivious, was still talking, and becoming smugger with each passing moment. "After that, it was just a matter of getting your confidence. My father always told me to hit them where they can't see you coming. He's a real ass sometimes, but I guess he knew what he was talking about.

"So now I have you where I want you. I thought the book was a nice touch; the shock of finding out the truth was going to great to watch. Look at you! Your doggy over there is too scared of me to do much. Right Niko?" He looked over, but the Samoyed was nowhere to be seen. "Hmm. I guess he ran away. That's loyalty."

239

"What are you going to do now," asked Misty in a whisper.

Nick shrugged. "Well, that kind of depends on you, now. I could just sit here and taunt you some more, but that's going to lose its charm real quick. No, I'm hoping for something more here." He reached behind him, and pulled out a long hunting knife. "Gift from my grandfather," he said by way of explanation. "Never got to use it, yet.

"So I thought we would just wait here for your little friends to show up, and find out just how much they really like you."

"I don't know what you're talking about, Nick," said Misty defiantly, and it seemed to Kelsey that she was stronger now.

"I don't know what you're talking about, Nick," answered Nick, mocking her in a singsong voice. "Please don't insult me. We'll wait here for your friends until. . ."

"Until what?"

Nick grinned evilly. "Until I get tired of waiting, and find something to pass the time with." His leer made Kelsey sick.

She could take it no longer.

The Choice

"Oh, it's you."

Misty had been hoping, praying actually, that Kelsey would have the good sense to stay hidden. Maybe if Nick didn't notice her she could have a chance to get away and find help. Of course, when Nick had made his intentions towards Misty clear, there was no way that her friend could have been expected to stand by and do nothing.

Misty would have done the same thing.

"Yeah, it's me, you slime," said Kelsey through gritted teeth. In her right hand she gripped a sturdy branch. "Now you can just back off, and run home. If you touch her I'll beat you to death. I swear I will." Her hands shook, but she was trying to keep it together.

Nick sucked on his lower lip, showing mock concern. "Well, I'd say you have me in a pretty tight spot, there being two of you and all," he admitted. "Still, I am a guy. Oh, and there's also this," he added, pulling a pistol from the front of his pants to add to the knife in his other hand. "This one is my dad's. Nine millimeter, his favorite kind."

Misty grew cold. "So you're going to kill us, is that it? Since when does following in your father's footsteps lead to murder?" Despite her calm tone, her stomach was doing somersaults. Nick was obviously unbalanced, and there was no telling what he might do.

"You really need to read that family history," he said, indicating the book that Misty still clutched in her hand. "You'd see that killing was sort of a pastime. But, no, I'm not going to shoot you. This is just to make sure your little friend over there doesn't try anything stupid.

"So, if you would be so kind," he said to Kelsey, pointing with the pistol at the log where the two girls often sat as they talked to Connell and Siobhan, "we can just wait around, like good kids."

Kelsey moved over, eyes narrowed. When she had reluctantly taken a seat, Nick grabbed Misty roughly and shoved her over. Kelsey had to move quickly in order to keep Misty from falling. As Misty came close, she was able to see into Kelsey's eyes, and to see the fear they contained.

Just what type of men where the Greens, that they would inspire so much terror?

"Where's Niko?" whispered Kelsey.

Misty looked around. "I never saw where he went," she said.

"He's not related to Lassie, is he?" said Kelsey, weakly attempting a joke.

Misty shook her head, marveling at her friend's ability to lighten up almost any situation. "No, I think he was just scared and ran home, and I don't think my mom knows how to speak dog." She remembered, again, that Nick had once owned Niko, and that the Samoyed had run away from the Greens right before being adopted by Christina. She tried not to think of the cruelty that would have driven such a loving, loyal animal to such a desperate action.

"Hey, Nick," she called, "what are we waiting for anyway?" Even if they were doomed, she would be damned if she was going to show any more fear. Now that the initial shock at what the Greens did had worn off, she was starting to think more clearly.

"We're waiting for my father. He's the one that accepted this job in the first place." Nick was leaning against a tree then, not seeming to pay much attention anymore.

Misty had figured that Nick's father was somehow connected to this. After all, he had been the one leading that expedition the day she had found them trespassing on her land.

"Guess that rules out calling the police," quipped Kelsey.

"Looks like," said Misty, for some reason feeling better. Maybe the fact that Kelsey was here was making this tolerable. "Let's just hope it's going to be a while."

Nick ignored them.

Things quieted down then, so Misty took the opportunity to further read the book Nick had "given" her. It contained a fairly detailed history of the family, going back dozens of generations. If it was accurate, it represented an incredible example of record keeping. It was really too bad that it was devoted almost exclusively to the family tradition of hunting and killing elves.

Misty read on. Interestingly enough, Nick's ancestors came to America on one of the first boats, masquerading as Puritans in order to gain passage. After arriving in Massachusetts, they quickly struck out on their own, steadily heading west. It was as if they knew exactly where the elves were headed.

It was only after she had skimmed through over twenty pages that she found out how they knew, and the truth chilled her.

"They had an elf," she whispered to Kelsey.

"What?"

Misty pointed out the relevant entry. "Not all of the elves had gotten away, it seems. They kept one captive, and they were using him."

"How?" asked Kelsey.

Misty glanced through the book. It was strange how she could now be so calm. It was as if she had all the time in the world. Not ten feet away Nick lounged indolently against a tree, carelessly twirling his gun around his forefinger, and she was reading one of the most gruesome tales she had ever encountered, made even more horrific because it had actually happened.

"Hold on," she said, "I'm finding it." What luck it was, realized Misty, that Nick had not thought to take the book back. Maybe he was getting a thrill out of knowing that she was digging deep into his family's dark history. Maybe he just wasn't thinking that clearly. "I think I've got it figured out."

Misty felt Kelsey lean closer. "Well?"

Misty traced the lines. Finally she found what she was looking for. "Oh my God." Suddenly, she was feeling sick again.

"What did they do?" Kelsey asked urgently.

Misty took a calming breath, trying to separate herself from the reality of what was written in stark black and white. "I think...I think they figured out that there is a connection between elves, some kind of psychic link that draws them to each other."

Kelsey frowned. "I don't see how that could—."

"They tortured him, Kels," said Misty, reading through the grisly accounts. The members of Nick's family, for all of their faults, were meticulous record keepers, and that included noting the details of every single indignity they had inflicted upon their helpless captive.

"According to this, before all of the Sidhe had gotten away, one of them had been captured by a Fomorian."

"The giants?"

"Exactly. It's something I had been wondering about for a long while, actually." Misty began to remember her first bits of research. Now that she was able to pull the threads of this mystery together, she was able to forget, for the moment, about her very real danger. "Both races are important to Celtic myth, and we know that neither of them are supposed to exist today."

Kelsey nodded, and Misty saw that she was beginning to understand.

"Right," said Kelsey. "We know what happened to the Sidhe, but we never found out about the Fomorians."

Misty closed the book. There was really no choice of whether or not she should tell Kelsey what had happened to them. It was just a matter of finding the right words.

"Hey over there," called Nick. He had stopped playing with his gun, and was now staring hard at the girls. "What are you two talking about? Don't get any stupid ideas. My dad taught me how to shoot before I was five years old. You won't get far."

Misty said nothing, and Kelsey, showing similar strength, only put her arm around her friend in a grim display of friendship.

"You know, Misty," said Kelsey. "I don't think we could leave even if we wanted to."

"You're right," agreed Misty. "Whatever happens, this needs to end here." She looked at Nick, who had gone back to ignoring them, whistling off-key. "But first I have to tell you about what happened to the Fomorians."

Kelsey laughed nervously. "What? Did Nick's family kill them off too?"

"Not really."

"Hmm. Why do I get the feeling I'm not going to like hearing this next part?"

"I don't blame you; I didn't like reading it. No, actually the Fomorians weren't killed off. I think they were smarter than a lot of the legends really gave them credit for. They were as in tune with the changing nature of things as were the Sidhe. After all, they were both creatures of the earth, just on opposite sides of the spectrum. One day, a Fomorian decided to do something about it.

"Okay, about the Fomorian who captured the Sidhe." Seeing Kelsey's nod, Misty went on, "He approached Nick's family with an offer. He would give them the elf if they gave him and the other Fomorians something in return."

"Ugh, I'm not going to like this," muttered Kelsey, holding her head in her hands.

"Just let me finish, okay? The Fomorians were few in number, and they were growing fewer. Eventually the humans would have wiped all memory of them from the world. There was only one way to ensure their survival. They would have to mix with the humans."

"They were bred out?"

"Yes they were. Nick's ancestors started the process with their youngest daughter."

"So Nick's part Fomorian," said Kelsey. "That explains a lot, actually."

Misty closed her eyes. She really didn't want to say this, but how could she look her friend in the face again if she didn't? "No, I don't think he's read that far, or he wouldn't be so cocky. But Kelsey," she whispered, agonizing over every syllable. "So are you."

***

Christina glanced up from her scribbles as the sound of wheels over gravel alerted her to a car coming into her driveway.

"That's strange. I wasn't expecting any visitors." Curious, and a little lonely with Misty gone all day—she assumed that Nick must have found them by now or he would have come back—she went to the back door and unlocked it, poking her head outside.

It was a police car. For a brief moment Christina's heart constricted, but then she remembered that Misty had mentioned that Nick's father, also named Nick, was a policeman. And besides, her daughter was in the woods she had tramped across these past five months, and with friends. There was nothing that could really happen to her, not to mention that there was no way the police would learn of any accident on her own property before she would.

So when Nick Sr. stepped out of the vehicle, she allowed the last of her apprehensions to drift away. "Good afternoon, Officer Green. Nick's in the woods with Misty and Kelsey right now, if you were looking for him."

The man stared a little too deeply, and Christina felt a little vulnerable and silly under his gaze. After a moment's pause, he spoke. "I know, Ms. Montoya. He told me he was coming here." As he walked up

247

to her, Christina checked herself from taking an involuntary step backwards. "Actually, I came here to see you about a friend of mine. A legal matter, if you don't think it would be a bother."

Christina shrugged, trying to appear nonchalant. This was a little too bizarre for mere coincidence, but there was little she could do. "I'll see if I can assist," she said. "Why don't you come inside."

Officer Green touched his cap. "Thank you, Ms. Montoya. It would be helpful." He walked in through the door Christina held open for him. "And Ms. Montoya, if you don't mind me asking, just where exactly in your woods did my son get off to?"

"It's Mrs. Montoya, actually, but you can call me Christina." Somehow, allowing this man, who was making her more uncomfortable by the second, even this courtesy felt wrong, but it would have been impolite not to.

"Oh. Sorry about that, Christina. I thought that with your husband dea…."

"I'll always be married to Carlos. Nick, is it?" He nodded. "And I don't really feel like talking about that, if you don't mind." There were certain things she shared only with her daughter, and others she trusted. This man didn't meet this criterion.

"Now," she went on, "why don't you show me what you have." She had seen the large poster case he had brought with him, and assumed that whatever he needed to talk to her about involved building plans of some sort. In her meetings with Thomas Keller she had seen enough poster cases to know what it was they held. Who knows, maybe Misty had told Nick and Nick had let slip to his father that Christina was

248

something of an expert in the legal issues surrounding acceptable land use.

"They're plans, actually," said Mr. Green, confirming Christina's guess. "I don't understand too much of this myself, but I thought you might." He rolled the blueprints out on the empty kitchen table and Christina grabbed some coffee mugs to help keep the corners down. "I think my buddy's having problems with zoning. Do you see anything wrong with this?"

Christina bent over to peer at the plans, and without even checking the corner for the name of the architectural firm, she recognized them immediately, her mind filling with a sudden sense of dread. "Where did you get these?"

The silence that filled the space after her question spoke volumes. She heard a strange sound, the click of a holster strap, and she knew that when she turned around a gun would be pointed at her.

As she pivoted she saw she was right.

"You know, I've never killed anyone," said Mr. Green matter-of-factly, "and quite frankly, I don't intend to start. So why don't you tell me just exactly how to find your daughter, and my son. You see, I'm used to coming at them from the other side. Afraid I might just get a little lost."

Christina stiffened, filled with a maternal instinct to protect her daughter. "She has nothing to do with the environmental groups working against Keller, and I don't know how much he paid you, but it couldn't possibly be enough to justify in your mind what you're doing." She was being the lawyer now, trying to find crack's in her opponent's armor, weaknesses she could exploit. But this time, the stakes were much higher. To her surprise, the man laughed derisively, the evil sound echoing through the kitchen. Christina, in the face of his mockery, grew red-faced.

"You think those piddling tree-huggers have anything to do with this? Mr. Keller could crush them in an instant. No, the problem runs a lot deeper than this, and goes back a lot longer than you think."

***

"The elves cursed Nick's family," said Misty, her voice taking on the rhythms of a storyteller's unique cadence, "and every family that helped them. A lot of Irish families have Fomorian blood in them. Including yours, Kelsey, the McMollens."

Kelsey closed her eyes. "It's a lie."

"Kels, it's right here. This is a family journal. Why would Nick's family lie to itself?"

"It's not. I can't be." Kelsey was on the verge of tears now, and Misty put a comforting arm around her friend. "What does this mean?"

"It doesn't mean anything," insisted Misty. "It happened so long ago that any Fomorian blood is so diluted it makes no difference. Even I probably have it."

"Except it's not your family that's been cursed all this time, now is it?" retorted Kelsey, anger flashing.

Misty felt her heart break, wishing there was some way to make it better. She thought of Carlos then, the father who had been everything to his little girl, and how he was abruptly torn away from her. "I don't know, Kels. Maybe we're all cursed, every one of us. Maybe we all share a little of the blame for the fate of the Sidhe."

And then she thought of the forests being felled daily, replaced with homogenous rows of the same trees, planted close together so that would grow upright so they could be easily harvested again. She thought of the strip-mining she had seen on her road trips through the country, and of the oil platforms that always seemed to threaten California's shores. She thought of a lot of things in those few moments.

"Maybe we always will be."

***

"What are you going to do?"

"Me? Nothing," answered Mr. Green. "I just need to find some information. If your daughter cooperates, none of this is going to hurt her. I promise." Somehow, Christina doubted that she could put much faith in the word of a man who was still pointing a gun at her.

"You're just going to leave us alone. How do you know we won't report you?"

He pointed at his badge. "It'll be my word and my son's against yours and your daughter's."

"And Kelsey's."

"Right. Who are they going to believe, a decorated officer or a bunch of loons claiming that fairies live in their backyard?"

Christina checked herself. Could she have possibly heard right? "Am I to understand," she asked, fearful that she was now dealing with someone not only armed but suffering from extreme psychosis, "that all of Mr. Keller's problems have to do with what, the little people?" She managed to keep any derision from her voice, but it was difficult. If the man wasn't holding a gun at this very moment she would have laughed at him outright.

"I'll admit that it does sound farfetched," he replied calmly. "Hell, if I didn't have the experience I do I would be the first to be calling for the crazy wagon. But, sadly for you, I do have some background with this, and this is no joke.

"Now, if you'll just point the way, or come along if you feel like it—I don't care which—we'll get this settled for good and you can find out the truth for yourself. Or try to."

Swallowing her fear, Christina took a chance. "Assuming that these, what did you call them?"

"Elves. Call them elves. If I had the time and the inclination I could give you a complete history with all of their ancient names and the places of power that they came from; I know a lot for a street cop. But I don't have the time, and you're making me lose my patience. So just call them elves and get to your goddamn question already."

All this time, Christina had been frantically searching the room and nearby kitchen for anything she could possibly use against the man, but she was too well organized, was too good at putting things away, for there to be anything that would help. About the only thing she could think of was her cell phone on the kitchen counter, and it was too far away.

And face it, you'd be dead after the "9" and the "1." No, she was pretty much helpless; all she could do was buy her daughter some time.

But time to do what?

She got back to her question. Truth to tell, she needed to know the answer anyways. "Assuming these elves exist," and boy, she was having a hard time with that, "what are you going to do to them?"

"Kill them, of course. I'll need to use your daughter's friends to find the others first, but eventually, yeah, I'll have to kill them all."

Christina had figured as much. "And my daughter? And Kelsey?"

Mr. Green chuckled. "I told you before, I ain't going to do a damn thing to them. It's like I said, no one's going to believe you anyways. You have my word, when this over you can go back to your normal lives and believe whatever you want to believe."

"Somehow I just don't find you all that trustworthy."

"Sorry to hear that, but I could have just killed you and found my way to your kid on my own."

So that was that. If she could trust this man to keep his word, her daughter would be safe. Wasn't that all that mattered? Still….

"Why are you doing this?" asked Christina, not really wanting to hear the answer.

Nick Sr. squirmed a little then, and Christina could tell that here was a man who was not used to answering to anybody. She could also see that he was struggling with a desire to unburden himself. Finally, he holstered his pistol and wiped his face, which had begun to show beads of sweat.

"Look, it's not like this matters anyway. Your kid's not going anywhere, so I'll tell you.

"I first saw Misty when I pulled her over. Standard speed trap, but she wasn't really speeding," he began, and Christina frowned at his casual use of Misty's name. "Something tipped me off, a gut feeling that she was important. Couldn't tell you why, but I know now that it's because of her connection to those creatures. She's got a bond with them, same as me. Well, not exactly the same," he muttered, and the hatred in his tone set Christina's teeth on edge.

He had a reason, she could see that easily enough just looking at him. The vitriol practically steamed from every pore, like a thing visible floating around his body, absorbing his spirit. What a terrible thing, she thought, to carry such a burden. It must have been eating at him for a long time.

Not noticing her appraisal, apparently unaware of anything save his own voice, he had continued speaking. "I followed her, that day, all the way to where the red-headed one, Kelsey, works. Don't know if she saw me."

Christina couldn't remember either. Guiltily, she understood that if she had been around for Misty to talk to, she might have heard about this. But she hadn't been and it was looking like it would take the balance of her life to redress this wrong.

"So you stalked her."

"For a time." The man was unapologetic. "Later, I ran into her in your backyard. My son and I were looking for them, and instead we found her. Not a coincidence, but there wasn't anything I could do about it then."

Christina frowned. All this talk about Misty being watched was making her stomach tighten painfully. "Just answer the question, please." She didn't want to hear any more of this. She just wanted to know why. No tangents. No drawn-out narrative. Just a simple reason.

"I'm trying to give you a little background," said Mr. Green impatiently, "but I can see that's not enough for you.

"Well, what can I tell you? If you want philosophy, talk to Keller. I've got two reasons for doing this. The first is money. The second is personal. Maybe you could guess just how if I gave you long enough to work at it—I've certainly given you enough information to pick at—but I'm not going to do that.

"Tell me where your kid is, now."

Christina's mind worked frantically. How much time could her refusal buy her daughter? Five minutes? Ten?

When it came down to it, she could not betray her daughter twice. She made a choice.

"Go to hell." She deliberately turned her back, and waited for the click of the hammer, the explosion, the darkness.

***

"Kels, I wish there was something I could say."

Kelsey smiled purposefully, a forced thing. "Forget about it. I'm over it. We've got other things to worry about." She hugged Misty, and for a moment Misty believed the words.

There was a sound from above, and Misty and Kelsey looked up simultaneously. It would be too much to hope.

It was too much; Officer Green came climbing down the hill, smiling.

"Good of you to get them, son. I'm proud of you."

Kelsey got up, all defiance once again. After all, it really couldn't get worse. And just where were Connell and Siobhan?

"What do you think you're going to do now?"

"It's time to end the curse," answered Nick's father, all smiles. Moving over to Misty he took the journal away. She offered no resistance. "It's been a long time coming."

And then he hit her.

It wasn't a slap, it wasn't a push. It was a closed-fist bare knuckle slug right into her cheek. Dropping to her knees, the only thought she could keep a hold of was that it was going to be one hell of a bruise come tomorrow.

Misty had never been hit, not really. There was the occasional spanking by her father, who had what she considered at the time to be decidedly ancient views on child-rearing, whenever she had misbehaved as a child. And there was one day in sixth grade when she tussled with Monica Jackson over some boy who, many years later, she had realized was really not worth the bother. So this was the first time.

She began to cry, and Kelsey rushed to her side, heedless of the danger, and put her arms around her, forcing back tears of her own. Watching the whole time, Nick said nothing.

"God, that felt good," said Mr. Green, flexing and wiggling his fingers. "Now get up and get moving."

Misty regained her balance, supporting herself on Kelsey's arm. "Where are we going?"

"We need to move on, girl. It's time to take things deeper. Nick, get behind them, and shoot them if they try to run. In the leg, mind you."

Nick nodded, taking his place behind the two girls.

"How far are we going, dad?" asked Nick.

For a moment, Mr. Green said nothing. Then, looking back while still moving, he answered, "A couple of miles. It's a place I found. A special place."

"You never told me."

"Because you weren't a man, yet!" snapped his father. "I had to wait to see if you were ready to take on this load. Your granddad did the same thing for me, 'cept it was a different place. Now it's your turn."

"My turn to what?" Nick sounded almost like a kid. Misty heard the uncertainty in his voice, and filed it away for future use. It was what her mother would have done.

Her insides iced up when she thought about her mother. Nick's dad had come from the direction of her house. That meant that he would have run into Christina.

She tried not to think of the rest, instead concentrating on putting one foot in front of the other, hoping that the end of this would bring some peace. At least they hadn't been permanently harmed yet, and that was a sign of hope. Of course, Nick's father had said something about a test.

***

Kelsey's mind was a riot of questions. Where had Niko gotten off to? Where were the elves? What happened to Christina? What was going to happen to them? It was enough to drive anyone to distraction, so she tried to ignore the persistent nagging and instead concentrated on finding any way out of this mess.

Sticks, sticks, and more sticks. Well, as they say, sticks and stones may break their bones...*unless they have guns*, she finished grimly. Never mind.

She nudged Misty, who was walking alongside. "Hey."

"Hey." Misty sounded like she'd swallowed a bug.

Kelsey was determined not to give up. They could be more proactive than this!

"Look, why are we just going along with these guys? We should make a run for it or something. Go and get help." She kept her voice to a whisper, hoping that if the Greens noticed they would just consider it foolish girl-talk.

"You don't get it, Kels. They'll just shoot us if we try."

"And what do you think they're going to do when they have what they want?"

"I know."

Kelsey took a deep breath. This was too much. For as long as she had known Misty, and sure that wasn't very long, she had never imagined that she was one to give up. Now, seeing her like this, shoulders slumped, feet dragging along the ground, kicking up dirt and dust, well it was almost enough to break her heart.

I guess I have to be strong enough for the both of us. *Don't worry, Misty, I'll think of something.*

A brave thought.

***

Actually, though, over the last mile, Misty had found something inside of her that had calmed her down. The defeated attitude she presented was just on the outside, and if Kelsey, the consummate drama queen, was buying it, then the Greens surely had to be as well.

Never give up, never give up, never ever ever give up. Winston Churchill said that after the German Blitz that had nearly brought England to its knees. Surely this situation was nothing compared to that.

And she was remembering her first dance recital, which could have gone a lot better, but what could a person expect from an eight year old except tears when things go badly. She hadn't meant to fall; she just spun one too many times. It wasn't like anyone noticed. Most parents were just watching their own daughters, too preoccupied to see any of the other dancers.

But other girls, after their instructor had left them to get changed back into their street clothes, had been brutal. There are fewer things crueler than eight-year old prima donnas in training, and their cutting remarks, whispered just loud enough for her to hear, were harder to take than the slippery wooden floor had been. Harder by far.

Her father had been waiting for her outside—her mother was presenting a case—and gave her a hug and those famous words.

Still, she gave up dancing after that night.

Her father, who never judged, said nothing more about it.

It was funny, walking to what would most likely be the end of her, that she would remember that day. Of course it must have been what her father told her. What was even funnier was that she regretted giving up dancing only now. Who knows what more she would have in common with her friend, who had persevered to become a dancer in her own right, if she had not allowed the cruel remarks of girls who really didn't know any better to squash her desires.

But they had found each other anyway, and that was a comfort.

"We're here." The announcement came with such quickness that Misty almost ran right into the older Green. She did take a little satisfaction back by giving him a little jab in the back while pretending to try to stop. Luckily, he only glared at her.

The place was a wasted field, a small meadow actually, in the middle of the woods. It couldn't have been more than forty or fifty feet across, and it had seen better days. Even with the winter rains pelting the area relentlessly these past weeks, there was little sign of life in the wilted grass and the scraggly bushes that still stubbornly clung to the tough ground. If Misty had been forced to make a guess, she would have compared it to an abandoned house, for there were no signs of inhabitants. It was a dead place, in a lot of different ways.

"This doesn't look special," complained Nick.

"It's not supposed to, boy. That's the point."

Nick said nothing, but Misty could feel him tense up at his father's chastisement. For a second she felt sorry for him. It could not have been easy growing up with this kind of pressure. From what she had been able to tell from her brief reading of the journal, the pursuit of the elves that had cursed their family had obsessed Nick's ancestors for hundreds of years.

It was strange that Kelsey's family, the McMollens, had not also been consumed by this obsession. Of course, they didn't know the source of their incredibly bad luck.

She looked at her friend, searching for the same anger she could see smoldering in the eyes of Nick's father and, to a lesser extent, Nick's as well. Kelsey had known about the connection between her family and the Sidhe, at least for a little while, yet had said and done nothing even

260

remotely close to what she was witnessing with the Greens, even though she learned that her own family had also suffered for generations. Perhaps the McMollens, whose blood flowed through Kelsey's veins, were made of better stuff.

She broke the silence. "Why are we here, then?" she asked. She wasn't expecting much of an answer, or one at all.

To her surprise, the elder Green spoke. "I can't cross into the field there," he said, pointing into the blighted area. "Something stops me, always had. Give it a try, Nick," he ordered his son.

Cautiously, as if he was expecting to burst into flames at any moment, Nick walked up to his father and tried to walk past him, into the field. He stopped suddenly, pushing against an invisible barrier.

"I can't do it," he said after several moments of trying to get his left foot to go past his right. "It's not a wall or anything. My foot just won't move."

Mr. Green nodded, having obviously expected this information. "I'd imagine she and her friend could," he reasoned, "though maybe not the McMollen girl, for all her family's as tied up in this as ours."

This gave Misty an idea.

"I know what you're thinking," said Mr. Green, sounding bored. "Whatever protection that place will give you doesn't stop a bullet. Watch." To illustrate he pulled his revolver from its holder and aimed carefully at a tree across the way. He pulled the trigger and a sound louder than Misty would have expected erupted from the weapon. Pieces of the trunk flew apart in a thousand directions. "So don't even think about it."

Misty didn't, instead maneuvering back to her previous question. "You still haven't told me why we're here."

"We're waiting."

"For what?"

Beside her, Kelsey nudged her arm gently. "Don't push him so hard."

But the man was apparently willing to talk, perhaps glad at having finally found an audience after so many years. "I think this is where those abominations come from. Now they're going to see you, and we're going to find out just what their friendship means. After that," he added, "I'll take care of the rest."

"Dad, this is a stupid place for elves to live," complained Nick. "It's dead here."

"You see what you are meant to see, human," came a voice from directly in front of them, out of the nothingness.

Materializing from the absent air, Connell and Siobhan stepped towards the four, grim looks on their faces. Behind them, Niko padded up, a low growl in his throat.

"Connell! Siobhan!" Misty could almost kiss them, if she dared to step away from her captors. Surely with them here everything would be fine now. "Niko, you found them." Now that it had come true she allowed herself to accept as real the secret hope she had been hiding, that Niko had not run away in fear of his former masters, but to get help.

Kelsey could barely control her grin, and after a moment stopped trying. "You are so going to get it," she said gleefully.

Nick stepped back a bit, uncertainty cascading over his face. His father, though, seemed not the least bit impressed.

"I knew you'd come for them. You are weak in your regard for your friends, like many people I know," said Mr. Green, displaying the confidence of a man who held all the winning cards.

Siobhan just stood there, and not even Misty could read her features. "Yes, we have come. It was our choice to help our friend."

Reasons

Christina awoke to pain emanating from the back of her head and spreading itself rapidly to other parts of her body. Gingerly feeling with fingers she located the newborn bump where Officer Green had struck her with the butt of his pistol. It was going to be a big one.

Grimacing, she managed to get her hands beneath her, slowly pushing herself off of the floor. When she had gained the dining room table, she took a moment to rest, using the time to search the rest of the room with her eyes.

He was nowhere to be found.

"It could have been worse," she said to the empty air. Maybe he couldn't find the resolve to pull the trigger.

But where did he go?

Misty. He had been asking about Misty, she remembered. That meant he had gone after her, into the woods. The thought sent a cold shudder through her. *What will he do if he finds her?*

She had a feeling that whatever scrap of conscience that had stopped him from killing her would fail utterly when it came to her daughter. The man's mania seemed to run deep. His ravings about elves and faeries certainly proved that he was certifiably nuts.

And none of this really matters, she reminded herself. *All that matters is that he wants my daughter. He probably already has her.* She forced herself to move, and despite the aching pounding in her head she managed to make it to her phone.

She took a breath. "Have to think of something." She couldn't very well call 911 and tell them that an officer had come to her house looking to kidnap her daughter and use her for bait to catch some supernatural beings.

Christina had spent the bulk of her career working to disprove the statement that all lawyers are liars, and for the most part she had succeeded, when it came to her at least. However, there were times when she had had to tread the edges of honesty, and she certainly had experience dealing with people who told lies as easily as a snake sheds its skin. From her years she had learned one important lesson in the art of deception: keep it as simple as possible.

She dialed the numbers.

"911. What is your emergency?" asked the voice on the other end of the line, exuding the calm of one who has heard it all and has all the answers.

"A man came into my house," started Christina. Her mind was already working ahead to find a pretense to send the police scouring the woods. "He must have come up behind me and hit me with something, because I just woke up and the back of my head is killing me." She worked hard at applying just the right type of worried tone to her words. Thinking of the danger Misty might be in at that very moment helped in this.

The operator got right to work. "Relax, ma'am. We're sending a unit over right now. Did you see your assailant? Is he still in the house?"

"No, he's not. I looked. But my daughter's gone too. I think she ran off into the woods. Maybe he chased her."

"Are you sure?"

"The screen door's been kicked off its hinges, so I think, yeah," she blurted.

She would have to remember to bust down the door after she got off the phone. It was a good thing it was pretty flimsy.

"Besides," she added. "Misty's always hiking around back there. She knows it pretty well, so I think that's where she'd go."

"We'll have the officer check," assured the operator. "They're on the way right now, so—."

"Thank you so much!" said Christina, hanging up the phone. She knew that the operator would have wanted her to stay on the line until the police arrived, but she had to take care of the door.

Right after she managed to beat it into submission, she heard the cruiser pull up. A minute later there was a hard knock at the front door. She opened it to find two officers, hands on their pistols.

"Ma'am," said the older of the two, a sergeant, "is another officer here already?"

Christina put on her most confused expression. "No. Why do you ask?"

The other officer, who was a younger woman, muttered, "It's Green's vehicle."

The sergeant nodded, looking grimmer. "We'd better take a look around."

***

"You shouldn't have come."

"But we did," stated Siobhan matter-of-factly.

"You needed us," added Connell, moving to stand beside his sister.

266

Misty hung her head, blinking back tears. Kelsey grabbed her hand and squeezed it tightly, the two of them a mirror image of the fey creatures across from them, who had now stepped from the boundary of the blighted field and onto the dirt path.

"Yes," said Misty, choking, "I did, and now it's going to cost you everything."

For reasons only he knew, the elder Green chose to say nothing at this moment. Perhaps he was soaking in his victory. Now that Connell and Siobhan had revealed themselves, he would use them just as his ancestors had used the elves.

"You don't know what he's going to do," protested Misty, as her friends came even closer. She had learned enough about the gruesome tortures inflicted upon that poor creature when she had read the journal. No doubt the methods today would be even more refined. It was going to be a brutal existence for her friends. "You can still get away. It's my fault that you're here."

"Yeah," said Kelsey, "she's right. You need to go. Don't worry about us. Just save your people."

Mr. Green chose that moment to speak. "Can this be true?" he asked, feigning shock. "After all that these…these things have done to your family you are still willing to throw away your life to protect theirs. What are they to you?" he demanded. "You betray your family, girl."

Kelsey stood tall. "I don't care what you think of me, Mr. Green, or what you think I owe my family. I'm angry about what's happened to them, sure, just like you are. But I'm not like you," she said slowly, working each word out with a deliberate bite, "I don't trade revenge for justice. It's not for me to judge whether the elves did right or wrong.

267

Maybe it's really worth all the crap they put my family through, or maybe it'll never add up.

"All I know is that these two are my friends, and that they've given me kindness, which is a whole hell of a lot more than a lot of us humans do for each other. So I'm with them, and I'm with her," she said, putting her arm around Misty, who could only watch in growing admiration for her friend's courage. "And I'm not going to abandon or hurt any of them."

And because she was Kelsey, she couldn't help but add, "Your family probably deserved what they got anyway."

"Enough!" spat the older man. "You can all go to hell if you choose, and I'll be happy to send you there. But," he added smoothly, looking back at the elves, who had listened to Kelsey's speech with the same astonishment as Misty had, "I don't imagine they're going to let that happen. Are you?"

"No. We made a choice, and a promise to each other. We will keep it. Do with us what you will. We will not resist," said Siobhan, seeming perfectly calm.

"But you will get no satisfaction from this," added Connell, his voice taking on the same rhythm his sister's did whenever she traveled into the past.

Misty, who knew that Connell's gifts did not extend in this direction, tilted her head in puzzlement. Perhaps Connell was changing. Not that he was going to get a chance to change much further.

Tossing a rope to his son, who seemed unsure of what to do with it, Nick, Sr. walked up to the elves. "I only need one of you," he said.

268

"But you have us both," stated Siobhan stubbornly. "We are brother and sister, and have walked all of our days together. This will not change now."

"Fine." Looping the rope around the diminutive waists of the elves, Nick, Sr. motioned to his son. "Get the other rope tied around the ankles. Move it now," he added, seeing that Nick was slow to act. "We've got to get them away from here before sundown."

"What happens at sundown, dad?" asked Nick, sounding all of twelve years old.

"Things," answered Connell, again in that eerie voice. He looked at Misty when he said it, making sure to catch her eye. Then, to Kelsey, he added. "I am sorry for what your family has gone through. For what it is worth, you have redeemed them, in our eyes at least."

Misty looked to the west. The sun was already sinking below the treeline, but it was moving too slow. What was supposed to happen at sunset?

Mr. Green wasn't paying attention to that. Something else had caught his interest. "There's a funny story about that, actually." He waited until he had everyone's attention, then continued. "We never did like those McMollens anyway."

Beside her, Misty felt Kelsey stiffen.

"What's that supposed to mean?" asked Kelsey.

"Here, let me show you something," he said. "This is gonna make this all the better, now that we've got ourselves some new elves to play with." He rolled up his sleeve, revealing a birthmark on the inside of his elbow. It consisted of two dots, side by side. One was considerably larger than the other.

269

"What's that supposed to be?" asked Misty, curiosity getting the better of her.

"Mismatched eyes, one large, one small. The mark of the Fomorian. My son's got it, which is why I know he's mine."

Absently, Nick rubbed his arm. "So that's what that is."

"What's that have to do with me," blurted Kelsey. "I don't have that mark on my...oh," her voice trailed off as she considered what the absence of this distinguishing characteristic meant.

Though the shock of what this meant moved through Misty like a tidal wave, she was too busy watching the sun set to see the implications.

Keep talking, Kels, she silently urged her friend.

The sun seemed to freeze in the sky, and she cursed under her breath.

Next to her, Kelsey was sorting out different things. "What happened?" she finally asked.

Seeming to take a perverse delight in the revelation, Mr. Green smiled widely, reveling in the memory. "I was the one that finally ended up breaking him, you know. He was pretty far gone by then, just a blubbering mass. Just a matter of snipping the last little threads, really. After that he just faded away."

"What does this have to do with my family?!" demanded Kelsey once more, this time with even greater urgency.

"I'm getting to that," answered Mr. Green, "but if you try my patience much more I reckon I'll just let you die not knowing."

"But you promised they would go free," blurted Connell, running forward and actually getting a few feet before Siobhan managed to catch up and place a restraining hand on his shoulder. She whispered something in his ear, looking pointedly at Misty, and he calmed down.

Nick, who had pulled out his pistol once again at this incident, seemed to settle down as well, replacing the weapon and watching his father for any cues. Still, he seemed a little shaken from his father's threat.

Another piece of information, Misty thought, filing it away. She was getting calmer now. For all his talk, Nick seemed to be a little squeamish when it came to shedding blood.

"They will, as long as they don't push me," said Mr. Green, his gritted teeth biting off each word, "but I don't owe you elves anything. You were stupid enough to get caught, and that makes it all fair in the end.

"Now where was I? Oh, right, the little bastard. As I was saying, he was pretty much done with. My grandpa told me what had happened right after we caught him though, sort of to pass on the story."

"Your grandfather?" asked Misty. "But this must have happened over two thousand years ago. How could he know?"

"Fomorian blood, girl. I'm older than you think or than I can remember. I've had more jobs, more lives, and yes, more names than you've had years. Nick here is gonna get it too, in a couple of years, once he stops growing. Unlike other Irish families," and he looked at Kelsey when he said this, "*we* kept the bloodline pure."

Nick looked down. "I always thought it was in my head, you never seeming to change." He didn't know whether to be happy or

271

miserable at this new information. Long life was a mixed bag, realized Misty, watching his face flit between wonder and despair. She didn't want it, if this was the cost.

Mr. Green had already moved on, ignoring his son. "My grandfather was the one who first planted the seed. He's always hated the McMollens. One of those feuds that goes so far back not even his father could tell him what really happened to start it all. It was only after a year or two of 'playing' with the elf that he learned of the elves' mental connection to each other. And he used it, telling his captive that our families were working together. He knew the elf would let the others know. A bit of a bonus."

"So it was a lie," said Kelsey in a dead tone. "All that suffering, the poverty, because of a lie."

Connell and Siobhan stood open-mouthed at this news, unable to contain their sorrow and their collective guilt.

"Kelsey...there is nothing I can say. We did not know. How could we know?" Siobhan looked as if she wanted to shrink into herself and fade away. "The Sidhe are as much to blame as the Greens, or whatever they called themselves. There is nothing we can do to repay the debt we owe your family for the centuries of suffering we have placed upon them. Oh, we are a lost race, to do such things to innocents," she wailed, placing her face in her hands and weeping.

Connell said nothing, but the crystal tears that had begun to flow spoke all the words that needed saying. Behind the mask of sorrow, though, his eyes were steadily watching the sun, which had now begun to dip below the horizon.

Misty, so tuned in with her friends that she noticed this small detail, said and did nothing, not even daring to look to the west now, for fear that Mr. Green would realize the time he had allowed to pass with his ramblings.

She tried to delay him further. "So what are you going to do now? Your job is surely lost when this comes out. And it will," she promised. Even if it meant her death she could not allow him to get away with what he had done and what he planned to do.

"Oh, I know, and believe me we won't be here long. I never liked it here anyway, and I was despairing of ever finding my way out. Then I met your Thomas Keller, and the things he told me set me back on the right track. It's funny how everything ties up so neatly sometimes. He has a need, and I have a need as well. Finding each other was fate.

"So I'm going to use these two," he said, jabbing a thumb in the direction of the elves, who still hadn't recovered from their earlier shock, "to find the others, and I'm going to wipe them out. All of them, even Keller's pests. I'll need to the money to get back home."

"Home?" asked Nick.

"Ireland, you stupid boy," he snapped, turning towards his son, who became smaller under his father's wrath. "The family waits there for us, for the curse to be done. Long life ain't nothing without the luck to make it worth something, and we've had little enough of that. With the last of this lot wiped out, the curse'll be lifted and we'll be free to spend our lives as we choose."

"We will not allow that to happen."

273

Mr. Green turned around abruptly. "You don't have a choice, girl!"

Misty turned to Kelsey, confused. Kelsey, equally flustered, could only shrug. Neither of them had said anything.

Nor had Connell.

Nor Siobhan.

For the sun had fallen just about far enough, and they were no longer alone.

"Uncle!" cried out Siobhan.

Misty turned around and saw Eogan, the elf she had rescued from the entangling branches those short months ago. He looked much the same; as it was with his niece and nephew, who wore the same clothing every day, he was dressed in the same manner as he was that first day.

He was not alone. Next to him stood another, slightly taller. She seemed old, even as elves go. This then, must be Diahan, and it was she who had spoken.

Kelsey, who had never known any elves besides Connell and Siobhan, nudged Misty in the ribs. "You know this guy?"

"Yeah," said Misty. "If it wasn't for me falling down the hill and bringing the forest down on top of him with me none of this would have happened."

Kelsey nodded calmly. "I'm still trying to decide whether or not that was a good thing. I'll let you know tomorrow."

Misty smiled in spite of the situation. She was impressed and baffled by Kelsey's attitude. She was certain that if she had just gone through the roller-coaster that her friend had been subjected to—

believing that you were some half-breed, and learning that it was a lie, that your family had been subjected to a horrible curse for nothing, and all in the past few hours at that—she would have ended up a blubbering wreck. For some reason, Kelsey was fine now. Should they get through this, Misty promised, she would seek to learn more about her friend.

Mr. Green seemed not the least bit disturbed by the new arrivals. "That took less time than I thought. So you must be the clan leader, then." He addressed Diahan as he spoke, ignoring Eogan completely.

"You are knowledgeable for one of your kind," said Diahan. "Yes, the care of the clan is my responsibility. All members of the clan," she added, eying the young elves.

"Had we known of what they were up to," said Eogan sternly, "we would have put a stop to their nonsense. But," he added, "we are not normally creatures of the day. Not anymore, though I may take the occasional daylight ramble. Too many of your folk about, prying and poking. So their adventures went unnoticed. This will not happen anymore."

Mr. Green pulled a little on Connell and Siobhan's rope, and they stumbled towards him. Niko growled in protest, but was calmed by a look from the young Sidhe. "I think you're right about that. Things are about to end quite soon. You, the leader, over here," he ordered imperiously. Calmly, Diahan stepped away from Eogan, who made no protest, and began to walk deliberately to the man.

Suddenly, it became clear to Misty. The old elf was timing things. And looking around her, Misty saw. Nick was standing way to the side, a lost little boy in a story too big for him. Mr. Green was ignoring her and Kelsey completely now; Diahan had his full attention. Connell and Siobhan had taken a hold of their bonds, their slender fingers holding them tightly now. Niko had moved off to the side, out of their captor's line of sight. And behind him, in the fields was a new sight.

She gasped. They were there, every last one of them.

When Connell and Siobhan had spoken of the dying out of the Sidhe, Misty had always imagined that they were the very last of a vanishing species, perhaps a few dozen at the most. But now...there were hundreds of them, moving as silently as the night around them. And this was only one clan.

Mr. Green, so fixated on the clan leader, his prize, never even looked past her to see his doom sliding towards him.

Perhaps things weren't as bad as she had thought. There was still hope, if this many still lived. There must have been thousands upon thousands at one time.

She blinked away her tears at the sight, and made a choice she knew her father, wherever he was, would be proud of. She would save them, even if she died.

And she would not do it alone.

"Niko!" yelled Connell.

The big dog, impelled by the years of beatings he had suffered under the hands of the man now before him and by the love he bore his new owner, this girl who had shown him only affection and care, gave a throaty bark and charged, fangs bared.

Then several things happened at once.

Mr. Green turned, distracted by this new threat. As he did Connell and Siobhan pulled as one on the rope that attached them to him. Stumbling he fell, his pistol firing. Then a bundle of fur and teeth was all over him, tearing and raking.

When Niko charged, Nick woke from his inner thoughts and raised his own weapon, driven by filial loyalty to defend his father. He never got the chance. Misty grabbed his arm with both hands, and with more strength than she thought she had she managed to raise it above the boy's head.

Then Kelsey, with the grace of the dancer she was, spun and delivered a solid kick to his stomach. Grunting in pain, he allowed the gun to slip loose from his fingers. Abruptly letting go, Misty dived for it, snatching it up and bringing it to bear before he could recover.

"Don't move, Nick! Just don't!" she screamed, aiming the gun right at his head. He didn't run, but slowly put his hands in the air. After a moment, Misty calmed down. "Thank, Kels," she said.

"Hey, no problem. I always knew that ballet class was going to do me some good. Of course I thought it would be on a college application, not a life or death kind of thing." Kelsey went to Misty, helping her to her feet. Through her calm exterior, Misty could see that she was shaking inside. Even the resilient redhead had her limits.

"You were great," she said.

Then she looked over to where the others had been, and her heart broke.

Mr. Green lay on the ground, unmoving. Next to him, Niko had collapsed, feebly trying to lick the ragged hole in his shoulder where the bullet had entered. It was a testament to his courage and his love that he had not slowed when hit, but had done what needed to be done to protect his family, all of them. Now he was paying the price.

Choking, dropping the gun, Misty ran to him, sinking to her knees and taking his large head in her lap. He whined softly, and licked her hand. "Oh, Niko, no!" He had given everything for her, and now she could do nothing for him. "I'm so sorry," she murmured over and over again. Niko's patient brown eyes held no condemnation, just endless love, the kind that only a dog knows how to give.

"He is a brave cu. Let me see him." Misty looked up and through the haze of her tears she saw Diahan. "It is okay, my dear. Let me see him."

"What are you going to do?"

"She is going to help him. It is what she does. She has taught Connell the art, but I have my doubts whether or not the lesson stuck with him." It was Eogan who spoke, and now he looked at Misty more directly. Misty remembered her broken ankle, deciding to keep Connell's proficiency a secret, for now. "That was a brave act, what he did. And you as well, the both of you. I had wondered why Diahan insisted on the entire clan coming this night. We ourselves could have handled it quite well, but I suppose she wanted us to see."

"To see what?" asked Misty. Beside her, Niko's body had begun to glow. Diahan was humming a familiar tune.

"To see that not all humans are as bad as the tales have told. I might have been guilty of those same thoughts myself," he added.

Misty remembered their first meeting, his startled cry of "Fomorian!", and smiled. "Some of us are," she said, glancing over at the still body of Mr. Green, and at Nick, who was now under the guard of Kelsey, who had, thinking quickly, picked up the gun that Misty had dropped when she saw Niko.

278

"There is hope," said Eogan so softly that Misty was unsure of what she heard, and did not ask. "As for you, Kelsey," he called out, loud enough for all to hear, "we owe you a great amount of gratitude, and your family a great debt, one which will never be repaid. Still, we will try."

"I lifted the curse myself, Eogan." It was Diahan, who had finished doing whatever it was she had been doing. Niko still lay on the ground, but he was resting peacefully now, his breathing regular. "He will sleep for a while, but he will be fine," she added, seeing Misty's questioning look.

"Then I will add the blessing," said Eogan, "and the rest will add their own." With a wave of his arm he indicated the gathered throng.

Misty looked at them now, and was surprised. While none of them stood taller than Siobhan, there existed within the group a remarkable variety of shapes, sizes, and looks. The colors alone boggled her mind, for her only experience had been with Connell, Siobhan, and for a brief instant their uncle, and they all wore shades of green. She had assumed that each elf did the same. She could not have been more wrong. Also, they had each chosen a distinctive pattern to follow, and wherever Misty's eyes looked from one to another, she was reminded by each one of a particular bush or flower or tree. They were all unique, yet each shared a part of something larger than themselves. It was the most beautiful display she had ever seen.

"As for you two scamps, we shall have to have a talk," said Eogan, wagging a finger at Connell and Siobhan, who were now turning a bright red. "Although," he said, softening, "I imagine that we shall talk about the good that your acts of truancy have brought to us."

279

"Yes, there is much to discuss," agreed Diahan, "but there are people coming now, and this is becoming a human matter. Somehow," she said, a twinkle in her eye, "I imagine things are going to work out just fine. For all of us."

"What about him?" asked Kelsey, pointing at Nick with the pistol.

But Diahan, Eogan, and the rest were already gone. Only Connell and Siobhan remained behind, and it was Siobhan who spoke first, coming to stand next to Kelsey.

"He has lost his father and his identity in one night. It is a large price to pay. Do you not agree?"

"I do," said Kelsey. Misty, who had more reason to hate him, decided to let it go, and nodded her head as well.

"Good. Nick?"

Nick, seeming much younger now than before, pulled his gaze from his father. "What do you want?" he asked dully.

"I am sorry for what has happened and for your pain," said Siobhan gently, "but you are free now."

"Free?" Nick muttered bitterly. "How am I free?"

"You are free from your father's will. You are free to decide what type of person you want to be in this world. It is more than most are given. And," she added, "you are free from your family's curse."

"Siobhan," said Connell, "are you sure?"

"Have we not all suffered enough? Nick?"

He looked at them, and now the tears came. "Yes," he whispered, his voice wavering.

"It is not in me to grant you the grace we have given the McMollens, for you do not deserve that. But I will give you this mercy."

Nick hung his head. "I don't know what to say. It's been...it's been hard."

"You say nothing. You earn this. Become your own person. That is all."

Walking up to him, she placed a hand on his arm.

"Misty, Kelsey," added Siobhan, "I hope to see you tomorrow."

"You will," promised Misty.

"Good. There are people coming. It is time to go. Connell?"

"Right away. Goodbye, you two. Keep your story simple." And they faded away.

Answers and Ends

"What in the hell happened here?"

As one, Misty, Kelsey, and Nick turned around. Even Niko, his fur showing no signs of trauma, and apparently forgetting his fear of Nick, trotted up. Running up the dirt path were two police officers, their uniforms dusty from the trail. Behind them came Christina. Misty had never before seen her look so worried. She met her mother halfway, and they hugged silently and fiercely, tears streaming down Christina's face.

"I was so worried, I was so worried," repeated Christina, over and over.

"I know, Mom, but it's okay now."

"I thought I lost you, just like Carlos. Tell me: what happened here? Who is that on the ground? Oh." She stiffened, recognizing Mr. Green's body.

"I'm hoping to find that out myself," said the male officer. "What are you doing here, Nick?" As he was speaking his partner ran over to Mr. Green's side, and rolled him over. She placed a careful finger on his neck, and shook her head.

"He's gone, but we're going to have to call the paramedics anyway. Looks like an animal attack." Getting up, she wiped her hands off on her pants. "It's a shame; he was a good man." To Misty, he sounded hollow and unconvinced.

The other officer, by his graying whiskers and his sergeant's chevrons the obvious senior of the two, shook his head. "You didn't know him," he muttered softly, but Misty and Kelsey were close enough to him that they heard anyway.

But they let it pass, for the man's son was standing not five feet away.

"Well," said the sergeant, "I guess that rules out most of our suspects." He looked at Niko. "That dog never seemed to me to have much bite in him, though. I wonder what set him off. Better alert Animal Control while you're calling that in, Officer Morgan."

"You knew this dog?" asked Christina, at the same time Misty and Kelsey were crying out, "No!"

He answered Christina first. "Yeah, I saw him around a few times. He used to belong to the Greens. And, I'm sorry, miss, but in the event of a dog attack, it's standard operating procedure to lock the animal up until this gets figured out. I don't know. Attacking a police officer. That's about as serious as it gets. They're probably going to order him put down."

Niko whined softly, moving to hide behind Misty, who quickly stood in front of him, like a protective mother.

"Wait!"

The sergeant looked back. Misty's eyes widened in surprise. It was Nick who had spoken.

"Do you have something to say, son? I've been holding off asking you your part in this, but I've got enough of a story from Mrs. Montoya here to make for a real interesting report, unless you care to add to it."

283

"The dog was protecting her. My dad…he, he was going crazy. Said he had some job to do for a friend of his. Thomas Keller, I think his name was. I guess he has…had…some grudge against her," he said, pointing at Christina.

"Something to do with those plans you showed me?" asked the sergeant, looking at Christina.

Christina nodded. "He was my former employer."

"Former?"

"His business practices were unethical."

"I'd imagine," said the officer drily.

Officer Morgan strode up, carrying Mr. Green's pistol in her gloved hand. "It's been fired recently," she said.

"In the air," said Nick quickly. "He was pointing it at Misty, telling her he was going to make her family pay, then Niko got his arm, and it went off."

The sergeant stroked his mustache. "It will be a job of work to find the bullet, seeing as it couldn't have hit any of you."

Misty threw Kelsey a significant look, and the redhead, whom she could tell had been on the verge of saying something sarcastic or witty, snapped her mouth shut, eyes gleaming.

Instead, she stooped down and picked an object off the ground. "Will this be enough?" It was the shell.

"Good enough, though I'd have preferred you left it there. Helps for placement."

Kelsey dropped the casing. "Sorry."

"A little late now, but I don't think it matters. We have three material witnesses, plus Mrs. Montoya's testimony. That, along with some other issues, will seal this up well. We'll have to talk to Keller, though, see what we can get out of him."

Misty could not believe that this was being wrapped up so neatly. Still, she had to ask, just to make sure that everyone would get what they had coming.

"Will he go to jail?" She was trying not to sound too hopeful.

Christina shook her head.

But it was the sergeant who spoke. "No. But it'll probably give him enough trouble he'll have to pull out of whatever he's got planned. He'll take a hit where it counts: in the wallet."

"You seem to know a lot about him," said Christina.

"Drove my father out of business, but that's old news."

Now Misty understood why he was being so calm.

The six stood in silence for a moment.

Misty broke the quiet. "So what's going to happen now?"

"Well," said the sergeant, "now we wait for the paramedics. Probably come by helicopter. Hang on a second." He activated his radio on his shoulder, muttered a string of numbers and said "Cancel the Animal Control."

"No, no," he said, waving away Misty's thanks. "We know what happened. But you'll need to wait here until the detective arrives. Tell him what you told me."

***

Three hours later, they were walking back, slightly behind the officers, who were lighting the path with their flashlights.

Misty watched Nick carefully. His back was slumped, and he seemed to have lost all fight. Even Niko showed no fear of him anymore, walking surefooted through the night.

"Nick."

"Yeah." It was barely a whisper.

"Thank you."

He nodded.

Kelsey shouldered her way up. "Why did you do it, go against your dad like that, after all the crap you did to us?" she whispered fiercely.

"I couldn't do it," answered Nick.

"Do what?"

"I couldn't let him pull the trigger. All that talk of his, I guess deep down I never really believed it. He was telling me that this Keller guy was going to take care of him and that we wouldn't have to worry about money, not anymore."

"Since when did you ever worry about money?" asked Kelsey.

"It was all he talked about, our family never really making it. Our house is mortgaged to the limit, and we're about to lose it. I just never let on, especially to Briana; she would have told the whole school." Nick sounded ashamed as he said this, and Misty began to feel a little sorry for him, again. Parents can be a terrible burden sometimes. And he chose to value the opinions of a group of people whose thoughts didn't really matter. In the end, it was not in Misty to judge him in this too harshly.

Kelsey was another sort. "No one would have cared, you know," she pointed out angrily.

"Yeah they would," said Nick, his tone utterly self-defeating.

"We wouldn't!" yelled Kelsey. At this outburst, the two officers turned around, prompting a hasty "sorry" from her, but after they had turned their backs, she wasn't relenting. "We're a bunch of geeks who spend their lunch hour goofing off. Do you think we ever cared who was rich or who was poor?" she asked. "Hell, it's not like my family's swimming in the dough."

"But you had to know they talked about you," argued Nick.

"Who? Briana and her little clones? If I learned one thing, it's that those bubbleheads don't have any control over my future, or any say in who I am. In six months we'll be leaving high school and I'm never going to have to see them again, except at reunions, but I'll just go to laugh at the nothings they end up becoming."

"And what do I become, then?" asked Nick, straightening up amidst Kelsey's onslaught.

"Well," put in Misty, "the elves have dropped the curse on you. Why don't you try becoming yourself?"

***

"So that's it?"

Christina pushed the remote and the image on the screen flicked off. She looked at her daughter, and tilted her head slightly. How was she supposed to explain the harsher realities of the world? Then she remembered a day three months earlier. Misty would be able to handle this.

"Yeah, that's it, honey. Sometimes the bad guy gets away. I'm sorry." Maybe it was time to go into environmental law. Less money, sure, but at least she would be able to sleep at night. Looking at Misty, though, she realized that she had missed out on the joy of being her mother for too long. She had spent three months trying to remedy that, just being there, totally available. It was magic.

So, not yet.

"It sucks," said Misty, "but at least that plan of his for the riverside got canned."

She must get her optimism from Carlos, Christina thought, smiling. "He is most definitely persona non grata in the Pacific Northwest," she agreed. "I'd like to think that I had something to do with it, but I imagine his hiring of Mr. Nicholas Green and the fallout from that did more than my resignation."

"Maybe it pushed him over the edge," offered Misty.

"And that was a good thing?" asked Christina, mock serious. Then she laughed, and it felt good. "Well, it ended well, so I suppose it was. Still, I wonder what the man must have been thinking, to hire that lunatic. To think, elves!"

Laughing again, she missed Misty's half smile.

* * *

Summer came almost too quickly, and along with it graduation: blue robes for the boys, white robes for the girls, invitations—Misty invited only her mother, Kelsey her entire family (the Irish contingent, in the middle of what would be an extended and totally inexplicable streak of financial luck, even managed to come)—and, when all was finished, goodbyes.

Nick avoided them for the rest of the year, although from time to time, in the middle of a vicious game of four-square, Misty would look up and see him eating his lunch alone. Occasionally he would watch them and wave hesitantly, and she would wave back, but for the most part she allowed him to figure things out on his own time and in his own way.

After that winter day, she later found out, he had moved in with his uncle—his mother's brother—and his wife, who lived in Gresham. He graduated on time, and Briana and her friends were never the wiser.

Briana graduated as well. Her type, while preferring shopping and boys over academics, generally manage to just squeak by. Misty overheard during one of their too-loud lockerside conversations that she was going to junior college, but wasn't sure what major she wanted to choose. She assumed that her friends would faithfully follow her, but that was really about all the mental space she gave them. She knew Briana and her crew would be forgotten in a month.

And they were.

As for the elves, Misty (and most of the time, Kelsey, though her parents could never figure out why) still took Niko for his daily walks, and Christina never questioned why her daughter continued to go to the same place where her and her friend's lives had taken such a nearly-tragic turn. Connell and Siobhan were always there, but the difference now was that more often than not they were not alone. Every young elf took the opportunity to get reacquainted with humans by starting with the only two who, in their memory, had never betrayed them. Even Diahan and Eogan stopped by once, just to inquire of Kelsey how her family in Ireland was getting along. Eogan had a twinkle in his eye when he asked.

Misty and Kelsey even managed to survive Amanda Mattos's class, despite the teacher's efforts to prepare them for postgraduate study with research papers of ever-increasing length and complexity. Ms. Mattos swore up and down that her students would thank her later. Misty was sure she was right, but kept it to herself, unwilling to infringe on the teenage student's time honored right to groan and gripe about every little thing.

All in all, it had been a really restful six months.

But now the two friends, bonded by something much deeper and infinitely stranger than blood, found themselves standing at the foot of the stage they had just walked across as high school graduates, wondering what was going to happen to them.

"University of Washington."

Misty fingered the golden braid that snaked around her neck. "Yeah. Out-of-state tuition's a ton, but my mom says it's not a problem, so I guess it's not. A problem that is."

"Well, she got that job working for Greenpeace," said Kelsey. "I guess they're pretty well funded."

"Yeah, I guess so." Misty changed the subject. "So you're heading to the University of Oregon. I think that means that we're supposed to hate each other now." She put her arm around her friend. "Are you excited?"

Kelsey shrugged her shoulders. "I should be, I guess. After all, it's where my parents went, and they said it was really great. Still, sometimes I wonder."

"Wonder what?"

"How you're going to make it through the next four years without me watching your back. We're family now, you know," said Kelsey.

"Always will be," agreed Misty. "But look, it's not like Seattle's so far away. We'll be able to see each other almost every weekend, if we make the time."

"We will, especially since," said Kelsey as, with a flourish, she pulled an envelope from the folds of her robe, "I'll be joining you."

"Kels!" screamed Misty, clutching at her friend in disbelief. "You never told me!"

"What would be the surprise in that? Duh!"

Misty was worried, though. "But what about the tuition? I mean, your family...." How could she ask without insulting her, or sounding condescending? She grasped for the right words, but as they seemed to elude her.

Kelsey waved her hands in the air, until Misty finally noticed and calmed down. "Thank the elves, Misty. Thank the elves."

"What do you mean?" asked Misty. She was becoming more confused by the moment. "Do the Sidhe have some kind of scholarship I didn't know about? Oh, wait, there really is a pot of gold, and they just didn't want to tell me about it, for whatever reason," she finished, allowing her last words to trail off.

Kelsey laughed, her red curls shaking. "No, you dork, they don't have a scholarship, or a pot of gold. Hmm, but maybe we should ask them about that."

"Kelsey!"

"Fine, fine. My Irish relatives, those from Ireland, that is, offered to pay my way through school."

"That was nice of them,"

"Wasn't it, though? Of course, they've won three of the last six Irish lotteries, so I think they can afford to swing it."

Misty caught on. "Eogan's blessing."

"Eogan's blessing," repeated Kelsey, merriment in her eyes, "and it's made up for a lot of lost time. And that means that I'm not going to leave you. Not for a while at least."

"Hey girls!" It was Christina calling them. Next to her were Kelsey's parents, and an entire herd of redheaded, befreckled folks, all beaming, and all of looking very much like her best friend.

Linking an arm through Kelsey's, Misty said, "I can't think of better news."

"Neither can I."

Rainbow's End

Four Years Later

The sun had climbed past the trees by the time Misty pulled herself up from the log, brushing off the dust of the forest from her college graduation gown, which she had every intention of removing for the long drive to Seattle the next day. Beside her, Connell drew tiny patterns in the dirt with his shoe. From time to time, a drop of water would fall past his nose and muddy the outlines.

"Why are you crying, Connell?" Reaching into her purse, she pulled out a tissue and began to dry his face. "You'll get streaky. Here, let me help."

Connell turned away quickly, "It is alright. I am alright." His voice shook, and more tears came. "Okay, maybe I am not alright!" He stamped his tiny foot on the hard earth. "What is this? Why am I doing this?"

"They're tears, that's all. Everyone gets them," answered Misty. "Trust me."

The elf rubbed his cheek, this time in awe. "Tears. I know of them. I have seen them from you many times." He suddenly was seized with another fit. "They come when you're sad."

"Yes, and sometimes they come when you're happy." She stared into the forest, collecting herself from the wave of sorrow that had now threatened to overcome her. "But not usually."

Connell finished wiping his face, and stood calmly once more. "I have never...cried, before. I do not know why I do it now."

"Because you knew what has to happen, and so does she." Both girl and elf turned jumped slightly at this new voice, and relaxed as Siobhan stepped into the small clearing.

Misty kneeled down and reached out to hug her friend, and Siobhan, after only the smallest hesitation, dashed forward to wrap her arms around one of the only two human friends she had ever had. "I didn't think you were coming."

Siobhan pulled away in a little twirl. "Connell told me that you wanted to see us, and I knew what you were going to do." She jabbed her brother in the ribs, and Connell yelped in complaint. "Even though this fool pretended for the longest time that he did not. I did not want to be here when you did what you were going to do. What you are about to do." She let this last sentence trail off into a whisper, followed shortly after by a sigh. For one who was hundreds of years younger, Misty found it easy to see Siobhan as a little sister now, in need of comfort.

Misty smiled warmly. "I'm not so sure I knew either," she replied, then added, "but I think I know now."

"Well I guess that just leaves me then," interjected Connell, "who still seems not to have a clue!"

"Oh, pipe down," retorted Siobhan, "and stop playing stupid. You know exactly why she is here, and those tears you shed, and appear to be shedding again as we speak, prove it."

"Prove what?"

Misty put her hand on the distraught creature's shoulder. "That I came to say goodbye. And Connell, I think that it will be for more than a year this time. Much more," she sighed.

"Is it to be forever? I thought you were just leaving for a small while."

"Yes, Connell, goodbye forever." Siobhan shrugged her shoulders in futility. "He is as dense as the Stone. Sorry, Misty, but the Sidhe do not part very well. Saying goodbye reminds us of our home, of Erin. And it is not an easy thing to think of." She eyed Misty thoughtfully, "Do you know that in all the books of recorded American Elven history, some two thousand years, you were the second human that we had come into contact with that had not asked us for a pot of gold."

Misty chuckled softly at hearing this, remembering the conversation she had had with Kelsey on that graduation day four years earlier, and then slowly the laughter let itself out. It felt so good to be able to laugh again, even over something so silly. It had been the first genuine laugh in some time, through many years of study, of college boyfriends, and college drama, with only Kelsey as her constant companion and confidante. By the time she had managed to stifle herself her sides were aching. Several moments later, she was able to sit again on the log, but every now and then her shoulders shook.

Connell was the first to speak. "While I am glad to see the joy restored in you, I fail to see what is so funny." He had by now fully recovered from his crying jag, and was his old self again, a near-perfect mirror of his sister.

"I'm sorry, I really am," apologized Misty, still red in the face, "but I thought all that pot of gold stuff was just some stupid joke."

"Well, it cannot be done, if that is what you mean," answered Siobhan, "but try telling that to all the farmers who would go out with their pitchforks every night, waiting to catch one of us by the glow of the full moon."

"And catching some of us, too," added Connell.

Misty remembered the story of Nick's family and shuddered.

"Yes, brother. But that is all in the past now. We are here now, and it is what it is."

"My father used to say that, every time I would complain about something that couldn't be changed," said Misty, "I try to remember it, in difficult moments."

"Moments like this?"

"Exactly like this," answered Misty, and this time the tears that fell to the ground were her own.

Connell came near, to stand by his sister. "I will not cry again," he promised. "It hurts a little too much. However, the day is growing late. You have someplace to be, do you not?"

"I do," said Misty. Now that the time had come for her to make her own way in the world, she found herself hesitating, her resolve for what she knew had to happen beginning to melt away like the morning dew at the coming of the dawn.

There was at that time a frozen moment, and this moment was better than the one shared by Misty and Connell alone. This time three friends stood together, surrounded by the forest that the world had created just for them. No words were spoken. And none were needed.

Indeed, there was nothing that could be said to make it all okay. Instead, there was infinite understanding, and with that came a little bit of peace. This moment, like so many that came before, seemed to dwell in eternity, promising to never end.

And all moments end. It is just what they do. And this is never forgotten, though the knowledge remains a burden for a time.

"Misty?" said Connell quietly, breaking the silent spell.

Misty blinked her eyes, and the tears were gone. "Yes?"

"That place is not here. Not anymore."

"I know," said Misty, "but I can come back, you know. To visit." She wanted so badly to turn back now, to hear her friends tell her that, of course, she could visit, and that they would be there, but she knew before she finished her sentence what the answer would be.

"Yes, you could," admitted Siobhan, "but we will no longer be here. For it is time for the elves to continue the long sojourn. Once again, the West calls us."

The West again. Misty had forgotten about all of that.

Misty was unable to speak for the ache in her heart. Finally, she managed to ask the question that she had kept inside of her for five years. "Why did I see you the first time?"

Siobhan chewed her lip, trying to find the right words. "I think it was because you were alone, I mean truly alone. In every possible way. Maybe you needed us.

"When Connell told you that you found us because you were looking for an answer, I think he was right. Maybe you did not know the question. Perhaps you still do not. Let me give it to you now: can you survive on your own?" Siobhan looked hard at Misty, and Misty caught her breath, because the question was so right in its simplicity. "You could not then. Now, at this time, you can. You have gained strength in yourself, strength enough to walk on your own. You no longer need us."

"How are you so sure of that?" asked Misty, trying not to let anger take control. Connell and Siobhan were two of the best friends she had ever had, and having to give them up, after all she had gone through, seemed the act of an uncaring universe. Sure, for the past years, she had been unable to see them as often as she liked, although she had visited at least every other weekend, but she had always assumed that the Sidhe, timeless beings that they were, would be there, always. It wasn't fair!

The elves sensed it, and began to visibly tense. "Please do not make this harder than it needs to be, Misty," pleaded Connell. "What Siobhan is trying to say is that you have entered a new phase of your life, and the steps you now take will be your own.

"Look," he continued, "you are not alone anymore. Your mother has discovered her daughter again. You have found friendship. You have made connections again with the real world. You did all of this on your own. Somehow, that has to be enough."

Misty crumbled, flinging up her hands. "I know! I know! It's just that I didn't think it would be so hard."

"Has parting ever been easy?" asked Siobhan gently. "For if it was, of what real value are these friendships we form? But we will not forget you, for a part of you shall stay with us, just as a part of us will go with you. And that is a comfort."

Suddenly, there was a loud rustle of leaves, as Christina's voice penetrated the forest air. "Misty, we're going to be late."

Niko came bounding up, preceding Misty's mother by just moments. He barked a farewell to his funny friends, and they waved. Connell came up to scratch the dog's ear one final time, receiving a generous lick in return.

Misty turned around, then looked back to offer one final goodbye to Connell and Siobhan.

They were gone.

Made in the USA
San Bernardino, CA
17 June 2015